"That's my boy," Nick cried, holding out his arms to the child and hugging him tight.

Carlee winced. She did not want that. Heaven help her, she did not want Scotty crazy about Nick, and that was wrong. She had no right to feel that way.

"Carlee, listen to me…."

She had turned her back on him and stood wooden and silent.

"I want to be your friend. I want to spend time with you and your son, because I'm crazy about him. And I promise that what happened the other night will never happen again unless you want it, too. But the way you've hardened your heart to romance…to love…it won't."

Tell him now, a voice within commanded. *Tell him and get it over with.*

It was what she *should* do. But what she could *not* do.

Dear Reader,

Do I have a sweet lineup for you—just in time for Valentine's Day! What's more enticing than a box of chocolates? The answer lies in the next story, *Cordina's Crown Jewel*, from *New York Times* bestselling author Nora Roberts's CORDINA'S ROYAL FAMILY series. This gem features a princess who runs away from royal responsibility and straight into the arms of the most unlikely man of her dreams!

Another Valentine treat is Jackie Merritt's *Marked for Marriage*, which is part of the popular MONTANA MAVERICKS series. Here, a feisty bronco-busting beauty must sit still so that a handsome doctor can give her a healthy dose of love. And if it's heart-thumping emotion you want, Peggy Webb continues THE WESTMORELAND DIARIES series with *Bittersweet Passion*, a heavenly opposites-attract romance between a singing sensation and a very handsome minister hero.

In *With Family in Mind*, Sharon De Vita launches her gripping SADDLE FALLS miniseries. One Valentine's Day, this newlywed author admits, she wrote a heartwarming love poem to her husband about their first year together! Our next family tale is *Sun-Kissed Baby*, by Patricia Hagan—a darling tale of a new single mom who falls for the man she thinks is her little boy's father. This talented author shares her Valentine's Day dinner tradition with us—making "a heart-shaped meatloaf" and at the end of the pink meal, "a heart-shaped ice cream cake, frosted with strawberry whipped cream." The icing on the cake this month is Leigh Greenwood's *Undercover Honeymoon*, a passionate tale of two reunited lovers who join forces to stay ahead of a deadly enemy and care for an orphaned little girl.

Make sure that you sample every Special Edition delight this month has to offer. I wish you and your loved ones a warm and rose-filled Valentine's Day (and that box of chocolates, too)!

Best,

Karen Taylor Richman
Senior Editor

Please address questions and book requests to:
Silhouette Reader Service
U.S.: 3010 Walden Ave., P.O. Box 1325, Buffalo, NY 14269
Canadian: P.O. Box 609, Fort Erie, Ont. L2A 5X3

Sun-Kissed Baby

PATRICIA HAGAN

Silhouette®

SPECIAL EDITION™

Published by Silhouette Books

America's Publisher of Contemporary Romance

For Barb Ralph, one of my favorite Floridians.

 SILHOUETTE BOOKS

ISBN 0-373-24451-7

SUN-KISSED BABY

This edition published by arrangement with Harlequin Books S.A.

® and TM are trademarks of Harlequin Books S.A., used under license. Trademarks indicated with ® are registered in the United States Patent and Trademark Office, the Canadian Trade Marks Office and in other countries.

Visit Silhouette at www.eHarlequin.com

Printed in U.S.A.

Books by Patricia Hagan

Silhouette Special Edition

Bride for Hire #1127
My Child, Our Child #1277
Race to the Altar #1397
Sun-Kissed Baby #1451

Yours Truly

Boy Re-Meets Girl
Groom on the Run

Harlequin Historicals

The Daring #84
The Desire #143

PATRICIA HAGAN

New York Times bestselling author Patricia Hagan had
written and published over 2,500 short stories before
selling her first book in 1971. With a background in
English and Journalism from the University of Alabama,
Pat has won awards for radio, television, newspaper and
magazine writing. Her hobbies include reading, painting
and cooking. The author and her Norwegian husband,
Erik, divide their time between their Florida retreat in
Boca Raton and their home in Bergen, Norway.

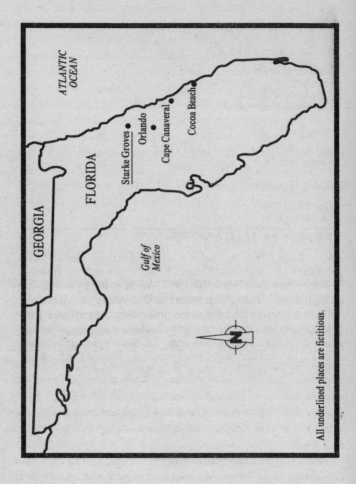

All underlined places are fictitious.

Chapter One

Carlee held Alicia's thirteen-month-old baby in her arms as she stared through her tears at the grave.

She still found it hard to believe that Alicia was gone. It had happened so fast. One minute they were having their Sunday-morning treat of Danish pastry with their coffee and looking forward to taking Scotty to the beach that afternoon, and the next Alicia gasped, clutched her chest and collapsed. Carlee had instantly dialed 911. After a frantic ambulance ride, Alicia was whisked into the trauma unit, and a little while later a doctor came out to say she had died.

He said it was her heart. Probably a congenital condition she'd had since birth. He asked Carlee if she knew about any heart problems in Alicia's family. She told him that Alicia had experienced a difficult labor and delivery when Scotty was born and afterward was told a heart murmur had been detected. Alicia had been advised to undergo cardiac evaluation, but she had no insurance and couldn't afford it. She didn't think the murmur was anything to worry about, anyway. She'd always been healthy. Besides, she was too excited about Scotty and wasn't thinking of anything else.

Too bad, the ER doctor had said. Had she been tested, there was a good chance the problem would have been diagnosed and corrected.

Alicia was dead, and Carlee suddenly found herself a mom, because after the paramedics had revived Alicia before loading her into the ambulance, she had asked Carlee to promise she would take care of Scotty if anything happened. Carlee hadn't hesitated and told Alicia not to worry. Then, while she was standing in the hallway of the emergency room, clutching little Scotty in a daze, the doctor had handed her a slip of paper. Alicia had asked a nurse to write a note declaring Carlee to be Scotty's guardian and managed to sign it before she slipped away.

The doctor had asked if they were sisters. "Best friends," she had whispered, not about to confide how their friendship had been forged by the worthless, cheating men in their lives, or how they'd clung together and vowed never again to be so foolish.

Carlee's parents had divorced when she was only ten. The court had awarded her mother custody, but her father had never paid the court-ordered child-support, and she'd refused to make him. She'd said that was begging and vowed she'd rather die. So times had been hard, and Carlee blamed her mother for her spinelessness and her father for shirking his responsibilities. The year she graduated from high school, her mother remarried and moved to the West Coast, leaving Carlee on her own in Florida. Carlee fell in love, married before she was twenty, and five years later her husband had driven them into bankruptcy and left her for an older woman who could support his extravagant lifestyle.

It was at the time of her divorce that she had met Alicia. They lived in the same apartment complex. Alicia was going to school during the day to study computers while working as a waitress at the Blue Moon Lounge on Cocoa Beach at night. She was also pregnant but didn't want to talk about the father, and Carlee didn't pry.

Carlee had been working in the gift shop at Jupiter Orange Groves since high school, but the work was seasonal. Still, she enjoyed it so much that during the rest of the year she took what jobs she could find so she'd be free to return. After her divorce, however, she needed more financial security, and Ben Burns, owner of the groves, had said he would give her a raise and put her to work year-round in the office if she would take a bookkeeping course and learn some computer programs. So when the season ended, she had enrolled in night school and worked at the cosmetics counter of a department store at a local mall.

Times were tough, and Carlee and Alicia decided to share an apartment to cut expenses. They became closer than sisters. Carlee went to Lamaze classes as Alicia's coach, and she was there for Scotty's birth. Later she helped with his care and came to love him as though he were her own. Alicia traded baby-sitting with another working mom in the complex, and life seemed to be going according to plan.

Now Carlee was left grief-stricken, wondering how on earth she was going to manage. She had to work and finish school in order to get a promotion, but she could not trade baby-sitting as Alicia had done. That meant she would have to pay for Scotty to go to a day-care center, and she just didn't have the money. Plus, she had taken on the added responsibility of the funeral, because there was no one else to take care of it, and she had not wanted Alicia buried like a pauper.

Though she hadn't had time to really think about it, Carlee had already tossed aside the idea of trying to find another roommate. The apartment was small, and the only reason she and Alicia had shared it was that they got along so well. She didn't want to take a chance on someone else not being so congenial.

"But don't you worry, little guy," she whispered in Scotty's ear as the funeral service ended. "We'll be okay." She pulled his blanket more tightly around him. It was spring, but the day was damp and cold, even for the central coast of Florida. They were near the Indian River, and a chilly wind was blowing in from the water.

Scotty awoke and started crying. She popped his pacifier into his mouth, promising to feed him as soon as they got home. Her own stomach gave a hungry rumble, and she couldn't remember the last time she herself had eaten. Coffee had been her only nourishment in the despair that had wrapped about her since that fateful Sunday only three days ago.

The hospital chaplain, James Barnhill, had offered to conduct the graveside services after learning Alicia did not have a minister of her own. He had been so kind that day in the ER, helping Carlee to fill out the forms, then driving her and Scotty back to the apartment. He and his wife had even come by later with food. He had also suggested that she see a lawyer as soon as possible about the necessary paperwork to have her officially named Scotty's guardian. The note Alicia had written would start the ball rolling, of course, but there were legal procedures that had to be followed.

As she turned to leave the gravesite, Mr. Barnhill said, "Miss Denton, the other ladies have told me earlier that they had worked with Miss Malden and would like to meet you. Do you have a moment?''

Carlee murmured, ''Of course,'' and he motioned to the four women standing nearby.

They oohed and ahhed over Scotty, talking about how Alicia was always bringing pictures to show them. Carlee thanked them for sending the floral blanket to drape over the casket. They said they were glad to, for they'd thought the world of her.

Then, as people are prone to do at funerals, they did not linger.

Except for one, Marcy Jemison. ''Alicia's baby is so cute,'' she said, gently patting his cheek, then holding her arms out invitingly.

Scotty promptly jerked away, growing crankier by the minute.

Carlee apologized. ''Sorry. He would normally go to you, but he's not feeling well today for some reason.''

''Well, who can blame him? It's his mother's funeral. Maybe babies sense things. Who knows? And this was such a shock. I mean, Alicia seemed tired at work lately, but heck, I've got a baby, and it's tough taking care of a kid when there's no man around. We heard that Alicia gave him to you right before she died. What are you going to do with him?''

It was a blunt question, but Carlee knew the girl meant no harm. ''Take care of him the best I can and love him like he was mine. I already feel like he is. I was there when he was born and lived with him ever since.''

''Well, I think you should make his father help. Everybody knows the creep was married, and how he dumped Alicia. I hate men like that. They have their fun and then take off, and to hell with what happens to the woman.''

''He didn't know she was pregnant when he went back

to his wife,'' Carlee said stiffly, not wanting to discuss Alicia's personal life but feeling the need to clarify the situation. ''When they met, he told her he was getting a divorce, and when he quit coming around the lounge, she figured he and his wife had probably worked things out. She never told him about the baby, because she didn't want to cause any trouble.''

Marcy frowned. ''That's what she told you?''

''Yes, and if you'll excuse me, I need to get Scotty out of this raw weather.''

''Sure. But think about what I said. If he can be found, you ought to make him pay. I wasn't working with her then, but she never would tell anybody his name.'' Her brows rose in question. ''Did she ever tell you?''

''Just his first name—Nick. She didn't like talking about him.''

''Well, that's a shame, but you know, he might not have been from around here. We get a lot of tourists at Cocoa Beach. Plus technicians from all over the country are always coming in to work at the Cape on temporary assignment, so who knows? But if it had been me, I'd sure as heck have put his feet to the fire for child support.''

Carlee agreed with Marcy but understood Alicia's reluctance. Her friend had also suffered a painful childhood. Her father had abandoned her mother and gone to live with another woman. But unlike Carlee's mother, Alicia's had been so determined to collect child support that she would go to the woman's door when payment was late and demand it. She dragged Alicia with her, and the older Alicia got, the more humiliated she felt. Then one day the woman opened the door and threw the money in her mother's face. Alicia had told Carlee, tears streaming down her face, that she would never forget the sight of her mother down on her hands and knees picking up the money from the ground.

Carlee had assured her things were different now. The father could be ordered to pay directly to the court, and if he failed to do so, the court would take care of tracking him down. But Alicia still felt that was demeaning. If a man had to be made to do something, she didn't want him.

Scotty cried all the way home, and Carlee felt as if the weight of the world was on her shoulders. She'd hardly slept a wink since Alicia's death, worrying how she was going to manage. She hadn't been to work in three days, and her manager had said she had to report tomorrow because her cosmetics counter was having a promotion and they would be extremely busy. In addition, she had used up all the absences from class that she was allowed. One more and she would be dropped from the course.

Scotty was still fretting when Carlee tried to give him his supper, but she was so exhausted it was all she could do to keep from falling asleep. Finally she gave up and put him in his crib, then phoned Fran Bremmer, the woman Alicia had swapped baby-sitting with and asked who was keeping her little girl.

"My neighbor. For twenty-five bucks a day. I can't afford that much longer. Do you want to work out a deal like I had with Alicia?" she asked hopefully.

Carlee told her she wished she could, but she had to go to work. "Do you think your neighbor could keep Scotty tomorrow? If I don't go in, I'm afraid I'll lose my job."

"I'll give you her number. You can call her and see."

Carlee was relieved when she called and the woman said she would—but only for that day. She really didn't have room for another child. Carlee was grateful but knew she would have to find time at work to call around for a baby-sitter.

Seeing Alicia's things scattered around the apartment was more than she could bear, so after moving Scotty's crib into her room, she gathered all the reminders and put them in Alicia's room, then closed the door. Later she would clean everything out, but there were too many other things to be done first.

Going over the bills spread out on the kitchen table made her sick with worry. The funeral home had said she could make payments, but there was also the pediatrician's bill. Alicia had fallen behind paying it, and Carlee wanted to take care of it in case Scotty got sick. So far he'd been a healthy baby, but there had been routine checkups and vaccinations to pay for.

Alicia hadn't left any money behind when she died. Her car, several years old, was financed and would be repossessed. A couple of credit cards were maxed out. The rent was due in a few days, and Alicia had spent her share on two recapped tires for the car and promised to make it up with her next paycheck. Carlee was pretty strapped, as well, having had to buy a battery for her old '93 Jeep. The apartment complex office would work with them but would charge a hefty late fee.

Carlee wanted to cry but knew it would only give her a headache. And that she didn't need, because it didn't look as though she was going to get any sleep tonight, either. Scotty had more or less drifted off, but every so often she could hear him fretting, making little thin, whimpering sounds. He was probably coming down with a cold—he seemed to have a stuffy nose. That could mean a trip to the doctor and a prescription. Plus, she'd be stretched thin till payday in order to pay the sitter. And what if a day-care center wanted some kind of deposit or registration fee? How could she take time off work to get Scotty to the doctor, anyway? It all seemed so hopeless.

Drowning in a pit of despair, she couldn't help but think of Scotty's father—whoever and wherever he was. If he had worked at Cape Canaveral, he undoubtedly made a good salary and could afford to help. But Alicia had been so stubborn she never once gave a hint about his identity, saying only that he was drop-dead gorgeous, and during the short time they'd been together, she'd fallen deeply in love.

"So he went back to his wifey-poo," Carlee said aloud in a voice thick with disgust. "Probably to a cozy house with a minivan and an SUV in the driveway, without a care in the world. A real selfish bastard—like all men."

Then she chided herself for being so judgmental. After all, he didn't know about Scotty. If he did, he might be willing to help with his support.

Carlee's eyes started burning, so she pushed the bills aside and went to bed. She was going to have to get up early to feed and dress Scotty. She would take him to the doctor if necessary even if it meant being late to work. As for class tomorrow night, well, maybe she could take him with her, and the instructor would understand. Finally Carlee drifted off to sleep.

The sound came from far, far away, and Carlee fought against it, wanting to sleep on and dream of happier times, like the trips to Indialantic Beach she and Alicia used to take; they'd been planning one the day Alicia died. There, seawater pooled among the coquina rock, making ideal spots for Scotty to sit and splash. They loved it there and…

It was a frightening sound, a thin, pitiful crowing. She sat up in bed and looked about wildly, trying to gather her wits. Turning on the bedside lamp, she was jolted by terror to see it was Scotty making the noises, his little arms flailing in the air as he fought for air. He was choking!

She grabbed him up, pounded on his back and then realized there was nothing stuck in his throat, and still he struggled to breathe.

Frantic, she raced to the phone and dialed 911, then paced about, fighting hysteria as she held Scotty and waited for the blessed sound of the ambulance's siren. It seemed like hours, but finally the paramedics arrived.

Never had she felt so helpless. They started him on oxygen, then loaded him into the ambulance, telling her to climb in with them. An IV line was started in his wrist, and she listened fearfully as she heard one of the paramedics radio into the emergency room that Scotty was in severe respiratory distress with a heart rate of 160.

"Please, tell me," she begged. "What's wrong with him?"

The man answered, "We won't know till we get him to the ER, ma'am. We're doing everything we can."

She watched as medications were injected into the IV line, and she wept to see how tiny and helpless Scotty looked, plastic tubes in his arms, an oxygen mask covering his nose and mouth. When the paramedics had arrived at her apartment, Scotty's face had been turning blue, but now a little color was returning, and her fear subsided, slightly.

At last they reached the hospital where a team was waiting to wheel Scotty into the trauma room. Carlee tried to follow, but she was told she had to remain outside. When she realized he was being taken into the same room his mother had died in only three days earlier, her knees buckled. Someone helped her to a chair, and when she was able, they took her to fill out the requisite admission forms.

When she was asked to give Scotty's last name, she felt a rush of panic. She didn't know what to write. How had Alicia listed him on his birth certificate? Had she named the father or used her own name—Malden? Carlee had never asked—never had reason to. Then she decided it didn't matter. Not right now, anyway. So she used her own surname and wrote Scotty *Denton*, and, on the line for parents, listed herself as mother and unknown for father.

The woman in the admissions office didn't bat an eye over that, but when she learned Carlee did not have insurance, she told her she would have to make a deposit.

Carlee only had the twenty-five dollars in her purse that she had planned on paying the baby-sitter.

The woman shook her head. "We need at least five hundred."

Carlee wrote a check and tried not to think about using most of the money she had left in the bank. The rest would barely cover the bank's service charge, and payday was not for another week.

Hurrying back to the ER, she took up her vigil once more. Finally a man wearing green scrubs, paper slippers over his shoes and a stethoscope looped around his neck came out of the trauma room. "I'm Dr. Vance. Your son is going to be fine."

Carlee bolted to her feet and burst into tears of relief. "Oh, thank God. Thank God…"

"He has croup, but we've got it under control. His heart rate is down to 120 and respiration to forty-eight. Those are good vital signs. He's also awake and alert and taking a bottle without wheezing."

"Croup." She mouthed the word. It was familiar, but she could not recall what it meant.

"It's a viral infection of the upper and lower breathing tract. It can come on suddenly, without warning, most often at night, and sometimes it's triggered by exposure to cold air."

Carlee blanched. *Cold air.* It had been damp and cold at the cemetery. She had not wanted to take him, but wanted to be able to tell him one day that he had gone to his mother's funeral. "It's my fault," she whispered, overcome with guilt. "I had him outside today. I shouldn't have."

Dr. Vance was quick to assure her, "Now, now. I said *triggered*, not caused. He already had the virus, only you didn't know it. There was no way you could have. So don't blame yourself. I deal with croup several times a night. It's one of the few diseases I can think of that can give the impression a child is going to die. Unfortunately some do, but you acted quickly and did the right thing in calling an ambulance, and now the danger is over. We're going to admit him overnight for observation, though, and keep giving him humidified oxygen and epinephrine every four hours as needed. By morning, I expect all the symptoms to be completely gone. We'll send him home with a prescription for prednisone and keep him on that for the next four days.

"You'll have a copy of his records," he continued, "so you can take them to his regular pediatrician. He's going to need a follow-up in about a week to make sure he's doing okay. I suggest you keep him inside, in bed if you can, till he's completely over this. Being weak, he doesn't need to be exposed to other children who might have another kind of infection. Just keep a close eye on him."

"I'll watch him every minute, believe me," she promised.

The door to the trauma room opened, and a nurse came out pushing Scotty in a rolling cradle. Carlee thanked the doctor and fell into step beside the nurse.

The woman smiled. "He's so cute. And such a good baby, too. You can stay with him in the pediatric unit if you like. They have recliners for parents."

Carlee wasn't about to leave Scotty's side. They'd have

to drag her out of the hospital if they tried to make her. And she didn't care about recliners. She would stand on her feet all night if necessary. She didn't want to take her eyes off him for one second.

The nurses in the pediatric unit were just as kind as the ones in the ER. They brought her a pillow and a blanket and said she should let them know if there was anything they could do to make her more comfortable.

Scotty was sleeping soundly, his breathing even and normal. Carlee watched his little chest rise and fall, and gave thanks that the worst was over. Tomorrow she would buy a book on child care and read it cover to cover so she'd be able to recognize illnesses.

Tomorrow.

She shuddered to think once again of the problems she faced.

Tomorrow she would lose her job, because there was no way she was going to leave Scotty with a sitter until he was completely well. And if she had to drop out of school, a new course wouldn't start until after it was time for her to report for work at the grove gift shop. There would be no promotion and no raise this year.

She was also going to have to tell the apartment-complex manager that since she had no job, she had no idea when the rent would be paid.

And what about the hospital bill and Scotty's medicine?

Leaning her head on the crib railing, she had never felt so alone or desperate in her life. There just didn't seem to be any solution. Asking for welfare or food stamps was out of the question, because she was afraid when it was discovered she was not yet Scotty's legal guardian, the authorities would take him away from her because of her inability to support him. He would be placed with strangers, and Carlee could almost hear Alicia crying in her grave if that happened.

Carlee was glad Scotty was in a semiprivate room. She did not want to be around anyone else. But then another baby was brought in, a little girl about Scotty's age, also recuperating from a croup attack. The parents looked as though they had been through the same traumatic experience as she had, weary and worn from the experience.

A nurse pulled the privacy curtain, but Carlee could hear the conversation between the couple.

"I'll stay with him, honey," the father was saying. "You go home and get some rest. Then you can come back and pick us up in the morning."

"Are you sure?" the mother responded, sounding doubtful. "You've got to work tomorrow."

"I can manage. I want you to feel up to taking care of Cindy and not be sleepy. So you run along."

"But tomorrow night you start that second job at the gas station."

"And I'll take a third job if that's what it takes to support you two. Now go home and go to bed, honey."

Silence. Carlee knew they were kissing. Then they said their good-nights, and the mother left.

There was a good father, Carlee thought wistfully. The kind she wished she'd had growing up. Who could say that Scotty's father wouldn't be like that if he knew he had a son?

If Alicia had told him she was pregnant, things might have been different. He might have agreed to help Alicia financially had he known about Scotty.

So maybe it was time he found out.

Carlee had reached the end of her rope and had nothing to lose by letting him know he had a son.

But first she had to find him.

Chapter Two

Carlee had never been to the Blue Moon Lounge but quickly recognized the decor Alicia had described—potted palms, ficus trees, hanging baskets of ferns and philodendron, and brilliant-colored tropical birds squawking in bamboo cages. Water trickled down a rock wall into a rock-bordered pool swimming with goldfish, and floor-to-ceiling windows offered a spectacular view of the azure sea beyond. Alicia had enjoyed working there, and had made good tips.

Carlee figured the late afternoon was a good time for her to drop by. She intended to be finished before the "happy hour" crowd arrived.

A man wearing khaki slacks and a bright floral shirt greeted her. "May I help you? I'm afraid the bar isn't open yet." He gave Scotty a questioning glance. "I hope you aren't planning on bringing him to Happy Hour."

"Oh, heavens, no! I was a close friend of Alicia Malden. This is her son, Scotty. I assume you knew her?"

"I sure did," he said, his tone instantly compassionate. "I'm Jim Martin, the manager. We all thought so much of her, and I want you to know how sorry we are. I wanted to make it to the funeral, but there was something else I couldn't get out of. I pitched in on the flowers, though, and I know that some of the girls here went."

"They did, and the flowers were beautiful. Tell me, how long did you know Alicia?" Carlee asked.

"I've only been the manager for seven months, so I knew her for that long. I thought she was nice, very hard-working." He looked puzzled. "Is there something you need from me?"

"No, because you didn't know her very long, you won't have the information I'm after. Is Marcy Jemison around?"

He motioned to glass doors opening out to a deck over-looking the beach. "She's outside taking a breather with some of the other girls before the rush starts."

She thanked him and made her way out to where Marcy was propped on a railing with two other young women, all dressed in the familiar white shorts and blue blouse that Carlee remembered Alicia wearing.

Marcy squealed with recognition and held out her arms to Scotty. This time, he went to her with a big grin.

"This is Alicia's baby," she announced to the others, whirling him around and hugging him. "Isn't he adorable?" Then to Carlee, "What brings you to the beach?"

Soberly, Carlee replied, "Our conversation at the cemetery."

Marcy's eyes went wide. "Oh, wow. That's great. So you're really going to nail the guy. Good for you."

Carlee hadn't thought of it in quite that way. All she

wanted was to ask Scotty's father to accept his responsibilities. If he refused to believe Scotty was his, then it would be a different story. She wasn't going to let another man mess with her life if she could help it. Besides, Scotty deserved the support of his father.

She turned to the other two women, who were obviously taking everything in. "Did either of you know the man Alicia was seeing?"

One shook her head and the other explained, "We've only been here a month and didn't know her very well, but we went to her funeral because we liked her."

"It was so sad," her friend added. "But we talked about it later, how tired she seemed all the time. She would sit down every chance she got, and I thought she was breathing heavy a couple of times."

If only Carlee had insisted Alicia see a doctor. *Woulda-Coulda-Shoulda,* as the taunting saying went. It was too late for regrets now.

Carlee felt her frustration growing. "Well, is there anybody working now who was here when Alicia was seeing her mystery man?"

"Bonnie Handel was," one of the girls on the railing said with a snap of her fingers. "I heard her say she's been here since the place opened four years ago. Others come and go, but not Bonnie."

"Why should she leave?" the other said with a snicker. "She's the hostess and the cashier and gets to sit on a stool behind the counter all night. She doesn't work her fanny off like we do."

Carlee, feeling a wave of excitement, cried, "Where can I find her?"

"Try looking over your shoulder," Marcy said, handing Scotty back to her.

Carlee guessed Bonnie to be in her mid-fifties. She was

attractive with silver-tinted hair and ice-blue eyes framed by shimmering turquoise shadow. The black satin blouse she was wearing with tight white slacks revealed the care she had taken of her figure through the years.

Carlee quickly introduced herself and explained why she had come.

"We can talk in the office." Bonnie led the way, and once they were inside, closed the door, leaned against the desk and flashed a big grin. "I want you to know I'm glad you're going to try and track him down. The creep deserves to have to pay through the nose for walking out on that poor girl. If it'd been me, he'd have never gotten away with it, and I told her that."

Carlee soberly agreed. "I know. I tried, too."

"She fell for him like a ton of bricks, and I can't blame her, because he was nice-looking. A real hunk. She lit up like a launch from the Cape the first night he came in. He was in her station, all by himself, and she hovered over him like you wouldn't believe. He started coming in every night, and I'd see them leave together and knew things were getting hot.

"She'd talk to me about him a little from time to time," Bonnie continued. "I'm older than the others are, and I've always been a good listener, so they come to me with their troubles sometimes. Alicia said he was married, but he was trying to get a divorce—only his wife was giving him a hard time. I told her I'd never known a married man yet who was fooling around that didn't say the exact same thing. But she said she believed he really cared about her, and even when he quit coming around, she held out hope he'd come back."

Scotty was getting heavy and starting to fret. Carlee sat down in a chair and poked his pacifier into his mouth. "How long were they together? Do you remember?"

Bonnie pursed her lips in thought, then said, "Oh, it was only a few weeks. She really fell hard and fast. It was something, all right. She totally flipped for the guy."

"And then he just disappeared," Carlee said, more to herself than Bonnie. "Maybe she was right in figuring he went back to his wife. She said she wasn't going to chase after him, that if he really loved her, he'd come back to her on his own."

"Oh, yeah, right." Bonnie rolled her eyes. "And he swore he did, too. She told me that. He said it was love at first sight, that he'd never felt like that about a woman before. He had a line, all right."

"Did she ever tell you his name?" Carlee probed hopefully. "She'd refer to him only as Nick, and once I asked her for his last name, but she wouldn't say."

"Well, she said that from the very beginning he made her promise to keep everything between them hush-hush, because if his wife found out, she'd make it that much harder for him to get the divorce. How come you're looking for him? To get him to take the baby?"

Carlee was taken aback. "No, no, of course not. I love Scotty and plan to raise him myself."

"Were you related to Alicia?"

"We were best friends, but she wanted me to have him. She signed a paper naming me guardian right before she died, and…" Carlee trailed off, embarrassed to share so much information. All she wanted was the name of Scotty's father and where to locate him. She didn't want to confide anything.

Bonnie gave a disgusted snort. "He wouldn't want him, anyhow. But since that's not what you're after, then it can only be money. Good luck there, because after he abandoned her like he did, I can't see him paying child support unless you want to take him to court. That means paternity testing, hiring a lawyer to go after him. You're talking big bucks.''

Carlee hoped it wouldn't come to that. ''I just want to find him and give him a chance to do what's right. After all, he doesn't even know he has a child and—''

''What's that you say?'' Bonnie stared at her incredulously, hands on her hips. ''I don't think I heard you right.''

Uneasily, Carlee repeated herself.

''Honey, is that what Alicia told you—that he didn't know she was pregnant?''

With a chill of foreboding, Carlee hugged Scotty a little closer. ''She said she never got a chance to tell him, because all of a sudden he just stopped coming around. And like I told you, she wanted him to come back because he loved her, not because he felt obligated, so she didn't go looking for him.''

Bonnie swung her head from side to side, laughing softly, sadly, then said, ''Boy, if pride could be bottled and swallowed, Alicia would have stayed drunk on hers. She was just too ashamed to tell you the truth—she *did* tell him she was going to have his baby, but he told her to get an abortion. They had a fight over it, right out there on that deck one night after we closed. I know, because I heard every word. It was real smoky in here that night, and I wasn't feeling good and went out to get some fresh air before checking out the register. They didn't see me in the shadows.''

Carlee felt sick. ''I...I don't believe it.''

''Believe it, honey, 'cause it's true. He told her to get an abortion, and she told him to go to hell. And that's the last anybody ever saw of him around here.''

Now she knew why Alicia had not wanted to talk about asking him for help. He'd been, in her mind, as shiftless and irresponsible as her father. And when he'd so cruelly and callously told her to have an abortion, it had been just as humiliating as when her father's lover had thrown money in her mother's face.

It all made sense now, and she was even more determined to find this guy and make him do right by Scotty. She said as much to Bonnie.

The woman nodded with understanding and allowed that she didn't blame her one bit. "The no-good creep should have to pay through the nose. I hope you do find him."

"Yeah, right," Carlee said bitterly as she stood and prepared to leave. "I don't even know his name."

"Well, I do."

She had already turned but whipped about to stare in wonder. "I thought Carlee never told you."

Bonnie smiled. "She didn't. But that doesn't mean I didn't know it. He was paying his bar tab one night and dropped his wallet. Everything fell out of it. I bent down to help him pick it all up and happened to get a look at his driver's license. His name is Nick Starke."

Carlee felt like shouting with joy. "And did you see his address—where he lives?"

"Just the town. He snatched it out of my hand like he didn't want me to see it. I thought that was funny at the time, but figured maybe he was afraid I'd find out who he was and call his wife and tell her about him cattin' around with Alicia."

"So what town? Where?" Carlee was shaking.

"I have no idea where it is, but I remember the name because it's so weird for Florida—Snow Hill."

"Snow Hill, Florida. Nick Starke." Carlee rolled the words around in her suddenly dry mouth. "Starke…" she whispered. "Starke…Groves…"

"What's that?" Bonnie asked.

But Carlee was halfway out the door. "Thank you so much, Bonnie. You've been a great help."

Carlee's head was spinning she was so excited. One day at the gift shop, her boss had been talking about all the big orange growers in the state, and now she recalled him saying that Starke Groves was one of the largest and most profitable.

He'd also said it was located in the oddly named town of Snow Hill, Florida. And if Nick Starke had anything to do with Starke Groves, he could well afford to help support his child.

The parking lot was filling up quickly as people getting off work arrived to unwind at Happy Hour. As soon as Carlee backed out of her spot, someone pulled in. Scotty let out a howl, and she realized she'd dropped his pacifier somewhere.

"Oh, baby, I'll never be able to find another parking place and go back," she told him, anxious to get home and get on with her search, now that she knew where to look and who to look for.

A voice called, "Hey, wait up a minute."

She slammed on the brakes and turned to see Bonnie running toward her, waving the pacifier.

When she reached her, she said, "I remember how my kids pitched fits when I lost theirs."

Thanking her, Carlee started to drive away, but Bonnie stopped her. "There's something else."

Carlee tensed.

"Have you thought about the possibility that Scotty's daddy might try to take him away from you once he finds out he's his?"

Carlee hadn't, but was quick to remind her that Alicia signed a paper giving Scotty to her.

Bonnie shook her head. "That doesn't mean a hill of

beans. Not if he can prove he's the father. Besides, are you the court-appointed guardian, or are you just going on the paper she signed?''

Carlee hated to admit all she had was Alicia's note.

''Well, maybe you should consider asking him to take him, anyway. You obviously can't afford to raise him yourself, or you wouldn't be trying to track the man down.''

Fiercely, Carlee fired back, ''He told Alicia to have an abortion, remember? I would never give Scotty to him.''

Bonnie sighed and leaned against the car. ''Look, I know none of this is my business, but I just like to try and keep young girls like you from making big mistakes. You try to keep Scotty on your own with the financial problems you've got, and sooner or later Child Welfare will take him away from you and stick him in a foster home. Wouldn't he be better off with his natural father if his father wants him and can take care of him?''

''If he didn't want him before he was born, he won't want him now.''

''That's not necessarily true. When a man is cheating on his wife and he finds out his girlfriend is pregnant, sometimes his first reaction is to tell her to get an abortion. He thinks it will solve all his problems. Things are different now. The baby is here, its mother is dead, and any decent man would want to take over and raise him.''

Carlee slammed her palms against the steering wheel. ''If he were a decent man, he never would have walked out on her. He'd have stood by her. So what makes you think I want somebody like that raising a baby I couldn't love more if I'd given birth to him myself?''

''Because you want the best for him.''

''And who says his father is the best?''

Bonnie shrugged. ''Not me. I'm just trying to make you

realize that whether you like it or not, Nick Starke might want Scotty, and if he does, you'll have a hard time stopping him. But on the other hand, you might be doing the best thing for Scotty. After all, Nick didn't seem like a lowlife. Sure, he breezed in, swept Alicia off her feet, then walked. But that doesn't mean he wouldn't make a good father. Think about it. And if you decide you don't want to take a chance on giving Scotty up, then leave it alone. Don't go looking for trouble.''

Carlee spent another restless night. Bonnie had given her a lot to think about. And even though she hated to admit it, as much as it would hurt to give him up, the reality was that Scotty belonged with his father if he was fit to have him. And that was where the problems began. If Nick Starke wasn't fit, she didn't want him to know Scotty was his, because she didn't want to fight him for custody. And if he was a member of the Starke Groves family, he'd have the money to hire lawyers to take him from her. As it was, she couldn't even afford to pay one to go through the necessary legal procedure of having her officially named Scotty's guardian.

So she was caught between the proverbial rock and a hard place.

The bills were mounting. She had no money coming in, and even if she went out and found a job, she would not get paid right away. And the apartment manager had let her know in no uncertain terms that if the rent wasn't paid within ten days, he would start the process to evict her.

Close to dawn, she decided to track down Nick Starke. If he were still married, he might not want his wife to know he had fathered a baby by another woman and be willing to quietly pay support and stay out of Scotty's life. On the other hand, if she checked him out and ultimately came to the conclusion he was a scoundrel, then she would not tell him about Scotty. Times might be tough, but she would manage somehow.

That morning, as soon as she got Scotty fed and bathed, she called information in Snow Hill and asked if there was a listing for Nick Starke. When told there wasn't, she asked for the number of Starke Groves.

A woman cheerily answered. Carlee took a deep breath and asked, "Does Nick Starke work there?"

"Indeed he does. He's the owner."

"The...the owner...," Carlee whispered in stunned echo. She'd thought he might be a family member, but not the actual owner.

"Would you care to leave a message? He's not here right now."

Now that she had found him, Carlee wanted to quickly learn as much as possible. "Can you tell me how to get in touch with Mrs. Starke?"

The receptionist paused, then crisply replied, "There is no Mrs. Starke."

So much for him quietly paying child support. Now to plan B, which was finding out what kind of person he was.

"I'm Elaine Streeter," the woman on the other end of the line said. "Is there anything I can do for you?"

When Carlee hesitated, not knowing what to say at that point, Elaine continued, "If you will leave your name and number, I'll have Mr. Starke call you back. But I should tell you that if this is about a job, he doesn't do the hiring. You'll have to see the grove manager, Mike Thurston. But he's not in right now, either, and he doesn't hire over the phone. You'll have to come in and fill out an application."

Carlee was surprised. "You mean you're hiring now? But the season doesn't start for months." Then she cried, "Valencias! You're harvesting Valencias." They were a late-season variety of oranges that matured from March to June, and she had often wished Ben Burns had grown them so Jupiter Groves would have stayed open longer.

"Well, isn't that why you're calling?" Elaine Streeter sounded as though she was becoming annoyed. "If not, then what—"

"Yes, yes, of course I am." It was the answer to a prayer. Working at Starke Groves would give her the opportunity she needed to find out everything she wanted to know about Nick Starke before letting him know Scotty was his.

"Good. Because we're desperate. The regular migrant workers don't show up this time of year. They've already gone to California, where they've got steady work till fall. We're short of women on the packing lines, but the pickers get paid more, if you think you're up to that."

"Of course I am." It sounded wonderful, but there was Scotty to be considered. "I have a baby that's a little over a year old. What kind of facilities do you have for child care?"

Elaine sounded pleased to tell her that they probably had the best of any grove in the state. "The Starke family has always taken care of their workers, whether year-round or migrant. We have a wonderful day-care center and one of the caretakers is even an LPN—licensed practical nurse. You won't have to worry about your baby at all. Just come on in today."

"It will be tomorrow morning. I have to pack."

Nick Starke stared at the stack of mail on his desk. He hated being inside doing paperwork, preferring to be in the groves. He enjoyed the whole process of growing fruit, from standing on a ladder and handpicking to watching the oranges roll along the assembly line for grading and stacking in boxes. He was a grower through and through and could not imagine any other kind of life.

Elaine peered through the open door to say she was going to lunch. "I'm going to Newt's place on the river. The word's out he's got fresh alligator tail. Want me to bring you a basket?"

"Do I ever." He loved the delicacy, which tasted like fried chicken but was sweeter, more succulent, and not nearly as greasy.

"Oh, by the way—some woman called this morning, and when she found out you weren't here wanted to know how she could get in touch with Mrs. Starke. I told her there was no Mrs. Starke."

He frowned. He and Gina had been divorced almost five years. He didn't even know where she was and no longer cared. It was strange that any of her friends, old or new, would try to contact her at the groves. "Did you get her name?"

"No. Actually, she was looking for a job. Maybe she thought your wife would hire her since you weren't around. I told her she'd have to talk to Mike."

"Good." He took out his wallet and gave Elaine the money for his lunch.

When she left, he leaned back in his chair, propping his feet on the edge of the desk.

Hearing that someone had asked to speak to his wife stirred up memories of Gina.

Bad memories.

He had met Gina in college, when he was attending Florida State to get a degree in agriculture. She was two years younger and studying to be a teacher, but when his father passed away right before Nick graduated, she bluntly said she wanted to marry him, quit school and help him with the family business. He was not resistant to the idea. Gina was pretty, and the sex was great. His mother had died a few years earlier, and he had not looked forward to going home to live alone.

But there was an obstacle—a painful, embarrassing secret he had kept to himself till the time he felt he should tell Gina. The sad news was that he could not father a child. Childhood mumps had left him sterile. But she said it didn't matter. They could always adopt.

And so they had married and everything had been fine—for a couple of years. Then Gina began to complain about living in a rural area. She didn't like the family home and complained it wasn't modern enough. Nick's grandfather had built it more than fifty years ago, and though it had withstood savage winds from several hurricanes, Nick agreed that maybe it was somewhat old-fashioned. So he'd given her free rein to redecorate, and she'd spent a fortune doing so, even putting in a swimming pool.

But it hadn't been enough. She was still miserable and began spending more and more time in Orlando, shopping, she said, with girlfriends from college days.

Then when they had been married about four years, Gina dropped a bombshell. She had been having an affair, had fallen in love with the man and wanted a divorce so she could marry him. Fool that he was, Nick asked her to reconsider, suggesting they go to a marriage counselor and try to work things out. Nick was not the sort of man to take marriage vows lightly.

Gina quickly dashed all his hopes and smashed his heart into little bits and pieces with the news that she was pregnant. To twist the knife, she cruelly reminded him that all the marriage counseling in the world couldn't change the fact he couldn't father a child.

At least he could be grateful Gina had not taken him to the cleaners financially. Florida was a no-fault divorce state, and, ordinarily, she would have been entitled to half of everything. But all of his assets had been premarital. They owned nothing jointly, so there had been nothing to divide. Still, she had asked for a mind-staggering sum of alimony. But when it was revealed that she was pregnant by another man, the judge had denied her.

Nick swiveled in his chair to look out the window at the rows of orange trees stretching as far as the eye could see. Perfectly straight lines like soldiers at attention.

Maybe he was a fool, but he just hadn't felt right about Gina leaving with nothing when he had so much. So he had written her a generous check, which she had snatched from his hand and walked out without a word. He hadn't heard from her or seen her since.

He had thrown himself into his work, and there had been plenty of it. Once in a while, he dated but never let things go too far. Never again did he want to feel the crushing humiliation of having a woman cut him down because of his sterility. So he tended the groves, went deep-sea fishing in his boat now and then, read a lot and told himself he was content with his life.

After all, being lonely was better than having another woman make him feel like less of a man.

Chapter Three

By the time Scotty's things were loaded into the Jeep, there was scarcely enough room for Carlee's few belongings. Alicia had worked almost up to her due date to make enough money to buy him everything she thought a baby might need. The crib had to be left behind in favor of the easier-to-pack portable crib, along with the playpen, but Carlee managed to cram in the bouncing swing he loved, along with the high chair.

She only hoped Elaine Streeter had not been exaggerating about Starke Groves' facilities for their migrant workers being so nice. It made her cringe to think of some of the conditions she had heard about—outdoor plumbing, windows with no screens, broken-down furniture and sparse appliances. Mr. Burns made a special effort to make his workers comfortable, but even he did not provide day care with an LPN in charge. That sounded too good to be true, especially when she found it hard to believe Nick

Starke cared about children in general. Knowing that he had been aware of Alicia's pregnancy all along filled Carlee with so much anger and resentment she wondered how she could even be civil to the man.

But she would manage, of course. After all, Scotty's welfare, as well as his future, was at stake here, and for his sake, she wouldn't blow it.

Give the man the benefit of the doubt, a part of her argued. Get to know him before forming an opinion.

Yeah, right, another side fired back. He was just one more selfish, self-centered man with the morals of a tomcat, possessing the same lack of conscience as her father and Alicia's father had. And, Carlee grimaced, her ex-husband, as well.

With Scotty sleeping soundly in his car seat, she headed north up Interstate 95 to Titusville, then west to the sleepy little town of Snow Hill near Lake Harney. The trip took about an hour. Very convenient for Nick Starke to drive down to Cocoa Beach to see Alicia. Had she not gotten pregnant, he'd probably still be seeing her and making her think he was still having a difficult time getting a divorce.

Several times she started to turn back, afraid she was wasting her time. After all, a man who had done what Nick Starke had was, in all likelihood, not going to turn out to be the answer to her problems. But she had nowhere else to go and couldn't have stayed where she was, not when she was being evicted. At least now she would have a job and a good place to leave Scotty while she worked.

But most of all, it was just something she felt driven to do, because she hated to see another man walk away from his moral and financial obligations.

Though she had been up before dawn, it had been almost noon before she was finally ready to leave. It felt strange not having anyone to say goodbye to. The only friend she'd had was Alicia. She did, however, take time to call Mr. Burns and let him know she was planning on returning to work for him when the season opened again. She regretted having to say she'd had to drop out of school. She told him about Scotty, and he said he understood and commended her for taking him as her own. He assured her that her old job would be waiting in the fall, and he'd also find room for her in one of his migrant cottages. She did not tell him where she was going, and he politely did not ask. There were meetings from time to time for citrus growers in the state, and he knew them all. She didn't want to chance him saying anything to Nick Starke about her. Or worse, mention how noble he thought she was to agree to raise her girlfriend's baby. Carlee intended to control any information given out about Scotty and her.

She did not have to ask for directions to Starke Groves. It was advertised on billboards all along the interstate and even more so as she drove across a bridge and into Snow Hill.

Once she turned off the main highway, a winding road led the way between lines of orange trees as far as the eye could see. At the end was a lovely two-story white frame house that looked like something out of *Gone With the Wind*, except there were towering royal palms swaying in the breeze instead of sheltering oaks.

The road curved around as she followed signs pointing the way to the office and the grove operations. Reaching a large clearing among the orange trees, she passed long, open-sided, tin-roofed structures that housed the processing belts and packing area. A paved road led in another direction, and she realized she had taken the tourists' way in.

The gift shop caught her eye. It had a garden in front,

bordered by a quaint two-foot wall made of coquina rocks with seashells embedded in concrete on top. Overhead, flowering baskets hung from a wire ceiling. There were benches and fountains, and she made mental notes to take back to Mr. Burns about how he might redecorate *his* shop.

She parked under a shady palm and took Scotty inside with her. Her first priority should have been reporting to the office, but she couldn't resist checking out the gift shop first.

It was larger and better-stocked than the one where she had worked but much of the merchandise was the same— orange marmalade, honey and candies, as well as bags of fruit that customers could take with them or have shipped anywhere in the world.

Scotty saw a stuffed teddy bar holding a tiny jar of orange honey, and he reached for it. "No, no, sweetie." She kissed his chubby little hand. "Even if I could afford it, there's nobody around here to sell it to us. Evidently they don't open this place when it's off-season."

"I'm afraid you're right. We're closed."

She whipped about to see a man standing in an open doorway to the side that she hadn't noticed. Beyond was some kind of huge storage area. Starke Groves was quite an operation, all right.

But as she focused on the man who'd spoken, everything else faded away.

He was tall and looked to be in his late twenties or early thirties. His eyes were a deep greenish blue, like the ocean above its darkest depths, and they seemed to glimmer with a focused strength. His sandy-blond hair was cropped close, the bill of his cap playfully reversed. And as he appraised her, the play of a smile on his lips revealed the dimples in his cheeks.

He was wearing white shorts, and his legs were long

and muscular. A tank top revealed bare arms and shoulders that showed he either worked out or did a lot of hard work. His dark tan glistened with perspiration, and as he turned to close the storage-room door, she couldn't help noticing he had a nice behind.

"I'm sorry," she said. "But the door was unlocked, and—"

"I know. I came in to do some inventory and forgot to lock it." He cocked his head to one side, and the smile widened, deepening the dimples she could not help finding so delightful. "Is there something I can help you with? We don't keep the shop open this time of year, but if you want some oranges, I can fix you up with some Valencias that were just picked this morning." He patted Scotty's downy head. "He's cute. How old is he?"

"Almost fourteen months. His name is Scotty."

"He's probably walking and getting into everything."

"No, he's *crawling* and into everything. He hasn't started walking yet. I think it's because he's so chubby. He tries to stand on his fat little legs and falls down."

"Give him time. He looks like he's going to be a strong little fellow." He kept looking at Scotty as he asked, "Did you want to buy some of the Valencias?"

"No, thank you. Actually I'm here to see about—" Just then Scotty's eye caught the bear again, and he strained to get closer. She pulled him back, and he started crying.

The man laughed. "He really wants that bear."

"Well, he can't have it. He'd get that honey all over him."

"Not if you don't open it." He took the bear from the shelf beneath the cash register where it had been displayed, obviously to entice the small fry as Mom and Dad paid for their other purchases. He untied the gold cord that held the little jar of honey in place and set it on the counter, then handed the bear to Scotty.

Scotty gave a delightful squeal, but it was nothing compared to his scream of protest when Carlee promptly took it away from him. "I'm sorry, but he can't have it." She had already seen the price tag and could not afford to spend twenty dollars on a toy no matter how badly he wanted it.

Scotty cried all the more loudly, kicking his legs and waving his arms in the throes of a temper tantrum. "I'm sorry," she apologized again, embarrassed. "It's time for his nap and he's cranky."

"But it's all right. He can have it as a gift."

She shook her head, not about to accept something from a stranger. "Thank you, but no." She saw the clipboard he'd been carrying and brightened. "You must be Mr. Thurston. I talked to a woman in the office—Miss Streeter—and she said you all were hiring pickers, and that's why I'm here."

"Well, we are, but—"

"I've had lots of experience working in groves," she interrupted, shifting Scotty, who had calmed down, so she could hold out her hand to shake the man's hand and introduce herself. "Mostly I worked in the gift shop, but I'd rather be a picker, because I can make more money.

"And she also said there were nice facilities for the workers," she rushed on, excited because he seemed so nice, but then so did everything else about Starke Groves so far.

"That's true. We have one- and two-bedroom cottages down by the lake, and the child-care center is air-conditioned, but—"

Again, in her enthusiasm, she cut him off. "Well, if you will point me to the office, I'll fill out my application, and as soon as I get Scotty settled in at the day care, I'll be ready to go to work. Just point me to where they're picking."

His gaze flicked over her but settled on Scotty once more, who continued to fret a little over the bear. He held out his arms for him and asked, "May I?"

Before Carlee could respond, Scotty lunged for the stranger as though aware he wanted to give him the bear.

"Oh, he's a big fellow. A fine little boy." He hugged him, then said, "I'm afraid we're through picking for the day, but you can start first thing tomorrow. We pay twelve dollars an hour, more if you're real fast."

Carlee swallowed a cry of delight. She didn't want to let on it was more money than she'd ever made before.

"We can use your husband, too, if he's looking for work."

She murmured she was not married and reached for Scotty. "I guess I'd better go fill out those papers now."

"Are you sure you won't let me give him the bear as a welcome present?"

Scotty was sniffling, which pulled at her heart. The man probably got a huge discount, so she said okay and thanked him. He handed the bear to Scotty, whose whole face lit up.

"The office is that way." He pointed to another door. "I'll be in to talk to you as soon as you give Elaine all the information she needs. Then I'll have someone take you to your cottage and show you around."

Carlee was thrilled to think how much money she would make and not have to pay rent. She would also be in a perfect position to secretly check out Mr. Nick Starke.

"We get started around six," he said, ushering her to the office door. "We don't have a lot of workers now, but there'll be somebody around to help you unload your car. I'll come by later to see if there's anything you need."

He started to say something else, but Carlee wasn't listening, quickening her pace to get into the office and start the ball rolling to put her on the payroll.

Nick Starke stared after her in somewhat of a daze. She was pretty, vivacious, energetic, and her baby boy was adorable. It was a shame that she was obviously on her own. He had seen her glance at the price tag on the bear as he came out of the storage room and how she'd winced and quickly put it back. Learning she wasn't married told him all he needed to know about her financial situation. Likely as not she wasn't getting any support from her son's father. He could tell she was trying to hide her excitement when she heard how much she would make.

Well, she'd come to the right place. Like his father and grandfather before him, Nick took pride in paying good wages for good workers. Providing much better living facilities than any other grove in the state kept the same ones coming back year after year. But Valencia season could not compete with California crops this time of year, regardless of the benefits he offered.

She had left the door to the office ajar, and he could see her at Elaine's desk, holding Scotty as he happily snuggled the teddy bear. Her chestnut-colored hair was pulled back in a ponytail, and her hazel eyes were glowing. She was wearing a stretch blouse that accented her small but shapely breasts and tiny waistline. Her khaki shorts hugged her hips and showed off her long, tanned legs. Carlee Denton, he decided, was not only pretty, but strong and spirited. Whatever life had handed her she would face, which, for the moment appeared to be raising a child alone.

Nick would try to make things as easy for her as possible, but only because of the baby. He was not about to open himself up for possible heartache again.

Not if he could help it.

He returned to the stockroom and finished the inventory, then went to the house and took a shower. He put on clean shorts and a light cotton shirt. Normally he didn't walk around in tank tops and ball caps, but there was no air-conditioning in the stockroom. So maybe it was just as well Carlee had been so enthused over her new job that he hadn't been able to get it across to her just who he was. Hopefully she wouldn't remember how sloppy he'd looked.

She was just finishing up the paperwork when he got to the office. Elaine was holding Scotty for her, bouncing him on her knees.

Carlee saw Nick and smiled. "You people are going to spoil my baby, I can see that." She turned to Elaine. "Mr. Thurston gave him that bear he refuses to let go of and wouldn't let me pay for it."

Elaine's brows lifted in surprise. "Mr. Thurston?" She laughed. "No, no, dear. This is Mr. Starke, the owner."

Carlee's hand froze. She'd been filling out the W-4 federal tax withholding form.

Mr. Starke.

Nick Starke.

The owner.

Alicia's lover who had abandoned her in her time of need.

Scotty's father who had wanted him aborted.

Hypocrite, liar and cheat.

These were the words that fired through her brain like bullets.

Her fingers began to shake, and she dropped the pen she was holding.

It fell to the floor, and Nick quickly crossed the room to pick it up for her, sharing Elaine's laugh as he did so. "I tried to tell you who I was, but you were too focused on the job to hear anything else. I'm really glad to meet you and happy you're going to be with us for a while."

He turned to Elaine. "Have you assigned them to a cottage yet? Be sure she gets one by the lake with a new air conditioner. We're in for some hot weather soon, and it will be nice for Scotty. He's a cute one, isn't he?"

Carlee wasn't listening, unable to hear beyond the roar of rage that swept her from head to toe.

Nick didn't notice. He was playing with Scotty again.

Carlee somehow managed to finish the paperwork, then gave it to Elaine, all without looking at Nick Starke. When listing her previous experience, instead of writing down Jupiter Groves, as a precaution she listed one in another part of the state that she knew had gone out of business. After all, Nick Starke might not show his true colors until she revealed the truth about Scotty. If that happened, she wanted to be able to say to hell with it, leave without warning and drop out of sight.

"Well, if you're done," he said when she handed the papers to Elaine, "I'll go with you to your cottage and make sure it's okay. You can follow in your car, and I'll carry your things in."

She tried and failed to smile or put any warmth at all in her voice as she responded, "That won't be necessary, Mr. Starke. I can find the way. I've imposed enough on you for one day. And I apologize for not giving you a chance earlier to tell me who you were."

He frowned slightly, puzzled by her sudden cool demeanor, and then decided she was just embarrassed and waved away her protest. "Nonsense. I'm glad to help. Besides, when I was on my way over here from the house, I saw the other workers leaving. Today is payday, and they always head for town.''

He took Scotty from Elaine, and Carlee bit her tongue to keep from protesting. He was just showing off as people did around babies, thinking it made them look so wonderful. And as she watched him, she ached to scream that he was cooing over the very baby he hadn't wanted.

Yielding to sudden impulse, she asked, ''Mr. Starke, how many children do you have?''

And was it her imagination, or did he wince ever so slightly as he turned his head before woodenly answering, ''I don't have any.''

She fell into step behind him as he carried Scotty outside into the warm Florida sun. ''Well, maybe you will one day,'' she said breezily, congratulating herself on recovering so quickly from the shock of discovering who he was. ''I'll bet you and your wife want to fill that big house with kids.''

''I'm not married.''

''Oh.'' She managed to sound surprised. ''A bachelor? You've never even been married?''

They reached her car, and he opened the door, then handed Scotty to her to buckle in the car seat. ''I was once. I'm divorced.''

''I'm sorry,'' she said, managing to sound sincere.

''It's all right. It was a long time ago.''

Longer than twenty-two months? she burned to ask. Because that was when he had been romancing Alicia while claiming to be going through a divorce.

She decided it was necessary to be downright nosy. ''So how long has it been?'' Then, because he gave her a strange look, she went on to explain, ''I only ask because I'm wondering about myself. I mean, I haven't been divorced very long, and I was wondering, you know, how long before you really get over it.''

"For me it's been five years, but I learned right away that life goes on, and you have no choice but to not look back.''

Carlee finished buckling Scotty in, glad that Nick had walked away to get in his own car, because right then she felt like slapping his face, dimpled grin and all.

Now she despised him all the more to know he had been divorced when he met Alicia. He had lied so he could tap-dance around any notion she might have had about getting married. He was nothing but a rich playboy, out to have a good time, use women till he tired of them—or got them pregnant—then move on to new conquests.

But despite her dislike of the man, Carlee could understand why Alicia had fallen for him so hard and so fast. He was not only attractive, he was smooth as French silk. He cleaned up good, too. When she met him in the gift shop, he'd been appealing in a rugged sort of way. Then later, in the office, when she was finally able to look at him through her red haze of fury, he was pure eye candy.

He led the way down a gravel road in an old Volkswagen that had been converted into a kind of beach buggy. Carlee sneered to think he probably kept a Porsche or two locked in his garage.

As she followed close behind him, she could relax a little; she didn't have to worry that he might put up a fight about paying child support. He could easily afford it, plus she had seen the Chamber of Commerce plaques on the office walls, along with plaques for contributions to the community. There were also a few trophies for a Little League softball team that Starke Groves apparently sponsored. He would definitely not want to risk a scandal. And once paternity was established, he would quietly do his duty.

Scotty was making happy noises as he chewed on the teddy bear's ear. Carlee wanted nothing more than to toss the toy out the window. But that would be immature and silly of her. Besides, she had to try to keep an open mind regarding Nick Starke. So she would hide her resentment of him and do what she had come to do.

Nick kept glancing in the rearview mirror. There was something puzzling about Carlee Denton. One moment she seemed friendly, but the next she was cold as ice. And then there were those personal questions. Normally all workers cared about was how much money they would be making and for how long. They didn't care about him or his life. But he reasoned that Carlee was not the typical migrant worker he was used to being around, because something told him she was smart and ambitious, and picking oranges was not going to be her life's work.

She had mentioned being recently divorced. She was probably spinning her wheels, passing time, till she decided what direction she wanted to go in her life.

It saddened him to see someone in her situation, especially with a child, and wondered where her ex-husband was and whether he kept in touch to see his boy. God knows, if he'd had one with Gina, he would never have relinquished his rights as a father. Maybe some men could just walk away and never look back, but not him. And he didn't like to think it was only because he couldn't have a child of his own when he wanted one so badly. It was just the right thing for a man to do.

He parked the beach buggy next to an empty cottage that had recently been painted and a new air conditioner installed. While Carlee was getting Scotty out of her car,

Nick went inside to make sure everything was as it should be. The same migrants returned year after year because the facilities and pay were the best to be had in the citrus-picking industry. They appreciated that fact and took care of things, so there was little maintenance to be done off-season. But some of the buildings were getting old, and refurbishment was needed.

He walked through the cottage and by the time he returned to the porch, Carlee was coming up the steps. "There's a slight smell of paint left, but I opened all the windows to let some fresh air in. Come on, I'll give you a tour."

Again he held out his arms to Scotty, who went to him eagerly.

Carlee pasted on a smile as though pleased he was so fond of her child.

"It's small but comfortable," Nick said as they stood in the tiny living room. There was a sofa that folded out into a bed, an upholstered chair and a television with rabbit ears. "The reception is pretty good from Orlando. I wish we had cable back here, but it would be too expensive, and nobody really has time to watch TV when we're working the regular season."

He led her through the other rooms. The kitchen had a table and four chairs, a small refrigerator and stove. There were twin beds and a dresser in one bedroom, and a double bed and chest in the other. "I can have the furniture moved out of the one where you want to set up Scotty's crib."

"He doesn't have a crib. Just a portable one, and it's small. It can go next to my bed."

"Well, we can get him a crib. Someone left one behind last season and—"

"No. Don't trouble yourself. We won't be here but a few months. We can get by. But thanks, again."

"Well, okay, it's up to you. I'll go get your things."

Again she was quick to protest. "I'd rather do it myself, really. I packed the car and know where everything is."

"If you're sure…"

She nodded. "I'm sure."

He did not insist. Her puzzling wariness had returned. Maybe she was uncomfortable accepting help from her employer.

He left her after saying he'd stop by later to see if she needed anything. That was met with yet another wooden *thanks-but-no-thanks*.

As he drove back to the office, Nick decided maybe Carlee Denton was just an independent sort, determined to make it on her own and didn't want anything smacking of pity or charity. After all, she hadn't wanted to accept the teddy bear as a gift for Scotty.

Scotty.

Nick really liked that little boy, even though holding him, feeling his chubby little arms around his neck, made him sad to think that he'd never have a son of his own. But maybe one day, with the right woman, he could adopt, and—

Forget it, a voice within warned. *You've been there, done that. And the bad memories are like a souvenir T-shirt wrapped around your heart.*

"Well, how did she like the cottage?" Elaine asked when he walked into the office.

"She seemed to like it. She didn't have much to say. I think she's tired. The little boy's sure cute. How's the day care doing, by the way?"

"I think there's six children there now, enough to keep it operating."

He gave her an incredulous look. "We'd have to keep it open even if there was only one child, Elaine. Migrants know they can always depend on having good care for their children here.''

''I know. It just seems expensive sometimes during Valencia season when there aren't many herc.''

''Well, regardless, we're keeping it open. Anything important in the mail?''

''No, but the Sheriff's Department in Brevard County finally got around to sending back your wallet and credit cards they retrieved from the guy who stole them.'' She handed him a large brown envelope.

Amazed at how long it had taken, he dumped the contents on the desk. There wasn't much. Just the wallet, his driver's license and a couple of credit cards. Things he had replaced right after the theft.

Elaine said, ''There's also a letter apologizing for the delay. How long has it been? Two years?''

''Almost. I was at that Growers' Association meeting in Cocoa Beach they have every year in June.'' He frowned to remember. ''The guy that picked my pocket sure had a good time using my credit cards till I could get all the companies notified and put a stop to it.''

Elaine nodded to recall. ''It was sad what happened to him, though.''

Nick put everything back in the envelope. ''Yes, it was.''

He went into his office and tossed the envelope on top of a file cabinet. He had some paperwork to catch up on and then later he wanted to make sure Carlee had settled in all right. Maybe if Scotty wasn't napping, she would let him take him down to the lake to see the ducks.

And even though every instinct told him to back off, Nick knew he also wanted to see Carlee again.

Chapter Four

Carlee braked to a stop in front of the day-care center. She had overslept and was running late. Nick had said they started work at 6 a.m., and it was almost that now.

A young woman who looked to be the same age as Carlee saw her from a window and was waiting when she carried Scotty to the door.

"Hi, I'm Becky Ivy. You have to be Carlee Denton, and you—" she caught Scotty's little hand and kissed it "—must be Scotty. I am so glad to meet you and your mommy."

"And we're both happy to meet you, Becky." Carlee followed her inside and looked about. It was a very nice room, decorated in blue, white and yellow with cheery animal-print curtains hanging at the windows. There were little tables and chairs, playpens and cribs, and sleeping pallets stacked in a corner awaiting nap times. Toys of every description and suitable for different age groups were arranged neatly on shelves or spilling out of wooden chests.

Becky explained, ''We have a kitchen where we prepare snacks and lunches, two bathrooms, and two small rooms in case a child is sick and needs extra attention. I have a girl who comes in around lunchtime to help me. We don't have a full house now, as you can see.'' She indicated two boys and a girl playing in a corner. They looked to be about two or three. ''If we did, there would be an attendant for every five children. Mr. Starke's rules.''

Carlee was satisfied that the facilities were as nice as she'd expected. She also liked Becky. She was neatly dressed in Bermuda shorts, a crisp white blouse and a blue smock appliquéd with dancing bunnies. She was friendly, cheerful and seemed very mature and capable.

As if she could tell Carlee was sizing her up, Becky volunteered, ''I'm a licensed practical nurse, and I studied child development at Florida State for a few years before deciding to go into nursing. Only, I found once I had my license, I missed being around children. I was lucky enough to get this job, and I can assure you that you don't have to worry about leaving Scotty with me.''

''No, no, of course not.'' Carlee didn't want her thinking she was overprotective. She was just worried that being left with a stranger was going to upset Scotty. Other than Fran Bremmer, she and Alicia were the only ones who had ever looked after him, and now he was clinging to her tightly and staring at Becky with fearful eyes.

''Come on,'' Becky said. ''I'll show you around.''

Carlee decided that perhaps Scotty would calm down if she didn't leave right away.

At Becky's suggestion, she put him in a playpen with some toys, which instantly caught his attention.

"Is there anything I need to know?" Becky asked. "Is he allergic to anything?"

"Not that I know of." Carlee showed her the bottles of formula in his diaper bag. "He's really a good baby. You shouldn't have any trouble, but if you do, I guess you'll know where to find me."

"Sure. I can call the office, and they'll send for you, but don't worry. He's going to be just fine, and after you leave I'll see if he wants to play with the other toddlers."

Carlee told her he would probably be better off in the playpen. "He hasn't started walking yet. I think it's because he's so chubby." She felt a stab of sorrow to remember Alicia saying that the day she died. "He can't even stand alone for more than a few seconds."

"Well, don't be concerned about it. One of these days you'll come in from work and find him running all over the place."

Carlee remembered Alicia saying she wanted to be there when Scotty took his first steps, and now Carlee knew how she felt.

"Come on. Let's take the tour. It won't take long." She led the way through the kitchen with its gleaming countertops and the very latest in appliances. The two private nurseries were cozy and clean, as were the bathrooms.

Becky motioned Carlee to follow her out a side door where the other toddlers were playing. "As you can see, we have every imaginable kind of play equipment. Mr. Starke insists on the best."

Thinking she might be able to find out more about Nick from Becky, Carlee asked, "How long have you been here?"

"Almost a year."

"And you like everything about it? Including Mr. Starke?"

''Oh, yes. The pay is good, and the working conditions are great. And Mr. Starke is wonderful. Nice-looking, too, isn't he?'' Her eyes twinkled. ''Too bad I'm married, but then, I've heard he doesn't date much. Now and then he might take someone to a charity benefit dance in Orlando. The family has always been involved in things like that, but he's a workaholic. With him, it's all about the groves.''

''Strange. You'd think with his money and position in the community he'd be having parties all the time.''

''Well, I think when he was married his wife threw a lot of parties. At least that's what I've heard.'' Becky flashed a teasing grin. ''Why do you ask? Aren't you married?'' Her gaze lowered to Carlee's ring finger.

Carlee glanced about the yard, suddenly self-conscious. ''No, I'm not, and I was only curious about Mr. Starke since I'll be working for him. I'm certainly not interested in him. He's not my type.''

''Oh. Well, you probably won't see much of him. Mike Thurston is the foreman, and he's real nice. I met him at the end-of-season picnic a couple of months ago.'' She turned and headed back inside. ''I'd better get back to the kids.''

''And I'd better get to work and leave you to yours.'' Carlee went to the playpen and leaned down to kiss the top of Scotty's head. Engrossed in his toy, he paid her no mind. ''So much for him crying when I leave,'' she said, laughing.

Becky picked up his arm as Carlee walked away. ''Wave to Mommy, honey. Tell her bye-bye.''

Mommy. It still sounded strange whenever anyone called her that. But she would get used to it, just as she was becoming accustomed to having total care of Scotty. Sure, she had helped Alicia from the beginning, but that wasn't the same as being the primary caregiver. It felt more natural though, with every passing day. And she liked it.

No, she loved it, loved Scotty, despite worrying about money and what the future held.

But she was starting to feel better about things. Before leaving home, she had called the school and was told she could pick up where she left off in the fall. Her old job would be waiting, and by the time she left Starke Groves, she hoped to have a good handle on her finances, especially if she was ultimately able to persuade Nick to help with child support. Regardless of how she felt about him personally, so far he didn't seem to be mean-spirited. Perhaps he would listen to reason and be willing to help if she took Scotty and left without making a scene that would tarnish his family name.

She looked at her watch. It was almost six-thirty. Being late would not make a good first impression, but she would assure him it was not going to be a habit. Settling Scotty in on his first day was surely an acceptable reason.

No one was in the office. In fact, no one was anywhere around. The open tractor-trailers she had seen parked under nearby sheds the day before were gone. Elaine would not be in until probably nine o'clock, so she couldn't ask where they were all working.

Standing in the middle of the road, she turned in every direction, but all she could see were the long rows of orange trees, stretching as far as the eye could see. She had no idea which way to go and was leery of taking off to search because she could get lost out there, the place was so darn big.

Hope surged when she heard the sound of a car approaching. She ran to the corner of the building to look around, then groaned to see it was Nick. He was the last person she wanted to encounter right then, even if it meant the day wasn't lost, after all.

He eased the beach buggy to a stop beside her. "Good morning, sleepyhead. When I say we start at six, I mean six in the morning. Not the evening."

The dimples were showing. He was smiling. So she knew he wasn't angry. Just amused. But that didn't make her feel any better. "I'm sorry. I'm afraid I took too much time looking around the day-care center."

"I understand, but the trucks always leave promptly at six. Get in, and I'll take you to where they're working."

As they drove, he explained that in the future she would probably know where picking was going on. "But if you miss the trucks it might be a heck of a long hike. I've got over two thousand acres of trees, and the Valencias are way in the back."

She was impressed, having heard Starke was among the biggest but she'd had no idea just how big.

"Well, I don't plan to be late again. Besides, I don't like to think of losing pay wandering around looking for everybody."

As they bumped along between the orange trees, he wanted to know how she liked the day-care center. "Or, more importantly, how did Scotty like it?"

"He seemed to settle right in." Nick had a friendly way about him that made him easy to talk to, and she found herself chatting away despite her secret loathing for him. "The center is really nice, and I liked Becky, too. I don't think I have to worry about leaving him with her."

"No, you don't. She was carefully screened, has terrific references, and I've never had a complaint about her."

Carlee tried not to think about what a nice profile he had or the strength in his hands as he gripped the wheel to steer around a hole in the road. His every movement was effortless, and he exuded confidence.

Remembering it was her turn to speak, she murmured, "It's commendable that you provide such good care for the children, Mr. Starke."

"Oh, please." He laughed and let go of the wheel to throw up a hand. "Call me Nick. I intend to call you Carlee—if that's okay."

"Sure. That's fine with me." The friendlier terms they were on, the easier it would be for her to get to know him.

"So you've picked oranges before?"

"That's right. Down the coast a ways." It was not a total lie. She had gone out into the orchard one day with Ben to handpick some really nice oranges for a gift basket a special customer had ordered.

"And you don't mind climbing up and down ladders all day? I have to say I was surprised you wanted a job picking. Most women would rather work in processing and packing. I've got six women there for the Valencias. I could use another."

"No," she said firmly. "I'll make more money out here."

"It's hard work," he warned. "If you change your mind…"

"I won't." She took a deep breath to drink in the sweetness as they drove by trees in bloom. "I don't think there's a sweeter smell in the world than orange blossoms."

"Those are the Hamlins and the Parson Browns. They'll mature from October through January, but I guess you know that."

"Right. Those are the early varieties. But what about mid-season oranges like pineapple oranges? Don't you grow those, as well?"

"No. We concentrate on the Hamlins and Parson

Browns because we probably transport over fifty tons of oranges a day during full season to juice-processing plants. That's our profit. The Valencias are gravy. We bag them and send them to wholesalers who then turn around and sell to retail outlets.''

Carlee's thoughts were straying again, this time to the way his T-shirt stretched across his broad chest and shoulders. He was wearing shorts again, and she tried not to look at his rock-hard thighs. She understood how Alicia had fallen for him so easily. He was handsome and charming, and she could well imagine how irresistible he would be if he tried to seduce a woman.

Suddenly she asked, ''Do you ever go to the beach? Like Cocoa Beach, maybe? It's so pretty there. I was thinking about going to work there at the Indian River Groves. But then I heard Starke was hiring and how it was a good place for migrants and their children,'' she added the lie.

''As a matter of fact I do. There's a Growers' Association meeting held there every year. I really like the area. It's pretty. I haven't missed going since I took over the business after my father died.''

Bitterness flashed. How very convenient. She wondered where he'd hung out the last time he'd gone and whether he'd left yet another woman heartbroken and pregnant. ''What about the rest of your family?''

''It's just me. My mother passed away before my father. I don't have any brothers and sisters.''

''So you're all alone since your divorce?''

He threw her a wry grin. ''Looking back, I think I was alone when I was married. At least it felt that way. How about you? Any family?''

''My mother is somewhere in California. I haven't heard from her in years. It's just me and Scotty.''

"Well, what more could you ask for?" he cast her a mock incredulous glance. "He's all boy, too, I can tell. I came by to see you yesterday evening, by the way. I wanted to check on whether you needed anything and was going to ask if I could take Scotty down to the lake to see the ducks, but your car was gone."

"I found my way into town to get a few things I needed." She was glad she had missed him. Being around him from time to time while working and casually asking other workers about him would tell her what she needed to know. She did not want him coming around the cottage. Nor did she like being with him in a one-on-one situation, as she was now. After all, she was no fool when it came to men, and she was aware of how he looked at her sometimes. The man was a womanizer. No doubt that was why his wife divorced him. She had probably caught him running around and hit him for huge alimony, and as a result he had sworn off marriage. Instead, he would consider women a buffet—enjoy as much as he wanted, sample all the varieties, and then go his merry way.

But not with her, he wouldn't. Oh, no. She would hold him at bay and wait until the last minute to inform him he'd left Alicia with a souvenir of their love affair. The Valencia season would last till the end of June or first of July, and she intended to stay till it did.

"Well, would it be all right if I came by this evening?"

She snapped her head around to stare at him, wondering how to gracefully decline, then explained she had planned to put Scotty to bed early. "And I intend to turn in early myself so I won't be late tomorrow."

"It wouldn't take long," he persisted. "We've got some really pretty ducks down there. I even bought a pair of swans. Besides, it would give you a chance to unwind and catch your breath while I take him, unless you'd like to go with us.''

Realizing he would not be easily dissuaded, Carlee took a blunt approach. ''To be honest, I want to spend as much time with him as I can myself when I'm not working. So I'll take him down and show him the ducks first chance I get. But thanks, anyway.

''Now tell me,'' she continued, wanting to change the subject, ''how many hours a day can I expect to work? I want as many as possible.''

There it was again. One moment she acted interested in him, asking about his family. But the second he offered to do something for her…for Scotty, it was as if a wall sprang up between them.

''I really need the money,'' she said when he didn't respond. ''So I'm willing to work as long as possible.''

''It depends on how much fruit is ready.'' He felt rather chilled himself. ''But I'd say no more than six hours a day. Not everybody wants to work till they drop, Carlee.''

''I didn't mean to imply—''

He cut her off. ''The oranges have to ripen on the tree. They don't ripen once they're picked. Besides, I don't like workers getting exhausted, regardless of how much is ready. So I'm afraid you'll have to content yourself with the way we're used to doing things around here.''

He didn't mean to sound so huffy, and cutting her a quick glance, he could see she was annoyed, as well as embarrassed. He was wrong to have been so short with her, but he was not about to apologize, not when she seemed to have something against him while trying to pick him apart personally.

Something told him to be the wary one. Yet he found

himself helplessly attracted to her. He also thought her son was adorable and couldn't help wanting to be around him.

Hers was a sad situation—no money, no husband and a baby to raise. Nick wanted to do what he could to help because it was his nature. He enjoyed helping people and he liked children.

And he could like Carlee Denton, too—a lot—if only she would let him.

He turned at the same exact instant as she, and they both spoke at once.

"I'm sorry…"

They laughed to realize they were both trying to apologize at the same time, and Nick said, "You haven't done anything. I'm the one who was being cranky. I guess I got up on the wrong side of the bed this morning."

"No, I was being rude when you offered to do something nice for Scotty." Carlee had realized she was going about things all wrong. If he wanted to use Scotty to try to make a move on her, then let him. She didn't want to turn him away completely. After all, it would be nice if they became friends. It would make things much easier in the long run.

"But I had no right to impose on your privacy." He had never done anything like that before with one of his female employees, but then he'd never been so attracted to one, either. "And as for your being late, it's fine, really. After all, you're getting paid by the hour, and if something happens so that you can't show up on time, it's just money you won't be making. I can certainly understand that with a baby things will come up sometimes you can't help, and you'll need to be with him."

She thanked him, then in the awkward silence that followed, said, "Look, I mean it. If you'd like to come by later, it's okay."

"Maybe when you've had a chance to settle in. Besides, you're going to be tired at the end of the day. You won't want anybody coming around to visit your baby."

He was feeling rather stupid. A grown man wanting to visit a baby he had only seen for the first time a day ago. Still, he was cute, and Nick liked kids, but he needed to slow down.

He also had to wrestle with emotions churning within that he didn't like having—emotions he'd promised himself he wouldn't have for any woman ever again. Maybe it wasn't Scotty he wanted to see, after all. He was just trying to make himself believe that so he wouldn't have to admit it was Carlee.

Time to back off, buddy, before you come any closer.

"There they are," he said, relieved they had reached the pickers and the trucks. "Come on and I'll introduce you to Mike."

She quickly got out of the beach buggy and walked with him to where a tall, heavyset man was talking to some workers. He had a craggy face, his skin leathery from too many years' exposure to the sun. Now he wore a hat that shaded his eyes and a long-sleeved shirt, despite the early-morning heat.

Nick made the introductions, and Mike Thurston raked Carlee with an appreciative, yet respectful gaze before saying, "You mean to tell me a pretty young thing like you wants to climb up and down ladders picking oranges in this heat?" He turned back to Nick. "How come she's not in the packing plant?"

"She wants to make the extra money. Besides, she's had experience picking, so she knows what she's doing."

"Well, I hope so," Mike said. "I rode up and down the rows early this morning, and the Valencias in this section seemed to have ripened overnight. We need to get all of them picked today, because the temperature is going way up this afternoon, and they'll spoil. I promised everybody a bonus for each sack they pick over their quota."

"Quota?" Carlee echoed.

Mike heard her. "Yes, little lady. Quota. Didn't you have one where you worked before?"

"Uh, sure," she said, rubbing her hands together, nervously. She'd told herself there was nothing difficult about picking oranges, so it didn't matter that she'd fibbed about having experience. Now they were talking about things she didn't know about—like *quotas*.

"So what was yours?" Mike wanted to know.

Just then one of the women nearby yelled out, "Probably not the five bushels an hour you expect of us."

Others laughed, and Mike grinned as he called back, "Luanne, you know darn well most groves ask for six. You're just lazy."

"Hey, I'm the best you got."

Carlee seized the lighthearted moment to try to bluff. "Five was what we had, too. But if we didn't make it, our pay wasn't cut," she ventured to add.

"Well, of course not," Mike said, obviously surprised she would even suggest such a thing. "Quotas are just incentives to let workers know what we expect. But we offer bonuses when we're pushed for time. Like today."

He turned to Nick. "I've never heard of anybody docking somebody's pay for not making quota, have you?" Without waiting for a response, he walked away, shouting to a worker that he needed to reset his ladder in harder ground.

Carlee said, "Well, I guess I'd better get busy. Everyone is way ahead of me."

She could feel Nick's eyes on her and wondered if she had made him suspicious. After all, she probably hadn't picked more than a couple dozen oranges in her life. Then she decided she was just overly sensitive, because of her real motive for being there.

That, plus the way she felt every time he came near.

She was supposed to feel loathing, not experience a warm rush as she had when she stumbled and he'd caught her arm as they were walking toward Mike. And if she didn't get hold of herself, the next few months were going to seem like years of endless misery.

What was wrong with her? she silently grumbled as she took one of the short wooden ladders from the truck along with a canvas pick sack. She was burned out on men in general, and here she was having hot fantasies over the very one she'd like to ram with the ladder. But she defended her weakness with the reasoning that Nick was good at turning on women. He calculated every move, every word he spoke, and knew just when to flash those dimples.

The ladder was light but clumsy to carry; yet she struggled along to go beyond the other pickers—and also to distance herself from Nick and Mike as much as possible.

Setting the ladder was not as easy as she'd thought it would be. The ground was soft, and the legs kept sinking, but finally she got it right. Then she positioned the sack beneath her and proceeded to climb as high as she could, her head poked into the thick, leafy branches and the fat, sweet-smelling Valencias.

When she dropped her first one into the sack, she groaned to hear it hit with a thud and a squish. For Pete's sake, was she supposed to run up and down the ladder with one or two oranges at a time to keep them from bruising or busting? At that rate, she wouldn't be able to pick a bushel in a day.

She came down a few rungs and ducked her head beneath the branches to check out what the other pickers were doing and saw that they were all wearing a kind of apron with huge pockets. As they picked the oranges, they would stuff them into the pockets, and when they were filled they came down the ladder and carefully emptied them into their basket. Then they scurried back up to begin again.

She had to have an apron and dreaded going back to ask for one, because it was something she should have known about.

Okay, so she would wing it. She'd say she had forgotten her apron because she was running late that morning and needed to borrow one. Simple. Easy. Nothing to worry about.

She climbed down the ladder, but in her haste failed to notice Nick standing there and bumped right into him.

He looked from her to the ruined orange in the basket, then displayed those delicious dimples with a slow, teasing grin. "Looks like Miss Sleepyhead forgot she wasn't wearing an apron."

"I...I guess I'm not a morning person," she stammered. "I'm sorry."

"It's your first day, Carlee. Don't worry about it. Here, take mine." He took off his apron and put it around her waist. "Let me tie it for you."

She turned around quickly so he wouldn't see her face, sure that her cheeks were flaming red.

He tied the apron strings into a bow. "There," he said, stepping back. "Now you have no excuses for using my oranges like bombs."

She had to laugh, despite feeling like a fool. "Thanks. Now I really do have to work hard to catch up."

She scurried back up the ladder and did not look back, though she yearned to do so.

And was it her imagination, she wondered dizzily as she began to pluck the oranges and carefully place them in the apron pockets, or had his hands really been shaking a little when he tied the bow at her waist?

Chapter Five

As always, Nick had joined in to work alongside the other pickers for a while. He preferred being outdoors in the fresh air, instead of cooped up at his desk, and escaped to the groves every chance he got. Though Elaine was excellent at her job, he still had plenty to do in order to keep on top of things. After all, he was the sole owner. So even though he was tired from working in the heat and sun, he still had to spend time in his office before he could call it quits for the day.

He could not recall a time when he had ever thought about any other kind of life. Raised around oranges, he probably knew enough about growing them by the time he got out of high school without the need to go on to college to study agriculture. But his father had insisted, saying an education was something no one could ever take away from him. And if, God forbid, anything ever happened and growing citrus was no longer profitable, then he could find a job doing something else.

Nick felt secure about the groves, and while he wasn't super-rich, he supposed he could hobnob with Palm Beach society if he wanted to. But he didn't. Though he liked fishing and boating, he avoided the party scene, because basically he was a homebody. And some people might say he was downright boring.

Like Gina.

Laying paperwork aside, he leaned back in his chair and let his mind wander into the past. He never liked to go there, but Carlee Denton and her fatherless son reminded him that he had missed out on so much in life.

Not that he was ungrateful for what he did have. Far from it. He was happy with his work and gave thanks for good health. Things could have been so much worse, so never, not even for one second, did he curse fate. It just seemed that some of the simple joys of life were missing.

Like a family.

He tried to focus once more on the task at hand, which was checking the payroll records for the month before Elaine sent them off to the accountant.

It was no use. He couldn't concentrate.

Tossing his pencil aside, he got up and began to pace about the office, finally slumping down on the leather sofa.

Which also reminded him of Gina.

He had been happy with the way the office was furnished before they married. It had been good enough for his father and grandfather before him. Simple sofa, chair, conference table and a few bookshelves. But Gina, always insisting on the best of everything, hadn't liked it, saying it was old-fashioned and drab. She'd called in a decorator, and now the furniture was all leather, and expensive artwork hung on the walls, which she'd had painted a rich green, elegant drapes at the windows. Berber carpet covered the floor, and in one corner was a wet bar with a small refrigerator beneath.

But thoughts of Gina did not pull at his heartstrings and had not done so for a long time. Sometimes he wondered what he was working for. Having no siblings meant no nieces and nephews. He had an aunt in California he hadn't heard from in years and didn't even know if she was still alive. So after the divorce, he'd had his lawyer change his will directing that upon his death all his property would be sold and the profits used to help build a new hospital to be named after his family.

There were times when he thought maybe he should just go ahead and sell off everything, buy a yacht big enough to travel around the world and spend all his time fishing and sailing. Yet, when it came right down to it, he could not bring himself to do it.

Nick had not felt this depressed in a long time, and he was pretty sure of the reason.

Carlee Denton.

Not only did the sight of her set his pulses racing, but seeing her with her little boy reminded him of what he didn't have, which was a family—someone to love and belong to.

He found himself wondering about Scotty's father, where he was and whether Carlee was still in love with him.

He was also nonplussed over her chameleonlike demeanor.

And did he imagine it or did she sometimes look at him as if she despised him?

No, that was silly. She had no reason to have anything against him, unless her marriage breakup had left her so embittered that she hated all men.

He supposed he should avoid her. After all, he had never tried to get involved with any of the single female workers that came along, though he had found a few attractive. He just felt it was best. He hated to seem snobbish, but they did not share similar backgrounds or interests. However, with Carlee, it was different. Something told him she would be at ease in any social situation.

Going back to his desk and sitting down once more, he found his eye caught by a cream-colored envelope. His name was written in elegant calligraphy, and he opened it to find an invitation to the annual Children's Charity Ball in Orlando. He was a benefactor and a member of the executive board, but he had forgotten all about the event. His presence was expected, but he never liked attending, because he had to find a date. Going alone made him feel awkward. Plus, he was a target for every woman there who had an unmarried niece or granddaughter. They wanted to fix him up, and Nick didn't want to be fixed.

The damn mumps had done that.

Elaine had left the forms on the desk for the new hirees, and Carlee's name leaped out at him.

He smiled to think of her again and suddenly thought what a sensation she would make at the ball. As good-looking as she was in work clothes, he could imagine what a knockout she would be in a formal gown.

Forget it, a voice within warned. When it came right down to it, she would react the same as Gina if he told her about his sterility. He had seen right away how Carlee was with her baby—loving, protective, putting him before herself in any situation. Like now. She was probably exhausted from climbing up and down her ladder all day, but was, no doubt, taking Scotty down to the lake to see the ducks.

She probably wanted lots of kids.

And he couldn't give them to her.

So it was best he keep his distance when it came to romance.

A welcome knock on the door pulled him from his miserable musings. He looked at his watch. It was nearly six. Everybody should have left hours ago. "Come in. It's open."

He blinked in surprise to see Mike, his shirt smeared with grease just like his weary-looking face. "What happened to you?"

"Okay to sit down dirty as I am?" Mike looked wistfully at one of the comfy leather chairs.

"Of course. Let me get you a beer." Nick went to the refrigerator and brought out a frosty can, popped the top and handed it to him.

Mike took a long swallow before describing how he'd had to work on a tractor-trailer that had broken down, because there wasn't time to call anyone out from town. "It was loaded with about forty-five thousand pounds of oranges, which I knew couldn't sit there overnight. Man, am I glad I had experience in the motor pool when I was in the army, though I'm afraid I never learned how to keep from looking like a walking grease spot when I finished."

Mike was a good man, and Nick considered him his most valued employee, which was why he paid him top wages. "So how did we do today? Did anybody go over quota?"

"A couple of the guys went a few sacks over, and I'm satisfied we got all the oranges that were ready. But there's something I need to talk to you about."

Nick saw Mike frown. "Go on."

"It's that new female picker."

"Carlee Denton?" It was Nick's turn to frown. "What about her? She sure seemed eager to work."

"She's eager, all right, but the fact is, I don't think that little lady ever climbed up inside an orange tree until today. She did good to fill one sack in an hour. Twice she fell. The last time she sprained her ankle and I sent her home. It was almost quittin' time, anyway.

"And you should've seen her hands," he went on with a disgusted shake of his head. "Blisters like you wouldn't believe. I told her if she didn't decide to call it quits and showed up tomorrow, she'd have to wear gloves. But I bet she's packing as we speak and ready to get the hell out of Dodge. Nick, I swear, I don't think she's ever worked in a grove before. What on earth made her want to try?"

"Money," Nick said curtly. "She's obviously hurting financially, and when I told her how much pickers make, she didn't want any part of the packing department."

Mike snickered. "Well, I'll wager she doesn't want any part of picking after today."

"I'll check on her, and if she decides to give it another try, be patient, okay? She'll get the hang of it sooner or later."

"Maybe, but how long do you want to keep paying her the same rate everybody else gets for picking five times as much? I mean, she's pretty and all that, but you've never let anything like that stand in the way of business before."

"And I don't intend to now. All I'm asking is that you give her a chance. She's got a baby. She needs money. We'll keep her on a while longer and see how she does."

"Even if she keeps falling off the ladder and can't pick one measly basket of oranges an hour?"

"Like I said, just be patient. I'm trying to do a good deed by giving her the chance to make more money for her and her boy. But let me know if you think she's just deliberately being lazy, and I'll let her go."

Mike said that otherwise he found her nice to be around and thought she was smart as a whip. "She's too smart to be trying to make a living as a picker. There's a lot of jobs out there for someone like her."

"I think she just went through a bad divorce, so maybe she thinks doing something like this will get her mind off things, get her out in the fresh air and so forth. She'll probably move on to something she's more suited for once the season ends."

Nick began to straighten the papers on his desk, a hint that he was finishing up for the day.

Mike took notice, quickly downed the rest of his beer and stood. "It's your groves, your money. I just work here. And like I said, she's nice to be around, so I don't have any problem there."

"Maybe you could find time to give her a few pointers. Maybe show her how to use the ladder the way she's supposed to. I didn't pay her much mind." No, he hadn't, because he was trying so hard not to and had worked as far away from her as possible.

Mike moved toward the door. "Okay. I'll see what I can do. We shouldn't be under as much pressure tomorrow. I don't think we'll have more'n a quarter of a block ready to pick. Today we had to do half, and I don't need to tell you how rough that was."

A block of fruit consisted of forty acres, with around 450 trees per acre. With the small number of workers on hand, Nick figured that picking half a block a day was doing well. When it was the season for the early varieties, he'd have enough people on hand to sometimes complete two blocks a day.

Mike tipped his cap. "See you tomorrow. I'm going home, and I'll probably have to wash off in the yard with a hose before Rosie'll let me in the house. You're the lucky one, Nick," he said as he left. "No wife to nag you about comin' in dirty."

Right, Nick felt like calling after him, there was nobody to nag him about anything anytime. He was his own boss. Nobody cared what he did.

But, oh, how sometimes he wished someone did.

Carlee's ankle was throbbing something awful. It helped to sit on the bank of the lake and soak it, but she couldn't wait to get back to the cottage and put it in a bucket of warm water. She intended to do just that once Scotty got tired of watching the ducks, laughing and waving his arms at them. She had brought a blanket and spread it out for them, and he was content to sit beside her and enjoy the world around him. If he was walking, it might have been a problem. She wasn't sure she could keep up with him, hurting like she was.

She felt like such a fool. Picking oranges had seemed so easy. She hadn't thought about things like having to be careful how she set the ladder due to the soft sand in some places. Nor had she worried about blisters.

She looked down at her hands, covered in bright red patches from climbing up and down the ladder. She needed to wear gloves tomorrow, but she didn't have any. And till she got paid, there was no money to buy some. She had spent the last of what she had buying food and milk for Scotty and gas for the car.

She was exhausted, ached from head to toe, her ankle was swollen, her hands looked terrible and stung, as well, and all the miseries combined made her wish she could just walk right up to Nick Starke and tell him everything. But that was not the plan. So far, he seemed like a good guy. But she was taking no chances.

He also seemed to like children, but she had to be sure

about that, as well. Having no wife to be incensed over an illegitimate son, he could very easily insist on partial custody, at the very least. For the time being, she wanted only one thing from Nick—child support. It remained to be seen whether or not she would consider sharing Scotty. And packing her bags and leaving was still an option.

Except that she needed money. And the best pay around for the moment was picking oranges, which, she had discovered to her dismay, was something she was not very good at. But she would learn, she promised herself, and learn quickly. Despite her injury. Otherwise, Nick might tell her she had to go to the packing and processing sheds. Not only would she make less money, but probably not be around him as much.

She had been disappointed that he had worked in a different area all day. She could almost believe he had deliberately distanced himself from her. But it was silly to think that. After all, he had practically insisted on coming by later. And though she didn't want to admit it, she'd been tempted to say, "Sure. Please do."

But that would make her feel guilty.

After all, he had been Alicia's lover, he was Scotty's father, and he had abandoned them both. Therefore she had no business finding him either handsome or enjoyable company. To do so was not only asking for trouble but defeating her purpose. There was just no way she was going to let Nick charm his way around her.

Scotty clapped his hands together and cackled with delight as he looked away from the lake and beyond her.

She turned to see what had his attention. Nick was walking toward them, and she cursed the sudden wave of pleasure she felt.

"Hello there," he called. "I'm glad to see you're out and about. Mike said you took a bad fall."

Embarrassed, she tried to make excuses for herself. "I guess I was too busy trying to do a good job to notice how soft the sand was. I'm sorry."

"Mind if I sit down?" Without waiting for an answer, he dropped to the blanket, immediately turning his attention for the next few moments to Scotty.

Carlee watched him closely. He genuinely seemed to like the baby.

Eyes still on Scotty, he said, "I noticed on your application that you worked for Riverton Groves. I heard they went out of business. It never was a really big operation, anyway. Did you pick for them?"

Carlee tensed. No doubt Mike Thurston had reported she hadn't come near making quota, and now Nick was wondering about her. She had feared that would happen and was ready with an explanation she hoped would save her job. "To be honest, I fudged a little and said I'd had a lot more experience than I did. I only got to pick right before the season ended."

A duck came out of the water and waddled up on the bank nearby. Scotty took off crawling after him, and before Carlee could pull her feet from the water and go after him, Nick had already done so, taking him into his arms.

"Once you do start walking, I'll bet you're going to be hard to catch," he said, laughing. He turned to Carlee. "I think maybe we'd better switch you into processing. If you keep falling off the ladder, you could wind up with a broken ankle or worse and then you'll really be in trouble trying to keep up with this big boy."

She was quick to protest, "And I'll be in even more if you take me out of the groves. I need the money. Things will be different tomorrow, I promise." She hated to sound as if she was begging, but, in actuality, she was.

Nick continued to hold Scotty. "I'd like to help you

out, Carlee, but it isn't fair to the other workers to keep paying you the same wages they get. I think you should try the processing shed. You might like it better.''

"It's not a matter of liking it better," she said, biting out each word, the rage returning to boil within as she thought how if not for him, she wouldn't be in such a predicament. And neither would Scotty.

She felt another shudder, this one of loathing. "Please give me another chance.''

"I'd like to, but I can see your ankle is really swollen. You can't climb up and down a ladder like that. You need to give it a rest.''

"It's not that bad," she argued. "I just twisted it. By morning it will be just fine. Now I need to get Scotty ready for bed.''

She started to get up, and he held out his hand. Not wanting to seem stubborn or risk stumbling and falling, she took it. But when she was standing, their eyes met, and as his fingers continued to hold hers, it was as if she had touched a light socket. The feeling that raced all the way up her arm and down her spine was that intense.

She yanked her hand away, and then she did almost stumble.

"Here, I'll get the blanket.'' He put Scotty down long enough to pick up the blanket and fold it, tucking it under his arm. "Come on. I'll walk with you to make sure you're all right.''

Her ankle did feel better. The soaking had helped, and as soon as Nick left, she'd do it again.

They reached the porch, and she was about to take Scotty, but Nick said he'd carry him on inside if she didn't mind. She did but wasn't about to say so.

"I'll be glad to bathe him or do whatever it is you need to do so you can rest your foot.''

She wasn't about to allow that, but as she stepped inside, her ankle twisted again, ever so slightly. Not enough to cause her to fall, but enough that she had to bite her lip to keep from crying out. She feared that if she took Scotty right then, she might stumble or do something awkward that would make Nick declare there was no way he would ever allow her back in the groves.

"If you're sure you don't mind," she said uneasily. "He loves his bath. I fill up the tub and let him play with his boat. He likes that." She kept her head turned so he wouldn't see the guilt she was feeling mirrored on her face. She told herself that two could play the same game. If he wanted to use Scotty to get to her, then she would do the same to get what *she* wanted—which was making more money and having a place to stay rent-free for a while longer.

"I'd love to. I've never bathed a kid in my life, though, so you'll have to help me here."

She filled the tub with warm water, added enough bubbles to please Scotty, and then put in the little toy boat he loved.

As she undressed him, Nick remarked that he needed one of those little windup boats to run around in the tub. "He'd get a kick out of that."

Carlee was sure he would, but she didn't have the money to buy any new toys. As it was, she'd had to leave a lot of Scotty's toys behind. He'd have to make do with what he did have, but the truth was he did like things that moved and bounced around. "He's fine with the ones he's got. When he's older, I'll get him one."

When he was splashing happily about, Carlee sat on the edge of the tub, wishing Nick would leave. He was pleasant company and she enjoyed having him around, but that wasn't the way it was supposed to be. "I've imposed on your time long enough," she said carefully. "I know you'd like to get home."

When he didn't say anything, she chanced looking at him, hoping not to see anger. She needn't have worried. He looked—what? Sad? Wistful? She wasn't sure, but his expression was anything but resentment at her hint that he should go.

"Thanks for all your help," she went on. "I really appreciate it. But I can handle it from here on. And I really would like another chance in the groves tomorrow."

He shook his head. "Not tomorrow. I want you to give that ankle a rest. You can work on the belt, sorting the oranges. I'm sure you know how to do that."

She sensed the remark was more a challenge than question. "Yes, but I'd rather—"

"Carlee—" his voice was thick with sympathy "—I know you want to make the extra money, but putting in a couple of days on the belt won't matter that much, and you need to rest that ankle. Otherwise, you could wind up having to work in processing all the time."

She thought about that and finally, reluctantly, nodded to concede. "Okay, but you will give me another chance picking after that, won't you?" She felt the need for reassurance she could make the higher wages.

"Of course. I want to do the very best I can for my workers always. That's why I'm insisting you take it easy for a day or two. In fact, if your ankle is really bothering you in the morning, I'd like to take you into town to see the doctor that treats my workers."

"No, I couldn't, I can't..." She trailed off, hating to admit she couldn't afford it. Doing so would make it obvious that she couldn't afford medical treatment for Scotty either, should the need arise. She just didn't want Nick to be able to say anything later about her being unfit or unable to take care of Scotty should he decide he wanted him. The way he was acting around him was making her uneasy, because what if it *wasn't* an act?

"It won't cost you anything," Nick assured her. "If one of my workers gets hurt on the job, I always pay for it. Ditto if they're sick, as well. When you work for Starke Groves, Carlee, you're part of a family." He smiled. "Get used to it."

For one single, solitary instant Carlee thought how wonderful it would be to do just that. But it couldn't happen. When the time came for her to do what she had come to do, she would leave.

Besides, she was grimly aware that Nick was going to hate her forevermore once he found out what she was all about.

She took a washcloth and began to clean Scotty's face. He batted at it and fussed, busy splashing and playing with his boat.

"He sits up real good," Nick observed. "He's big enough to walk, isn't he?"

"He'll be walking soon." Carlee leaned over to kiss the top of his head.

"Do you have good walking shoes for him?"

"No, I don't." Since it was summer, she hadn't seen a need for him to wear shoes.

"Don't you think he should have them for support once he does start walking?"

"Well, when I get paid, I'll buy him a pair."

Nick was silent for a moment, then took a deep breath and bluntly asked, "Don't you get any help at all from his father?"

She had not expected the question, and it was only with great effort that she was able to quickly come up with a response. "I don't know where he is."

"That's a shame. Makes it rough on you both. No wonder you're trying to make as much as you can.

"But tell me," he went on, cocking his head to one side in curiosity, "what do you plan to do in the future? I mean, picking oranges is not exactly the kind of life's work I picture you doing."

"Really, why not? I like working with citrus, especially in the gift shops, because I enjoy the tourists, meeting people, things like that, and—" she caught herself. She was giving him too much information. On her application she had made it seem like her experience was actually in the groves. Not retail sales.

Quickly she tried to compensate for the slip. "But then, I didn't work in the gift shops much. Just filled in when they needed me."

"Well, who knows?" he murmured breezily. "Maybe you'll want to stay on here in the fall and work in ours. That way you'd be close to the day care and could run in and see Scotty during the day. That's kind of hard to do when you're way out in the groves."

He was making her nervous. "I really need to finish up with Scotty now." She reached for a towel. "So if you'll excuse me, I'd like to get him to bed so I can go myself.

"I don't intend to be late tomorrow," she added lightly, tossing a tight smile over her shoulder as she lifted Scotty from the water.

Nick rapped the door frame with his knuckles and said breezily, "Sure. I shouldn't have stayed so long, anyway. I guess I've just taken a liking to the little guy."

Carlee bit her tongue to keep from saying he *should* take a liking to him, since he happened to be his son. "Well, that's nice. It was good of you to drop by. Good night."

"Yes, good night. I'll see you tomorrow. And don't

worry. Once you give that ankle a rest, I'll put you back to picking.''

"I'd appreciate it.''

After he was gone, Carlee sat for a long, long time, holding Scotty and feeling so very, very torn—because she was finding it harder and harder to despise Nick Starke.

Chapter Six

The time Carlee spent in processing was terribly monotonous. At least when she was picking, she could move around a bit, not be in only one spot.

After the pickers dumped the fruit into plastic tubs that held approximately nine hundred pounds of oranges, a special truck called a "goat" would come through the grove and, using a hydraulic boom, pick up the tub and dump it into the back of the goat. Once it was out of the grove, the back of the goat was raised and its load dumped into a large open tractor-trailer that could hold about forty-five thousand pounds of oranges. Then they were brought in for processing.

It was after the oranges were conveyed by belt through a washing process that her work began. As they passed by in a steady parade, she would sort out those too bruised or overripe and drop them into discard baskets.

It all made for a long, boring day, but on a positive

note, she was near the day-care and could check on Scotty during breaks and lunch.

He always seemed happy and content, and Becky said she never had any problems with him. She did, however, emphasize how glad she would be when he finally started walking. There'd be so many other toys he would then be able to play with, like pedal and push cars, things like that.

Carlee would also be glad when he began to walk, but as always, hoped he didn't take those first, precious steps till she was there to witness them.

The morning after she twisted her ankle, she was dismayed that it still hurt terribly if she tried to put weight on it. There was no way she could have climbed up and down ladders, sometimes having to stand on tiptoe and stretch for an orange just out of reach, no matter how badly she wanted the extra money.

She had tried to keep from limping when she reported to the shed, but Mamie, the woman in charge, noticed and brought her a stool. Everyone preferred to stand, she explained, because they had a better view of the fruit, but it was okay for Carlee to sit if that was what she needed to do.

Carlee hoped Nick would not come by and see her perched on a stool, but she needn't have worried. The pickers were working their way deeper into the Valencia groves, and he was not around as much. Also, he had switched to driving his pickup truck, instead of the beach buggy, so he'd have more room for carrying water kegs and other supplies. Somehow that made him seem not quite so accessible when he did pass by.

But by her third day in processing, Carlee's ankle was no longer bothering her, and she began to stand like the others. She was anxious to return to picking and said as much to Mamie.

Mamie shook her head. "Honey, that's hard work. I know 'cause my husband, Ron, and our two boys are out there, and some nights they come in so tired they can't hardly lift a fork to their mouths to eat supper. Believe me, they'd rather be picking strawberries in California than climbing up and down in those trees all day."

Carlee found that surprising. "Then why are you all still here?"

"Ron has been working for the Starkes since he was knee-high to a bushel basket. He's always liked them, always been treated fair, and when Mr. Nick asked him to hang around this year to harvest the Valencias, he couldn't say no. So here we are.

"But what about you?" Mamie asked, flicking Carlee a curious gaze. "How come a young woman on her own with a baby wants to do this kind of work? Seems to me you'd want to get yourself a job in town around folks...men—" she grinned "—so's to find yourself a husband."

Momentarily caught off guard, Carlee couldn't help stammering as she tried to frame a response. "I...uh...I also heard how the Starkes take care of their workers...the day care for children and all...and I like being outdoors, and..." Her voice trailed off. It was a weak explanation, because Mamie was right. It was a bit strange for her to be doing that kind of work. The other women were either married or with their family.

From farther down the conveyor belt, Sandy, a girl about her age who hadn't been very friendly, smirked and said, "Maybe you also heard how Mr. Nick is divorced and what a fine catch he'd make if you could reel him in. I've seen how you look at him when he drives by."

The others laughed, including Mamie, who, after noting Carlee's look of dismay, quickly moved to give her a friendly pat on the shoulder and tell her to ignore Sandy. "Truth be known, she'd like to be the one to reel him in. She sure throws him enough bait. But then, her folks would be glad if she'd hitch up with anybody so's they could get rid of her."

Sandy ignored Mamie's sarcasm with a shrug. "Heck, I don't mind saying it. I'd be tickled to death if he asked me out. But this is my third season working here, and I've never known him to give any of us a second glance."

"Well, he sure as heck glances at Carlee," Mamie said. "He even went to see her the night she moved in."

Carlee didn't like hearing that, but should have known that, as close together as the workers' cottages were built, everyone knew everyone else's business.

"You can forget latching on to him with that kid, though."

Carlee threw a sharp look at Sandy. "Why do you say that? Not that I'm even remotely interested in the man." She plucked a bruised orange from the moving belt and threw it into the bucket so hard it splattered. Sandy was pushing her buttons, and she didn't like it.

Sandy looked smug. "I hear things, like why he and his wife got a divorce. Something about her wanting a baby and he didn't."

Mamie promptly told her that was the silliest thing she'd ever heard. "Of course he'd want a baby. Who's going to carry on the Starke name and take over the groves when he's gone?"

Sandy hooted. "You think a playboy like him cares about something like that? Why, that goody-goody act he puts on is just that—an act. All for our benefit. He goes out of town a lot, and I'll bet you he swings when he does. He doesn't care about being tied down to a family. He was probably glad when his old lady left him."

"You don't know what you're talking about," Mamie retorted, then turned to Carlee and lowered her voice. "She's just mad 'cause he ignores her, and believe me, she's practically made a fool out of herself over him, too."

Carlee didn't care about that, but wanted to know more about Nick's marriage. "Why *did* his wife leave him, then?"

"Who knows?"

Carlee persisted. "Well, does he go out of town a lot to swing like Sandy says?"

Mamie told her she didn't know about that, either. "All I do know is that whenever there's a big charity event in Orlando, he shows up with a different woman every time. I know 'cause I've seen his picture in the paper. But he never brings anybody to our parties."

"We have parties?"

"Oh, yeah. There'll be one this Saturday night. A barbecue down by the lake at the pavilion."

Carlee had noticed what looked like a recreational area on the other side, but hadn't been over there due to her injured ankle.

Mamie continued, "Sometimes he has a deejay come so we can all dance. It's real nice." Once again she leaned close to whisper, "That's when Sandy really goes after him. But he dances with most of the women, anyway, including married ones like me. It's all in fun. You'll see."

No, Carlee felt like telling her, she wouldn't see, because she had no intention of going. She was finding out things about Nick without dancing with him, for heaven's sake. "So what was his wife like?"

"I don't know. She never came around. But she was pretty. All I know is, one season she was here and the next she wasn't." Mamie saw that the last of the oranges had passed along the belt and threw the switch to turn it off, then told everyone to take a break till another load was brought in.

It was nearly three o'clock, and Carlee had a sinking feeling as she watched Mamie note on her clipboard what time they had stopped. When the belt wasn't running, they didn't get paid, because even someone as good to his workers as Nick couldn't afford to pay them to stand idle.

When a half hour passed, and there was still no sign of a truck, Carlee grew more and more anxious. She began to mentally count what she had made so far, her first week. It was not going to be enough to pay something on each of the bills.

Finally she couldn't stand it any longer and went to where Mamie was sitting and talking to a couple of the other women. "I think I'm going to go out in the groves and find where they're working and start picking. I need the money, Mamie."

"I understand, but it's going to take you a while to walk to where they are. Ron said last night they'd be picking one of the back blocks. Probably a mile from here. Maybe more."

"Do you know which direction?"

Mamie pointed. "That's where the trucks have been coming from all day. If you go between those rows, you ought to run into them sooner or later. But remember," she added with a frown, "neither Mr. Mike or Mr. Nick has said you could go back out there yet. You ought to just wait till tomorrow morning."

Carlee recalled how the day before Mamie had called it quits in midafternoon, saying they wouldn't have time to finish another truck. Carlee had pointed out that they could switch off the conveyor belt anytime, which meant they could put in a full workday even if they didn't complete processing a whole truckload. No one else agreed with her, so she gave up, figuring they just didn't need the money as badly as she did. After all, with her, every dollar counted.

She asked Mamie how much longer she was going to wait for a truck. Mamie looked at her watch and said maybe twenty minutes.

"Then I'm going to the groves," Carlee said.

"Better check those clouds up there," Mamie warned. "If it starts raining, they're going to quit, so you're probably wasting your time."

Carlee felt like saying that was what she'd been doing there—wasting her time—but didn't and started walking.

Ordinarily it was beautiful being among the verdant trees, shady from the relentless sun and fragrant with blossom. But there was no time to enjoy her surroundings. She had to hurry, because if she could put in two more hours' work at picker's wage, she could pay off some of the pediatrician's bill.

What Sandy had said about the reasons for Nick's marriage breaking up gave Carlee cause for worry. If it was true, if he had, indeed, not wanted children then, he would not be a happy camper to find out he had one now. In addition, it would confirm her suspicion he was only pretending to be crazy about Scotty to get to her.

Carlee could easily imagine Nick as a playboy, a womanizer, when he was away from home. Here, he played the role of the ideal boss—fair to his employees and concerned about their welfare. But when he was traveling, he was probably as wild as kids on spring break in Panama City Beach.

Alicia hadn't been experienced enough to hang on to her heart around somebody like Nick. And once upon a time, Carlee might have been just as weak. But now it was different. She knew men for the conniving, selfish jerks they were, and if she never married again she wouldn't have a moment's regret.

At least that was how she wanted it to be.

And the sooner she got away from Nick Starke, the better.

Panting, she quickened her pace and would have broken into a run if her ankle had not started throbbing again. The clouds had grown even darker and thickened as distant thunder rumbled closer. Orange blossoms torn from the trees created a blizzard of petals whipping about in frenzy.

She stumbled and fell, and when she got back on her feet wondered whether to continue on or turn back. Then she realized with a flash of panic she had got turned around when she fell and now did not know which direction she had been going or where she had been coming from. No matter which way she turned, everything looked the same.

She knew she'd been a fool to start out on her own with a possible storm coming in, but it was too late to worry about that now. Rain was starting to fall, and she had to seek shelter fast. Forks of lightning split the sky, and it was dangerous to be out among the trees.

Suddenly she hated them, their limbs clattering together as though taunting her. In a frozen moment of terror and indecision, she childishly wished them to be torn from the ground and flung up and away to disappear in the menacing clouds.

"Get a grip, Carlee," she yelled into the wind, then muttered, "and you aren't going to find a way out of this by talking to yourself, either."

It was then that hail started falling, the pea-size chunks of ice stinging her skin. She began running as fast as her injured ankle would allow, thinking there had to be a storage shed somewhere nearby. Most growers spaced them at intervals throughout the groves for easy access to often-used supplies so they would not have to go all the way back to the main buildings.

Her teeth were chattering but not from the ice. She was terrified. And not for herself but for Scotty.

Because if something happened to her, what would become of him? She was all he had, and now she did curse herself for letting money problems get in the way of being sensible.

And once more, she cursed Nick Starke for her lot in life.

Nick dashed from the truck to the processing shelter but still got soaked in the torrential downpour. Stamping his feet, shaking the water from his hat, he glanced about with relief to see the women had left before the storm hit. Then Mamie came out of the corner office, and he asked, "What are you doing still here? I came by to make sure everybody got home okay."

"I had to fill out the payroll sheet, and by the time I finished I knew I'd never make it home." Her face was drawn with worry. "What about the pickers? Did they get caught in it?"

"No. They're okay." He jumped as lightning popped close by. "Boy, this is a bad storm. I'm afraid we're going to lose most of the blossoms.

"But are you sure you sent everyone home in time?" he persisted, still worrying and hoping Carlee had been able to pick up Scotty and make it back to her cottage without getting soaked.

"Oh, yeah. We'd already quit for the day, because the hauler didn't come, and I didn't want to start another belt going."

"I know," he said, disgusted. "We've been having trouble with the one that was loaded and ready to bring in for processing. Mike's been working on it, but he can't seem to keep it going. I'm going to send it to Orlando for repair or else buy a new one. If this was our regular season, we'd be hurting, but we don't have to move so fast this time of year.''

He was talking more to himself than Mamie, trying to get his mind off Carlee. But it was getting harder and harder. He stayed away from the processing shed as much as possible so he wouldn't have to be around her. Because the more he was, the more he wanted to be, and from her chilly manner toward him, it appeared that trying to make friends was an exercise in futility.

"I'll bet Carlee was soaking wet when she got there," Mamie remarked.

He snapped to attention. "What did you say?"

"Carlee. She was upset about not putting in a full day and said she was going to work in the groves."

Nick stared at Mamie incredulously. "But she doesn't know her way around out there. And she didn't know where to find us."

Mamie's eyes widened. "You mean you haven't seen her? But she left here about twenty minutes ago, right before it got bad. You didn't see her when you drove in?"

"No," he cried, alarm ripping up his spine as sharp as the lightning that was streaking the sky. "Which way did she head?"

Mamie pointed. "The same way you came in. And you didn't see her?" she repeated, then cried, "She's probably lost out there!"

He bolted out and into the storm.

"Mr. Nick, you'll never find her in this," Mamie frantically called. "It's raining so hard you can't see your hand in front of your face."

Nick kept on going, leaping into his truck.

Driving slowly, he rolled down the windows on both sides in the cab of the truck, not caring about the rain blowing in as he strained to see left and right among the rows of trees. The main driving path was a little wider, but in the storm she might have gotten confused and turned down the wrong one.

He couldn't help blaming himself. Sensing she was desperate for money, he'd felt bad to have to take her out of the groves in the first place, but till her ankle healed there was no way she could work. His guilt came from avoiding her and not checking to see if she was able to start picking again.

Carlee was smart, mature and very pretty, and he couldn't understand how any man in his right mind could have left her, especially with a baby. She probably had good reason to be leery of him, and men in general. That was probably why she turned on the big chill around him. But maybe, if he could muster up enough nerve, he could change all that.

Because staying away from her just wasn't working.

He still couldn't get her out of his mind.

And why? he had asked himself over and over as he lay awake every night since they'd met. He'd dated a lot of beautiful women, but they never held his interest for long. But there was something about Carlee that just made him want to be with her and get to know her better.

Then there was Scotty. Nick could not deny he was already fond of the little boy. So he had double the reasons for wanting to melt Carlee's reserve.

Suddenly he saw her and slammed on the brakes. She was stumbling along in the wrong direction, away from the main path. He was out of the truck like a shot. He grabbed her, scooped her up in his arms and carried her back.

Carlee screamed in surprise, then realized it was Nick and seemed to melt against him in her relief. "Oh, thank God, you found me."

Her arms were around his neck. It was a good feeling, and he could not help thinking how he wished she did not have to let him go when he settled her on the front seat. "I've got a blanket here somewhere." He reached behind the seat and found it. "Here. Wrap up in this, and I'll get you home as fast as I can. Are you okay? You aren't hurt, are you?"

"No, just tired and soaked and feeling like a complete fool. I never should have started out walking with the weather like it was, but I actually thought I could find everybody.

"You see," she nervously babbled on, "my ankle is so much better, and I'm able to go back to picking. Mamie was about to quit for the day and—"

"You wanted to keep working to make more money," he finished for her with a disapproving glance. "You could've been hurt, Carlee, and looking for you in this mess I could have been hurt, too."

In a flash she became defensive about being caught in the storm. "Well, I'm really sorry about that, but I would have been okay. I'd have found a shed somewhere to wait it out."

"No, you wouldn't have. The closest one to you was in the opposite direction. If you'd kept going, you'd have wound up in the sand pits, next to a drainage ditch that's probably flooded by now. You could have stumbled into it and drowned."

She bit her lip, not only to keep from crying but also to keep from telling him to go to hell. "I guess you think I'm just some bimbo who doesn't know how to climb a ladder or stay out of the rain."

The annoyance Nick had so rapidly mustered dissipated just as quickly. He saw the stubborn tilt of her head, the way her lower lip turned down ever so slightly in a childish pout he was sure she wasn't even aware of. And in that moment, with the windshield wipers beating out a rhythm to match that of his heart, it was all he could do to keep from pulling her into his arms and kissing her till she smiled again.

Only something told him it wouldn't happen that way.

Carlee Denton was not going to smile easily for any man, and if he did try to kiss her, she'd probably slug him.

And, thinking that, he laughed.

She whipped her head about. "What's so funny? I know I owe you an apology for putting you to so much trouble, and you have it, but you don't have to make me feel even worse by laughing at me."

"Sorry," he said, his intent not to humiliate her. "I shouldn't have come down so hard on you. I was just worried, that's all."

She softened. "Well, thanks for what you did, and I do hope you aren't giving up on me. I'm ready to go back to picking, and this time I'll know how to spot soft sand."

"You better believe you'll know how to spot it, because this time I'm going to be right there every time you set that ladder to make sure." He grinned and thought once more how lovely she was, even with her wet hair plastered to her head. And he'd noticed before he wrapped the blanket around her that he'd been right about her having a nice figure. With her wet clothes clinging to her, that fact had been obvious.

"You...you don't have to do that," she said in a strained voice, shaking her head from side to side in protest. "It's not right that you should have to watch me every minute. You've got your own work to do. After all, you're the boss.''

"That's right," he said breezily, "and you remember that. Besides," he continued on a sober note, "I want to help you, Carlee. It's obvious you're going through a tough time right now, and I'd like to do whatever I can to make things easier for you—if you'll let me."

"Thanks. That's nice of you."

Her words were perfunctory, and once more she turned away. It was almost as if she could not bear to look at him. Again he wondered what had happened to make her so bitter toward men. And surely that had to be it—because there was no way he had done anything to offend her.

When they reached the shed, he parked next to her car. She removed the blanket. "I'll take this with me and hang it out to dry when the sun comes out."

"That's not necessary. I can take care of it later."

"All right. Thanks again." She reached for the door handle.

"Wait. I'd like to talk to you for a minute."

It was not his imagination. She actually cringed, probably thinking he was about to fire her, so he hurriedly continued, "I'd like to take you and Scotty out to dinner tonight. It's almost stopped raining, and I know of a great little seafood place not far from here. So why don't you go get him, and I'll give you time to change into dry clothes, and then I'll pick you up."

"No."

If the word had been a knife, it could have cut him in two.

"Thank you, but I'm too tired."

"Some other time, then…"

His words were lost in the slamming of the door, and he pounded his fist on the steering wheel in frustration.

And as he watched her get to her car, it was all he could do to keep from going after her to ask what on earth made her lump him with all the men who had hurt her. He only wanted to be her friend, and yes, maybe he wanted more than that. Something about her just kindled the fires he'd thought long dead—fires that burned with longing for love, a family and everything else that makes life complete.

It was sad for someone as young and lovely as Carlee to be so jaded. He wanted to help her and was going to whether she liked it or not. Probably she would tell him to go to hell, but he had to chance it.

Because he was going to find a way, somehow, to make her realize he had nothing to do with whatever pain and anger she carried in her heart.

Carlee was shaking, but not because she was soaked to the bone. It was from being in such close confines with Nick. Sitting beside him in the cab of his truck, the rain beating on the windshield, they might as well have been in a bedroom alone together. She could feel the heat of his body, and when he'd touched her as he covered her with the blanket, her toes had actually curled under as she fought to keep from trembling so he would not know what his nearness was doing to her.

It's not supposed to be like this, she told herself as she turned the ignition with fingers still shaking. *I'm not supposed to feel anything for the man except disgust and loathing.*

She shifted into reverse and backed away from the building, noticing out of the corner of her eye that Nick was still there. No doubt he wanted to make sure her car started and she was okay.

But why couldn't he leave her alone?

Because that's how he is. She knew his type, had him pegged for what he was.

The problem, however, was herself and how just now she'd feared she might be losing control of her emotions. They'd had a moment. Or at least *she* had. And, right there at the end, when she'd been about to get out of the truck and he'd told her to wait, she had, for a fleeting instant, thought he might kiss her. There had been something in his voice, and in his eyes when she'd dared to look at him.

Perplexing, though, was her inability to curb her attraction to him when she and Alicia had laughed over how they each liked different types of men. Alicia admitted to being drawn to the strong, domineering type—me Tarzan, you Jane—a definite weakness she'd tried to overcome. Carlee, on the other hand, although she'd sworn off men forevermore, had confided she liked the nurturing, protective kind.

Such as Nick seemed to be.

It was all so frustrating, but the only thing Carlee could do for the time being was continue to learn as much as possible about him—and keep a tight rein on her heart all the while.

When she arrived at the day-care center, Becky was waiting for her at the door. "I was so worried. All the other mothers have already picked up their children. One of them said you'd tried to find the pickers right before the storm broke."

Carlee took Scotty and hugged him. He patted her cheek and she kissed each of his little fingers in turn before explaining to Becky what had happened, confiding her embarrassment. "I just didn't realize how fast the storm would hit. It didn't look all that bad when I left the shed. Just a little thunder."

Becky told her that was how the weather in Florida was

and laughed to recall someone saying, "If you don't like the weather, wait five minutes."

"I believe it. But I still wish I hadn't done it. I was anxious to get a couple more hours in today. So how was my boy? Was he good?"

"Oh, he's always good," Becky said fondly. "Mr. Starke says he's never seen such a good-natured baby. You should see the two of them when Mr. Starke is pushing him in the toddler swings."

The words were like ice water in her face. "What is he doing taking Scotty outside?"

Becky's smile faded at Carlee's sharp tone. "He came by yesterday and asked if he could take Scotty to play on the swings. I said sure. I didn't see any harm. Scotty has to spend so much time in his playpen, because he can't walk yet, and I was busy with the toddlers and—"

"Sure. It's okay." It wouldn't do for Becky to pick up on her resentment of Nick. "It just surprised me that Mr. Starke would have the time."

Becky looked relieved that there was not a problem, after all. "Actually I think he made the time. I could see he's really taken a liking to Scotty. He's never done this with any of the other children. Oh, he'll stop occasionally to make sure everything is running smoothly, but he's never singled out one to play with. Maybe it's because you don't have a husband, and he thinks Scotty would enjoy being around a man."

Becky was quite the psychologist, Carlee thought sarcastically, then chided herself. The woman was only being nice. She had no way of knowing Nick Starke had an ulterior motive, which was to get to her through Scotty. But she intended to use that to her advantage and point out to him when the time came how crazy he was about his *very own son*.

"Whatever," she said finally, taking the diaper bag Becky handed her. "It's nice of him."

"He's always nice. The woman that gets him will be very fortunate."

Carlee seized the topic. "One of the girls who works in processing says he's quite the playboy when he's not around here."

"Mr. Starke? A playboy?" Becky threw her head back and laughed. "That's really funny. I can't imagine that."

"She said his wife left him because she wanted children, and he didn't."

Becky pursed her lips in doubt. "I can't imagine that, either, and I'll bet I know who told you this—Sandy. Everybody knows how she chases him every year and he doesn't pay her any mind. She's just jealous, because he's shown you a little attention."

"I guess there are no secrets around here, are there?" Carlee said with an exaggerated sigh.

"Not when it comes to the boss," Becky replied. "But if I were you, I wouldn't pay any attention to anything Sandy says. She's also a big gossip."

Carlee was glad it had stopped raining so Scotty would not get wet as she carried him out to the car.

Becky locked the day-care center door and followed. "By the way," she said, "I think if you'd get Scotty some walking shoes, it would help. I know lots of people think it's good for a baby to learn to walk barefoot, but I think in his case he needs the additional support around his little ankles."

"I'm going to see about getting him a pair when I get paid." She only hoped there was enough money left after paying the bills that were due. She hadn't worked a full week, so her pay was really going to be stretched.

If only she'd been in a better financial situation when

Alicia died. But there had been the unexpected car repair and she hadn't been working in the gift shop then….

She gave her head a weary shake. There was no point looking back on the reasons. Tragedy never struck at a convenient time, and Alicia's death had been just that—a tragedy. So Carlee had to face up to each and every problem, do the best she could and not waste energy looking back.

Scotty was bouncing around in his car seat, his bare feet kicking. He did need shoes, and she was going to have to buy them for him. If not this week, then surely next.

As she darted glances at him, she tried to see something about him that reminded her of his father, but couldn't, other than they both had sandy-blond hair. Nick had green eyes; Scotty's were blue, like Alicia's. But none of it meant anything, because babies as young as Scotty seldom resembled their parents.

"Don't worry, little guy." She reached over to pat his leg. "If your daddy gives us a hard time, we can always have you tested and prove you're his. But I don't think it'll come to that."

What it *would* come to, she thought resentfully, was her having to hold off Nick Starke should he be bold enough to make a move on her before she was ready to make one of her own. And she was going to take her own sweet time doing that, too. She liked the accommodations, liked everything about Starke Groves.

Besides, she had nothing else to do for the time being except remind herself whenever Nick was near how much she loathed him and—

She saw it the minute she pulled up in front of the cottage.

A tiny windup boat.

The man was nothing, she thought grimly, if not persistent, which was probably how he'd won Alicia's heart.

"But not mine," Carlee said through gritted teeth. "It just isn't gonna happen, Mr. Nick Starke, no matter how many toy boats you buy my baby."

Chapter Seven

Carlee was anxious to open the brown pay envelope. Though she had put in nine hours picking oranges the day before, it would not be included in this week's pay.

It was Saturday morning, and others were lined up at the pay window, so she hurried back to her car. When she saw what was inside, she was glad she had waited. She would not have wanted anyone else to see how disappointed she was, because, after deductions, she had less than twenty dollars to last the week once she paid the bills. Sadly there would not be enough to buy Scotty's shoes, because she needed a few groceries.

"Hi, Carlee." Mamie said as she walked by with her envelope. "Are you going into town today?"

"Yes, I'm got to find Scotty some shoes." She could at least look even if she had to wait another week to buy them.

"Drive into Sanford," Mamie advised. "There's a nice

shopping center there. You won't find much in Snow Hill, I'm afraid. All of us go either to Sanford or Titusville, and sometimes we'll even drive into Orlando.''

"Sanford it is, then.'' Carlee tried to sound cheerful, even though she was feeling terribly down. Titusville was a little farther in the opposite direction, toward the beach, and she wanted to save on gas.

"See you tonight.'' Mamie waved.

"Why? What's going on?''

"Didn't you see the notice on the bulletin board about the barbecue at the pavilion?'' Mamie pointed to the board hanging beside the payroll window. ''Free food and a dee-jay for dancing. Everybody's going.''

Carlee had been too focused on getting paid to care about anything around her. She got out of her car and went back to check the time. She didn't care about dancing, but free food sure sounded good.

"Oh, by the way,'' Mamie yelled, ''The day-care center will be open so you can leave Scotty there. Mr. Nick always has Becky work when he puts on these things so nobody will have to miss it because of baby-sitting. He's wonderful about things like that.''

Sure. Carlee smirked. He knew all about being a good guy. But she knew him for what he really was and re-minded herself of that every time he smiled and showed his dimples, making her heart skip a beat.

Carlee had not seen Nick standing just inside the open door of the main office. He had heard everything said between her and Mamie. And he had also seen the way Car-lee looked when Mamie made the remark about him being wonderful. Carlee's expression plainly said she thought he was anything but.

She obviously didn't like him, and he could no more

understand why any more than he could fathom why he was so attracted to her.

When she had curtly thanked him for the toy boat he'd left for Scotty on her porch, her eyes had been dark and cold, her smile stiff and forced. Yet when he had asked how Scotty liked it, she had warmed a bit as she described how she'd had quite a time getting him out of the tub because he wanted to keep on playing with it.

He hoped she had the money to buy shoes for Scotty. If he could have done so without Elaine knowing, he'd have put some extra money in her envelope.

Carlee backed out of the parking space and turned toward the main road leading out, Scotty strapped into his car seat.

Nick hurriedly went to his truck and followed, keeping far enough back so she wouldn't know she was being tailed. He planned to keep her in sight, and if she did find shoes for Scotty and couldn't afford them, he would see what he could do about it. When he had stopped by the day care, he had taken paper and pencil with him. When Becky was busy with the other children and not looking, he had traced Scotty's foot on the paper. Hopefully, a good shoe salesman could figure out his size by the drawing.

First she went to the post office. Nick watched through the windows as she appeared to buy several money orders and stamped envelopes. When she went to a counter to fill everything out, he wished he could help her with Scotty while she was doing it. She had the boy balanced on her hip as she wrote, and he was being a handful, grabbing at her hair and her pen.

Afterward she drove to the mall.

Nick was right behind her and, once inside, stayed as close as he dared.

She went straight to a children's shoe shop. She picked

up several styles on display, frowned and put them back. When a salesclerk offered to help, Nick moved in a bit closer, keeping his back turned so he could hear the conversation.

"Let's see what size he wears," the clerk was saying.

Carlee wanted to know if he had anything inexpensive.

"Sorry. Not in a walking shoe. We've got some little sandals that are cheaper."

"No. He needs walking shoes. Any chance these will go on sale?"

The clerk seemed sympathetic. "We never know. Our sale information comes from the home office, and they don't give us advance notice of when we're having one."

Nick could see Carlee was trying to hide her disappointment by making her voice too bright, too cheery. "Oh, well, that's okay. I can probably get them next week."

"We take all major credit cards," the clerk advised.

"No. I'll get them when I can pay for them. Thank you."

She started to leave, and Nick blessed the clerk for having the foresight to try to secure a future sale.

"Miss, we could go ahead and size your baby, and then if the shoes do go on sale, I can hold them for you."

Carlee was all for that, and Nick exited the store and remained a discreet distance away till she and Scotty left. Then he went inside, quickly bought the shoes Scotty had tried on, then went in search of Carlee.

She was at the food court, sharing an ice-cream cone with Scotty. She probably hoped in some way that it made up to him for having to wait another week to provide something he really needed.

Nick took a deep breath and walked over. "Hi, mind if I join you?"

Carlee nearly dropped the cone. "What...what are you doing here?"

He pulled out a chair and sat down, then gently tweaked Scotty's cheek. Scotty recognized him and giggled with pleasure. "Oh, I had a little shopping to do, and it's nice to get away from the groves once in a while."

"No conferences coming up in Cocoa Beach any time soon?"

He wondered not only about the question but the sharpness in which it was asked. "No. My next outing will be a charity ball in Orlando."

There was a moment of awkward silence, and then he mentioned Mike's reporting that she had done quite well since she returned to picking.

"You should know." She laughed. "You were right beside me almost the whole time."

He was glad to see that, for once, she was looking straight at him without dislike mirrored in her eyes. "Yes, but Mike is the final authority. He keeps up with quotas. I just wanted to make sure you didn't fall off your ladder again."

"I think I've learned my lesson about that. I hope so, anyway. I can't afford to miss any more work."

"So you think you'll stay with us till the Valencias are all picked?"

He thought for a minute she was about to give him that look again.

"I'm planning on it."

"That won't be till around the end of June. You're welcome to come back and work when the early varieties are ready around October, but what will you do till then?"

She licked the cone. Nick noted it was vanilla.

Finally she responded. "I don't know yet. Find work somewhere."

"Where's your home?" he chanced, making her angry in an effort to learn more about her.

Sure enough, there was the look.

"Sorry. I guess I'm being nosy."

"It's okay. Actually anywhere I am is home. I don't have family. Just Scotty," she hastened to add.

"Well, I'd be glad for you to make Starke Groves your home."

She sat up straight. "What do you mean?"

"We could probably find something for you to do around the place."

"Like what?"

Nick floundered to come up with something. He hadn't really thought about it till now, and she suddenly seemed suspicious. Then he remembered what she'd said about enjoying gift shops. "Maybe you could help get the gift shop ready for the regular season. It could use some fixing up."

"And you'd still let me live in a migrant worker's cottage?"

"Of course."

"But why would you want to do all this for me? Have you ever made such an offer to anyone else?"

"Uh, actually, no." He was caught completely off guard by her skepticism. He also realized he had put himself in an awkward position, because apparently she thought he had ulterior motives. "Look, Carlee, I don't want you to get the wrong idea. I told you before—I just want to help you."

"I know you did," she allowed. "But I can't help wondering why. You don't know me. You don't know anything about me."

"Maybe—" he met her intense glare with one of his own "—I'd like to. Is that so wrong? I mean..." Again he faltered, then decided to heck with it. She obviously didn't think much of him, so what did he have to lose? "The fact is, Carlee, you're a very attractive woman. You're single. So am I. I'd like to date you. What's wrong with that?"

She held the cone for Scotty to take a lick. "Nothing, except that I'm not interested in going out with anybody. All I want to do is work and take care of my baby."

"You can do that and still go out with me," he persisted. "But maybe you don't like the idea of dating your boss. Is that it? Because that doesn't matter. Not to me, anyway."

"Do you date a lot of your workers?"

"Why, no..." Why was she making him feel as if he had to justify something so innocent as asking her out? But then he didn't know how badly a man had hurt her in her past. Maybe she had every right to be suspicious. "Actually I don't date much at all. I'm a workaholic, in case you hadn't noticed."

"I noticed," she allowed. "But why are you asking me out—a woman with a baby? Seems to me you'd prefer someone without children."

He laughed. "What makes you say that? I like kids. I like Scotty. I'd like to take him places, too, if you'll let me."

She dabbed at Scotty's mouth with a paper napkin. He was tired of the cone and so was she. "It just seems funny, that's all."

Another awkward silence fell, then Nick pushed for an answer. "Will you go out with me? There's the barbecue tonight, but I thought tomorrow we could drive to the beach for the day. I know a place where I can call ahead and have a picnic basket ready for us to pick up when we get there. What do you say?"

"I need to rest. I want to make my quota Monday. In fact, if I can, I'd like to go over it. Mr. Thurston said something about a bonus, because the block we're supposed to pick is loaded with oranges about to fall on the ground. He wants the whole block done in one day, and that's going to be tough."

"And that's why you need to relax," Nick said, flashing a coaxing grin. He saw that she was finished with the cone and it was melting and running down her fingers. "I'll throw that away for you."

When he came back from the trash bin, she was lifting Scotty in her arms and getting ready to leave.

"What do you say?" he asked brightly. "Picnic tomorrow? The three of us?"

"Thanks, but I'd really like to rest." She noticed the bag he'd left on the chair next to him. "Don't forget this."

"I didn't forget it. It's for Scotty." Jamming his hands in his pockets, Nick turned away, shoulders slumped in disappointment.

"Wait," Carlee called after him. "You shouldn't..."

But he had already disappeared in the Saturday crowd of shoppers.

With a ragged sigh, she sat back down, putting Scotty back in the child's seat beside her. "Okay, let's see what toy he bought for you this time to get on the good side of your mommy."

She gasped as she saw the shoe box.

"I don't believe this," she whispered, taking out the box and opening it to see the very shoes Scotty had tried on. Then it dawned on her. He had been watching her, following her and had obviously seen that she did not have enough money to pay for them herself.

Her first impulse was to run after him and say no, she

couldn't accept them, but she was instantly amazed by her stupidity even to consider such a thing. Of course she could accept them.

After all, she thought with a satisfied smile, a father should buy shoes for his son.

And maybe she should chill out and let Nick do other things for Scotty, as well. What was the harm? Scotty needed the attention, and sure as heck needed shoes and anything else anyone bought for him. Also, if Nick was solidly attached to him before he found out who he was, that couldn't hurt, either.

She put the shoes on Scotty, tied the strings, then gave him a hug and said, "So, little guy. Want to go on a picnic tomorrow with your daddy?"

Nick knew he should give up, back off and regard Carlee as just another migrant worker. She was in and out of his life like all the others. She obviously wasn't interested in him, and if he continued to let himself get attached to Scotty, it was only going to hurt more when she moved on.

No more, he had told himself as he drove back from the mall. He was much better off focusing on his work and forgetting about any kind of a personal life.

When he got home, he went for a swim in his pool and once more was reminded of Gina. She had insisted on the pool, and they'd had some nice times there before she found someone who could give her a baby. Having no one to share it with now just made him feel all the lonelier. He had thought about inviting Carlee to bring Scotty some evening. He could get a little float for him to splash around in. But Carlee would never come.

He did his laps, then showered and dressed in khaki

slacks and a white pullover shirt, slipping on a pair of leather deck loafers.

He checked the messages on his machine. The deejay had called to say he would be setting up his equipment at the pavilion by seven o'clock. Then the caterers had called to say they'd be erecting tents for serving the grilled chickens, barbecued ribs, potato salad, coleslaw and pies he had ordered.

He had plenty of time before the party was to begin, so he settled back to read. However, he could not stop thinking about Carlee, arguing with himself that maybe he shouldn't give up so easy. After all, if he was able to show her he only wanted to be good to her and her baby and perhaps down the road have some kind of a relationship that might possibly turn serious, it was worth a shot.

Besides, what did he have to lose?

When Carlee left Scotty with Becky, he was almost asleep. "He probably won't want to play very long. Just give him his bottle and tuck him in and he'll be out like a light. He had a big day at the mall, and he's tired."

"New shoes?" Becky noticed. "Great. He'll be walking in no time, I'll bet. Want me to take them off when I put him in his crib?"

Amused, Carlee said, "If he'll let you. He keeps looking at them like he's so proud."

"Well, I'll leave them on if he really wants me to. Now you go on and have a good time. The barbecues are always fun."

Carlee could have driven around the lake, but instead, left her car at the cottage and walked. It was a beautiful night, a full moon making the water dance with a thousand diamonds. A soft breeze was blowing, crickets were chirping and in the distance an owl hooted from a stand of pine trees.

She was wearing a sleeveless print blouse, knotted at her waist and white Capri pants that came to just below her knees.

Colored party lights were strung around the raised wooden dance floor, where couples were already dancing to the music the deejay was playing. She could smell the smoked meats and barbecue sauce, and her mouth watered at the huge bowls of food and desserts.

No one had begun eating yet, so she helped herself to a glass of lemonade, then wandered around talking with the people she knew.

"You made it!" Mamie cried when she spotted her. "I'm so glad. You need to get out and meet some of these folks. There's never enough time when we're working.

"We're like a big family, you know. Sort of like a traveling circus. We'll go from here to Idaho to dig potatoes, and we'll see folks there we know. Want to come with us?"

"I'm afraid not. I'm hoping I'll have some money saved and go back to business school."

"Oh, you were in business school?" Mamie asked. "Then why did you quit? With an education you can get a good job. What happened?"

Carlee lifted her shoulders in a careless shrug. She had said too much and needed to gloss over it. "Things happen. Like marriage. Babies. Divorce. Life goes on. We pick up the pieces and try again."

"Well, sure, honey." Mamie patted her on her back. "You're young and smart, and I know you're going to do well. But what you need is a husband and a father for that boy of yours."

"Been there, done that. I'd rather make it on my own, Mamie."

Mamie winked and gave her a poke in her ribs. "You haven't been there and done that with Nick Starke, honey, and in case you haven't noticed him, *he* notices *you*. All the time. Like now." She cocked her head to the side, indicating Carlee should look in that direction.

Nick was standing beside the deejay, but he was looking straight at her with a bemused expression as if he wasn't sure whether or not he should wave.

Carlee raised her hand.

He grinned and waved back.

"See? He likes you." Mamie whispered. "I saw that when I saw how upset he got to find out you had gone out into the groves before that storm hit. He took off like a scalded dog, he did."

Carlee passed that off by saying that naturally he'd be concerned about an employee being out in such bad weather.

"Uh-uh," Mamie said. "It was more than that. Now why don't you walk on over there and ask him to dance?"

Carlee looked at her as if she'd lost her mind. "I can't do that."

"Oh, go on." Mamie gave her a little push. "Nothing ventured, nothing gained."

Very patiently, very politely, Carlee said she just wasn't interested. "But I do need to talk to him about something."

"Sure, sure," Mamie said, a knowing smile on her face. "You just go do that now. Maybe you can sit together while you eat. They're getting ready to start serving."

Carlee was not about to approach Nick, knowing Mamie would be watching. She did not want to be fodder for gossip among the workers. She also didn't want to eat with him. So instead of crossing to where he was, she got in line and helped herself to the food.

Everything was delicious, and she was famished. All she ever bought for herself to eat were bare essentials. Cereal. Bread. Fruit. A few TV dinners. Nothing like the food being offered in such abundance here.

She had just finished a second helping of orange pound cake when Nick walked over. She had found a place away from all the lights, a remote table in the shadows. She didn't want Mamie to see her and come over again to start playing matchmaker. Nor did she want Nick to find her. She wanted to talk to him to thank him for the shoes, but hoped to wait till later, when the crowd thinned out a bit.

"So this is where you're hiding." The table had a wooden bench on each side, and he sat down directly in front of her, rather than next to her. "I was afraid you'd already gone home. I'm glad you made it."

Carlee wiped her mouth with her napkin, sure she must have barbecue sauce all over her face, because she had really eaten the ribs with relish. "Actually I was going to find you later and thank you for Scotty's shoes. That was nice of you." She wasn't going to offer a perfunctory remark about how it wasn't necessary.

Because it was...

Only Nick didn't realize that yet.

"You were following me, weren't you?" She tried to make her tone light and not sound annoyed—which she was, regardless of the positive outcome.

He held up his hands in mock surrender. "Okay, I admit it. I overheard you telling Mamie you were driving into Sanford to get Scotty some shoes, and I wanted to make sure you did."

"I could have gotten them next week. My paycheck was

short this week, and I had some bills to take care of. I can pay you back."

"Not necessary," he said firmly. "How many times do I have to tell you, Carlee, that I want to help you? No strings attached."

"Okay," she said with a conciliatory nod. "If that's what you want to do, then I will accept on Scotty's behalf. But I want you to know it's not expected."

"I know that. It's just I feel guilty sometimes to..."

His voice trailed off, and she looked at him anxiously, awaiting his next words, but after a few seconds of silence, he murmured, "I just want to help, that's all."

Carlee put her hands under the table, squeezing them into fists so tight she felt her nails dig into her flesh.

Had he been about to slip and say he felt guilty because once upon a time he got a woman pregnant, told her to have an abortion and then disappeared?

She busied herself gathering up her plate, cup and napkins so she wouldn't have to look at him as she thought what a hypocrite he was.

She had no way of knowing that he had been about to confide that he sometimes felt guilty to have so much when others had so little. He was glad he'd caught himself, afraid he would sound condescending, and he was being extra-careful to not say the wrong thing around her.

Nick stood, sensing she had climbed behind her wall again and was not about to let her go so easily. "Carlee, would you dance with me? I like to see all the ladies on the dance floor," he added, so she wouldn't feel singled out. "Even though I've got two left feet and absolutely no rhythm."

Telling herself it was for Scotty, she allowed him to lead

her onto the floor, hoping he wouldn't notice how damp her palms were.

She was aware others were watching them, but told herself that was only natural. After all, he was the boss. He was single. Besides, he tried to dance with all the women there, married or not. Very congenial. Ever the gentleman. No one could accuse him of having a personal interest in the woman he held in his arms now.

But Carlee could not help herself.

She loved feeling his hand on the small of her back, and the caressing way he held her fingertips as they moved. She told herself she would have felt that way with any attractive man. Because, for the moment, it was easy to set aside animosity and go with the emotions stirring inside her.

They danced for a while without speaking. He kept an appropriate space between them, and Carlee cursed herself for wondering what it would be like if he held her so close their bodies melded together and she could feel the beating of his heart against her own.

Then he quietly commented that she was a very good dancer and asked, "Did you and your husband go out a lot?"

She saw no reason not to talk about her marriage to Jack Wheeler. "We did at first, but then he started going out on his own. I wound up staying home more and more by myself."

"Did you divorce before Scotty was born?"

When she hesitated, Nick said, "I'm sorry. I don't mean to pry. It's just that I'd like to know more about you, Carlee."

"It's okay," she said, because it was. Besides, once he found out about Scotty and how she planned to raise him, he was going to want to know a lot more about her background. "And yes, we were divorced before Scotty was born." *Which was, of course, not a lie.*

"That must have been tough on you. Didn't he want to have a baby?"

"No. Jack didn't want children." *Also not a lie.*

"That's a shame. Children are great. I'd love to have a houseful."

Well, you've made a start, she thought bitterly, *only you don't know it yet.*

The music ended, but he did not let her go, instead asking, "Can you give me one good reason why I can't take you and Scotty on a picnic tomorrow?"

She could give him a reason, all right. She could simply tell him she didn't want to go because it was becoming more and more unnerving to be around him. She was having trouble remembering why she should detest him. But of course she wasn't about to tell him any of this, and just gave in. "I guess not, Nick. Scotty enjoys the ocean, so we'd be happy to go with you."

For one alarming instant Carlee thought he was actually going to kiss her. He looked so happy, with his whole face lit up in a grin. Her apprehension was so great that she stepped back from him.

He was too elated to notice. "I know a nice place just north of Titusville where it's not crowded. The weather is supposed to be perfect. We'll have a wonderful time."

"Scotty will like that," she murmured, wondering what she was getting herself into. But it was too late to back out. Still, it was important she have some time alone with Nick.

That was the only reason she'd said yes.

At least that was what she wanted so desperately to believe.

Chapter Eight

It was perfect weather for the beach. Not too hot with a cool ocean breeze, and the breaking waves were far enough out that Scotty was not scared as he sat playing in the foam at the water's edge.

Nick had stopped at a convenience store on the way to buy him a pail and shovel. Carlee had not protested, having decided to let Nick spend whatever he wanted on Scotty.

She had slathered sunblock on Scotty so he wouldn't burn. As an added precaution, he was wearing a cotton T-shirt and a little baseball cap. He kept pulling that off till it fell in the water, so she'd put sunblock on his head to keep it from burning.

They had not been there long when Nick decided that despite her best efforts, the sun was too strong for Scotty. There was a resort a short distance up the beach, and he walked there and brought back a nice, big umbrella.

"How did you manage that?" Carlee knew from experience that resorts would only allow their guests to use their beach equipment.

"I bought it," he said simply. "Paid four times what it's worth, but it's a seller's market, right?"

As always, his grin showed his dimples. There was just no denying his appeal to her—to women in general. She saw the way bikini-clad girls looked at him as they passed by. He looked great in white swim trunks that accented his tan, as well as his nice buns. His stomach was flat. His chest was broad, with a sensual mat of hair that trailed down to below the waist of his trunks.

"How's this?" He had finished pushing the pole into the sand and stood back to make sure it was stable.

"You're the expert when it comes to sand, remember? I'm a real klutz."

"Oh, not anymore. You did great on Friday. I was pleased." He spread the blanket he'd brought, then reached for Scotty, who was squirming in Carlee's arms, anxious to get down on the sand again. "Okay, Scotty. Now dig all you want but stay in the shade."

He motioned to Carlee to join them. "You, too. Can't have you getting sunburned and begging off work tomorrow."

Carlee almost laughed to think she'd let anything keep her away.

Nick busied himself building a sand castle, much to Scotty's delight. He was good, Carlee mused as she watched. He appeared to be totally absorbed in playing with Scotty, paying her no mind. If she didn't know Nick for what he was, she would never have suspected it was all an act. She would think he was genuinely crazy about the baby.

"You know," Nick remarked, "it's amazing how much fun you can have with a kid. And I can't help thinking that when they get older, it just gets better. You're lucky to have him, Carlee.''

She didn't reply. What could she say? It was not something she wanted to discuss with Nick.

"So what are your plans for the fall? Can I talk you into staying on?''

She was lying with her legs sticking out from under the umbrella, trying to get some color. She had worn an over-size T-shirt over her swimsuit. The only one she had was a bikini, and she was reluctant to reveal so much skin around Nick. He hadn't said anything, but she thought he had looked at her funny when she kept the T-shirt on once they got to the beach.

"Probably not," she finally answered. "I may go to night school. I can't pick oranges for the rest of my life.''

"And what would you study?''

"Bookkeeping. Accounting. Computers. Anything to train me for an office job." She wasn't about to confide she already had one lined up once she finished school. Nor would she reveal that she couldn't wait to get back to work at Jupiter Groves.

Scotty began to fret, letting Carlee know he was hungry. She got his bottle, and he settled back with that. She was also hungry and told Nick so; he opened the basket he had brought. Fried chicken, pimento-cheese sandwiches, potato chips and cookies. He also had frosty bottles of soda packed in crushed ice.

Again she was impressed. "You really went all out.''

"I've bought lunches at that place before. They always do a good job.''

Carlee could not resist teasing, "So you bring lots of women with their babies out here, then?''

"No, no." He laughed. "Nothing like that. Sometimes Becky will get someone to help her take the older kids to the beach during regular harvest. I order their lunches for them. And there have been times I've come alone and bought my own. You're the first date I've brought here."

Before she realized it, Carlee blurted, "I didn't consider this a date."

Dammit, you did it again, Nick silently cursed himself. There was the look, like a curtain dropping over her. Why was she so sensitive? He had to watch every single thing he said. "I didn't mean it like that, Carlee. I just meant you're the first woman I've brought here."

"I see."

He decided to heck with it. He might as well plunge ahead and draw the curtain tighter, but at least he'd feel as if he was trying to reach some semblance of understanding between them. "Is it so awful for you to think of this as a date?"

"I...it..." she floundered. "It's just awkward, that's all."

"Too soon after your divorce?"

She seized on the excuse. "Yes, that's it. I haven't been out with anyone."

"And I guess it's strange to think of dating with a baby."

Another lifeline. "It sure is. Most men don't want a ready-made family."

He could have shouted, *This one does.* Instead, he cautiously opined, "I don't think that would matter if two people really came to care about each other."

She lifted her chin, staring at the distant waves cresting as they joined hands to roll toward shore. "I wouldn't want to get involved with any man who couldn't love Scotty like his own."

Nick gazed at the little boy. He was now sleeping contentedly. "You won't have a problem there, believe me. But tell me," he ventured, since she was opening up a little, "you said the other night you don't know where Scotty's father is. Have you tried to find him? He'd probably want to help with child support and even spend some time with his son."

"He doesn't know about him."

Nick was confused. "You didn't tell him you were pregnant? Or didn't you know you were when you broke up?"

She shrugged as if it didn't matter. "Okay, so he did know, but he didn't care and left, anyway."

Though she continued to stare straight ahead, he could see that her eyes were blazing with anger. He had obviously broached a very tender subject. Probably he should shut up and talk about something else. But this was the closest he'd ever come to getting her to talk about her personal life, and he felt driven to continue till she completely disappeared behind the curtain. "I'm sorry, Carlee. But maybe you should try to find him. If he saw Scotty, he might change his mind and—"

"And do what?" She whipped her head about to glare at him. "He didn't want him then. He wouldn't want him now."

She stood.

The curtain had dropped all the way.

"If you'll keep an eye on Scotty, I think I'll go wading. I need to cool down."

Nick told her to go ahead, thinking that was exactly what she needed to do, because he had struck a hornets' nest.

But at least he could be sure now that she carried no torches for Scotty's father, and that was a relief. What did bother him, however, was that her resentment and anger were slamming the door to any chance for romance.

And he wanted that. Very much. Because no matter how often he'd told himself he should stay away from her, he couldn't.

When she finally returned, he once more threw caution to the wind and said, "Look, Carlee. I've always been a direct person. I don't beat around the bush. I like you and I like your son. I'd like for us to be more than friends. And if you think I'm asking too many personal questions, it's because I'm afraid you're so mad at Scotty's father it's making you resent all men. But I'm not like him, and I'd appreciate it if you'd give me a chance to prove that."

She was sitting as far from him as she could get and still be under the shade of the umbrella, but he reached to cover her hand with his, and she did not pull away.

"Will you give me that chance?"

Carlee had done a lot of thinking during her hour-long walk and had actually been tempted to return and tell Nick the truth. But did not do so for a couple of reasons.

One, she was making good money and had a wonderful place for her and Scotty to live until fall. If she told Nick now, she would have to leave, for it would be too awkward to remain.

Two—and this bothered her deeply—she couldn't help the fact that she enjoyed Nick's company, maybe even liked him a little.

No, the reality was she liked him a lot.

And if Alicia were watching from heaven above, Carlee prayed she would understand and forgive her. After all, Alicia had not been able to resist him, either. But Carlee did not intend for things to go that far.

"Maybe you're right. Maybe I am bitter. But as for giving you a chance, let's just say I'm not ready for any kind of serious relationship, Nick. Besides, it's kind of awkward with you being my boss. If you get mad at me, I'm fired, and I can't afford that right now. So maybe it's best we keep things strictly business between us.''

''Uh-uh.'' He shook his head, an almost impish smile on his lips. ''None of that. Either give me a chance or you *are* fired.''

He realized at once she wasn't taking it as a joke. ''Whoa, wait a minute. I'm teasing, Carlee. If you really don't want to see me, then okay. We'll make it strictly business and forget today. But I want you to know that if you did agree to see me and things didn't work out, you've got my word it would not affect your job.''

He appeared to relax, and he moved to lighten the moment by adding, ''As long as you don't set your ladder in soft sand.''

She couldn't help laughing.

He was still holding her hand and squeezed.

''Okay,'' she said finally. ''I'll set the ladder like it's supposed to be, and you remember I'm not ready for anything serious. Just friendship.''

''It's a deal.''

She pulled her hand away and reached into the picnic basket for a sandwich. Taking it from the plastic bag, she took a few bites, then said, ''Okay, you've been asking me personal questions. Now it's my turn. What happened in your marriage?''

He was munching on a drumstick, and such a direct question took him by surprise. He swallowed, then took a sip of soda, stalling as he searched for a way to answer without revealing more than he cared to for the time being. Finally he said, ''She just wanted something I couldn't give her.''

Again he was bewildered by the look of loathing she

gave him, but it went away as quickly as it had appeared. "That was a pretty nosy question," she said. "I'm sorry."

"No, no, it's okay." He reached for her hand again, moving closer as he did so. "Listen, when we know each other better, I'll tell you all about it. Just like I'm hoping one day you'll feel close enough to confide in me all the hurts in your past.

"I just want you to remember one thing," he rushed to emphasize. "I'm not like Scotty's father. I'm not the one who walked out on you, okay?"

Carlee knew they were treading on dangerous waters. He was triggering emotions she was trying her best to control. For Scotty's sake, it would be nice if they could get to know each other and be friends before she divulged the truth. But it could not go further than that. She couldn't let it. But before they even got off the ground, she had to push back the resentments that were trying to surface. In a light, breezy voice, she suggested, "Let's not go there, Nick. There are things we both don't feel comfortable sharing right now, so why don't we leave it at that and enjoy the day...enjoy each other.

"And get ready to enjoy Scotty," she warned with a nod and a smile. The boy was awake and sitting up. Seeing the water again, he began crawling toward it, a determined look on his face. "Maybe we'd better let him splash around for a while. It won't hurt for him to be in the sun a few minutes."

Together they went to the water's edge. The tide was coming in. Nick scooped out a little hole for Scotty to sit in and, to his delight, the sea quickly rushed in to fill it.

As Carlee watched them together, she wondered not for the first time what Nick's reaction would be when the truth came out. Would he be angry and accuse her of extortion and a paternity test? If he was indeed using Scotty to get close to her, that might well be his response. She was also reminded of her other fear—that if he was sincerely becoming attached to him, he might argue for custody.

And that she didn't like to think about, because he could offer Scotty so much more than she could. Still, she knew she would fight him, even if she had no chance of winning.

Because she loved Scotty.

And because she had made his dying mother a promise she intended to keep.

Her mind also wandered to the two men in her past she had thought she loved, only to wind up feeling like the world's biggest fool. They had professed the best intentions, gained her trust along with her heart, only to ultimately turn out to be liars and cheats. So it was no wonder that she regarded someone like Nick with suspicion and doubt.

Besides, she wasn't supposed to have a relationship with him.

She wasn't supposed to have any desire for him.

And certainly not any love.

Still, she couldn't help feeling a wee bit guilty over treating him so coldly. As hard as it would be, maybe she should give him the benefit of the doubt. After all, he had gone out of his way to be nice to her, as well as Scotty. Still, she was wary, especially when she recalled Sandy's remarks about why his marriage had failed. And on top of that, his saying there was something his wife had wanted that he couldn't give her.

Couldn't? Or *wouldn't?*

It was mind-boggling. Carlee gave her head a brisk shake and vowed to stop dwelling on it. She was going to focus on her job and make as much money as possible. When the Valencias were all picked and there was no more work, then—and only then—would she tell Nick.

With that resolved, she settled back to enjoy the rest of the day.

Finally it was time for her to say they needed to start for home.

"Did you bring a change of clothes like I suggested?" Nick asked as picked up Scotty and they started back to where they had left their things under the umbrella.

"Yes, but I'll just wrap a towel around me and ride home like I am, if that's okay. I guess I thought there'd be a place to shower and change around here."

With a mysterious gleam in his eye, he confirmed, "There is. That's why I told you to bring some clean clothes."

Once they had packed everything in the truck, which Nick had opted to drive rather than the beach buggy, declaring it was safer on the highway, he drove north. When he passed the turnoff that would put them on the road to home, Carlee cried, "You missed the road."

"I know. We aren't going home just yet."

"But—"

"I have a surprise for you. The day isn't over yet."

Any other time Carlee might have enjoyed whatever game he was playing, but it was close to Scotty's suppertime, and she had only brought enough baby food for lunch. "Nick, we really need to get back. Scotty has to be fed on schedule."

"He will be. Don't worry. This is just a little treat I planned to cap the day off right."

She settled back and told herself there was no need to be annoyed, because she had a feeling Nick knew what he was doing.

About twenty minutes after leaving the beach, they turned into a curving paved drive. Ornate lanterns bordered, banked by lush hydrangea bushes with royal palms towering above.

Carlee glanced about, puzzled. "Nick, where are we? Who lives here?" They were passing a waterfall with a pool beneath and white swans gliding about.

"Nobody. It's a club. A private club. I belong to it. There are cabanas where we can shower and change. We could have come here for our picnic, but I thought we'd have more fun off by ourselves."

"So why are we here now?"

"They have a wonderful dining room with a terrific view of the ocean. And the food is excellent. I thought you'd enjoy eating here before we go home." He turned to wink. "And don't worry. I asked Becky what kind of food Scotty eats and called ahead and told them to make sure they had some ready."

"I...I don't believe this," she stammered. It was too much too soon, and she felt like saying so but didn't. "I just hope Scotty behaves. Some people don't like to have young children around when they're out for the evening."

"He'll be fine. And don't worry. I know we have to be up early tomorrow. We'll stay just long enough to eat."

A valet came out to park the car and could not have been more solicitous of Nick had he been driving a Rolls-Royce.

Carrying Scotty, Nick led the way around the building to the cabanas set back from the ocean. "We can take turns looking after Scotty while we shower and change. You go first."

Carlee was moving almost trancelike. Dear Lord, if Nick was doing all this to impress her, he was doing a real good job. There was no denying she was having fun...and fun was something she had not had much of in her life.

She was glad she had brought a nice pair of white slacks

and blouse. Still she felt a bit shabby and said as much to Nick when he came out of his cabana wearing a sport jacket.

"You look fine," he assured her. "Men are expected to wear a jacket at night here, but other than that it's strictly casual. If it weren't, I wouldn't have sprung this on you. I'd have told you it was dressy."

Which, Carlee was depressed to think, meant she would have had to decline, because she didn't have any dressy clothes. The few cocktail dresses she had owned when she and Jack were married were long gone.

They were seated at a window table with a gorgeous view. Nick ordered a bottle of wine. He said the steaks were really good, so she let him order for them both. And, as he had promised, a waiter brought Scotty's favorite baby food, all nicely warmed.

Halfway through her second glass of wine, Carlee was feeling so relaxed and mellow that, without thinking, she declared, "I could get used to all this."

Nick was enjoying himself, too. Scotty was being a perfect angel, and Carlee seemed to have raised that curtain and was as much fun as he had hoped. Her remark, however, had triggered something inside him that he'd thought he was over—as far as she was concerned, at least.

I could get used to all this.

She was glancing around the room, taking in the decor—potted palms, hanging baskets, seascapes on the walls, plush carpet on the floor. And it hit him then and there that the only way she could get used to such luxury was through him.

Could it be, he wondered as suspicion snaked up his spine, that her cold reserve was all an act? That she was actually playing the old game of hard-to-get? Maybe when he had given Scotty the honey bear at first meeting, she had seen he was a softie when it came to children. Especially babies. So what better way to get to him than through her son?

He shook his head to clear it, the movement so hard that Carlee noticed.

"Is anything wrong?"

"No, just tired I guess." He tossed down the rest of his wine. A waiter appeared instantly to refill his glass, but Nick declined. "No more. One glass is my limit when I'm driving. Coffee, please. Black."

Carlee had turned her attention to Scotty, who was playing with his creamed peas.

Surely he was wrong, Nick admonished himself. She wasn't like the others. No way. She acted the way she did because she carried a lot of baggage from her past. Still, she might just be one shrewd cookie. He would find out soon enough. Till then, he would just continue enjoying her company, enjoying Scotty and all of them having a good time.

And he would not allow himself to think about the future—not when Carlee seemed unable to let go of her past.

"I'd love a slice of that key lime pie," she said wistfully when the waiter brought the dessert tray around, "but I'm afraid we don't have time." Scotty was getting fretful, and she thought it was time they got him home and in bed.

"She'll have a slice to go, please," Nick told the waiter.

"No, really, you don't need to—"

"I want to."

"But…" She knew it was no use. He was determined to be as nice as possible, and she just had to relax and let him, even though it was so terribly awkward.

Carlee was quiet on the way home in the truck, her guilt rising once more. She should get it over with. But could not...and would not. Because she liked things the way they were for the moment.

And she liked Nick.

When they pulled up in front of her cottage, Scotty was sound asleep in the car seat Nick had fastened in the rear of the cab. He carried him inside, and Carlee led the way to her room, where she had set up the crib Nick had sent over.

"I'll just let him sleep like he is," she said. "I don't want to wake him up. And I can't thank you enough for his crib."

"Glad to do it."

They stood looking at each other for an awkward moment, then Nick said he'd better be going and walked out.

Carlee followed him to the porch, carrying the little box containing the key lime pie. It was dark and she hadn't turned on the light. If Mamie or any of the others saw Nick bringing her home, they'd have a field day gossiping.

"It was a really nice day, Nick. Thank you."

"I enjoyed it, too. We'll have to do it again some time."

Again they seemed frozen in place, eyes locked in a deep, thoughtful gaze.

Carlee knew she should run inside, but could not make herself move.

Then there was no more time to think, because suddenly Nick acted on instinct and the feelings rocketing through his body. He took her in his arms and kissed her.

For an instant Carlee stood motionless, then her own emotions took hold. Her hands went about his neck, and she clung to him. She shivered at the intensity of his body pressed to hers and at the delicious passion of his kiss.

And then he was pulling away from her, taking a step backward, staring in a mixture of wonder and apology.

"I'm sorry. You probably didn't want me to do that, but I just couldn't help it."

"It…it's all right." *All right?* Heaven help her, it had been wonderful. She'd never known a kiss could be so wonderful.

In the light spilling from inside the cabin, Nick looked at her as though he could not get enough of the sight of her. Then, with a muffled groan, he pulled her to him once more, cupping her chin as he lifted her face for yet another kiss.

This time he parted her lips with his tongue, and she sighed deep in her throat as she clung to him.

Later, as Carlee lay in her bed wide awake, unable to sleep and staring at the ceiling, she wondered what would have happened had someone not slammed a car door somewhere in the distance. The sound had made them spring apart.

"Good night, Carlee," he'd murmured, then quickly left.

And Carlee had stood there for long moments after the truck's taillights had disappeared, fingertips pressed to her mouth.

She knew then that no matter what the future held, she would always remember that kiss.

Chapter Nine

Carlee was perched on her ladder, picking the big ripe Valencias and enjoying the day. She had learned to wear gloves so her hands would not blister and was good at setting the ladder, so all was well.

Everyone was focused on what they were doing, especially those who had not made quota, as they neared quitting time. She was pleased to have met hers, because she was getting faster and better, and allowed her mind to wander.

It had been two weeks since the night Nick had kissed her. Since then, he had been friendly whenever they were together but someone else was always around. He had not come by the cottage or made any effort to contact her when they were not working.

That night Carlee had lain awake till nearly dawn. With her lips still warm from his, she had tossed and turned with mixed emotions.

It had been wonderful, and she had enjoyed it, but her conscience needled her—was she betraying Alicia? But who better than Alicia, she reasoned, to understand how irresistible Nick was? Besides, Carlee was not about to let anything compromise Scotty's welfare. He came first and foremost in anything she did.

It was a no-win situation for both Nick and her. Her purpose was to dig in her heels and work as long as possible before telling him about Scotty. His was, no doubt, to get her into bed, making yet another conquest. She would ultimately achieve her goal, while Nick would fail.

Still, she told herself to enjoy the ride as long as it lasted, and when she had finally drifted off to sleep in the wee hours, she had not felt so bad about what had happened. After all, it was just a kiss, albeit a *nice* kiss.

The next morning when the alarm had gone off, she had barely been able to drag herself out of bed. Even Scotty had overslept, and she had raced around to get them both ready.

She had also dreaded seeing Nick that day but needn't have worried. He had not shown up in the groves. As a matter of fact, she had not seen him until the end of the week. When she had, he was cheerful and friendly to everyone but made no effort to single her out or pay her any mind at all.

As the days passed and nothing changed, she told herself it was probably all for the best. She could now focus on work and Scotty, and look forward to the time when she could return to Melbourne and get on with her life. Besides, she reasoned, she had already accomplished what she'd set out to do—find Scotty's father—and concluded that if he should want visitation, she would work something out. Beyond that, she resolved to fight tooth and nail to keep anyone from taking Scotty away from her permanently. That was another reason she wanted to make as much money as possible—to be able to hire a lawyer if it came down to a showdown with Nick.

Still, in the quiet of the evenings, Carlee could not help remembering how much she had enjoyed the time she had spent with Nick. She would sit on the porch steps, arms wrapped about her knees as she watched the dancing fireflies, listen to the tree frogs and crickets, and loneliness would wrap about her like a shroud.

She told herself she was being silly. All they'd had was an encounter at the mall, a dance, a picnic...and a kiss. Hardly enough to wax nostalgic, but she could not seem to get him out of her mind no matter how hard she tried.

From somewhere below Mike Thurston yelled, "Okay, quitting time. Everybody down, and let's load up."

Scrambling down her ladder, Carlee emptied the canvas pick sack into one of the plastic tubs. They each held about nine hundred pounds of oranges, and in a few moments the goat would come through and, with its hydraulic boom, lift the tubs and empty them into its container.

"Carlee, you did real good," Mike complimented her as he helped her with the ladder. It wasn't heavy, but the male workers were real good about giving her a hand.

"Thanks. That makes four straight days I've made quota." She walked along with him as he carried the ladder to a truck for transport to the next block ready for harvest.

"Make it one more day, and there's a fifty-dollar bonus for you this week."

Carlee was thrilled. She had been making regular payments on the bills and started stashing away a few dollars every week. But money was still tight. If not for living rent-free, she didn't know how she and Scotty could make it. There were always things like welfare and food stamps, as well as organizations like Aid to Dependent Children, but she would never resort to that even if it meant working day and night. She was afraid Scotty would be taken away from her if it appeared she couldn't afford to look after him. But if she could hold on till harvest was over, everything would be okay.

She saw Nick in the distance, but if he saw her, he did not let on.

There were times when she thought it might be best if she just quit and hired a lawyer to confront Nick about child support. Let someone else be the go-between. But she always reminded herself that was not the way to do it. Besides, he might get the wrong idea and think she was afraid to tell him face-to-face, and that wouldn't do. Not when she might have to deal with him until Scotty was grown.

She climbed on the back of one of the pickup trucks for the ride back to the main area where she'd left her car. Everyone was talking about the coming weekend, glad Starke Groves did not require seven-day workweeks like some groves.

Unlike the others who looked forward to shopping, fishing or the beach, Carlee was happy to spend time with Scotty. She planned another picnic with him, this time at the lake, where he could watch the ducks and she could help him sail the boat Nick had given him, which had become his favorite toy.

Mamie was just coming out of the processing office and stopped Carlee as she was about to drive away.

Carlee bit back a groan. She had managed to avoid her since that night at the pavilion, knowing she would be full of questions.

"I was wondering how the romance is going, because I

haven't seen the big boss down our way in a long time. I hope things didn't come to a screeching stop.''

"No, they didn't," Carlee said breezily. "Because they never got started in the first place. We had one dance, that's all.''

"And a trip to the beach." Mamie's eyes were twinkling.

"How did you know about that?''

"One of my boys was out walking and saw the two of you driving up the road when Mr. Nick was taking you home. Also, Mr. Nick's housekeeper is a friend of mine, and she told me about the sandy shoes and wet clothes he left in the laundry room the next day. I just put two and two together.''

Though decidedly annoyed, Carlee was not mad. She knew Mamie meant no harm. In fact, she probably thought she was doing a favor by encouraging a romance. Little did she know how Carlee was fighting it, but there was no need to worry about things going any further. Not the way Nick had been acting. "Yes, we did go to the beach, and Scotty loved it. But that's it. Nothing is going on between us, Mamie, believe me.''

Mamie gave her arm a pat through the open window. "Well, you just be careful and don't get hurt, honey. He's already paid you more attention than I've ever seen him pay to anybody else. Just take it slow and easy. You might be playing out of your league.''

Carlee laughed to herself as she drove away. Nick Starke hurt her?

When she got to the day-care center, Becky was waiting to wave her in, bouncing up and down on her toes in excitement. "Just wait till you see, Carlee. Just wait till you see. Our boy took his first steps today, and he hasn't slowed down since.''

Feeling joyful and disappointed both at once, Carlee

rushed past Becky to go inside. She wanted to witness that very special moment when Scotty first walked, and she had missed it.

He was standing on the outside of his playpen, clinging to the bars as he swayed back and forth. He was grinning as if he knew he'd done something special he should be proud of.

Carlee dropped to her knees and held out her arms. "Come on, Scotty. Walk to me. Let me see you do it."

With a happy squeal, he let go of first one bar, then the other, and took one cautious step. Then two. Then three. And just before he reached Carlee, he lost his balance, dipped forward, then backward to plop down on his bottom.

She grabbed him and hugged him, and over her cooing baby talk praising him, did not at first grasp what Becky was saying.

Then she froze.

"…he'd been coming by every day, and today it happened. Scotty went to him. He took two steps, then fell. But he did it."

"Whoa, wait a minute." Carlee stood, then picked up Scotty to hold him as she fought for composure. She did not want Becky to see how upset she was. "You mean Nick has been coming by coaxing Scotty to walk?"

"He sure has. He's crazy about him."

Carlee realized she wasn't doing a very good job of masking her feelings when Becky asked, "Is there a problem? I mean…do you mind him coming by to see Scotty?"

"No, no, of course not." Carlee forced a smile. "I think it's great. I know you're busy with the other kids, and I always try to play with him as much as I can when I get home, but you know how it is when you're tired from working all day." She was saying too much, talking too much, but trying very hard to sound approving of Nick spending time with Scotty.

But the reality was, she was seething inside, because, without knowing it, Nick had witnessed his son's first steps.

And that seemed heartbreakingly unfair to Carlee.

She talked for a few moments more with Becky, all the while anxious to leave. And once she was back in the car with Scotty tucked in his seat and no one to watch, she slammed her fist against the steering wheel and cursed whatever game Nick was playing.

He was apparently ignoring her to keep her at bay, hoping she would wonder if he would come around again. And all the while he had been sneaking over to visit Scotty, knowing she would hear about it and be touched.

She was touched—but not in the way he had intended.

Nick was sitting at his desk when Elaine came in. "What are you doing still here?" he asked. "It's nearly six."

"Clearing up some odds and ends. I could ask the same about you."

She could, indeed, ask, but he would lie and say he was also catching up on things. The truth was, however, that he did not want to go home to an empty house. Especially today of all days, when he had finally coaxed a little boy who had captured his heart to take his first steps. While it had been a nice experience, it had reminded him of how he'd never have a child of his own. So that was why he was still in his office, brooding and, yes, feeling sorry for himself.

Elaine said, "Someone called from Orlando today about the Children's Charity Ball. They said you hadn't confirmed your reservation yet. I told them I'd check with you and call them back.''

''I should've done that before now. It just slipped my mind.''

''Then you're going?''

''Might as well.'' He sounded anything but enthused. ''I usually do.''

''And who will you be taking this time? They need to know for the place cards at the head table.''

He thought of Carlee. She was perky and cute in those short pants she wore, hair pulled back in a ponytail, but once again he could envision how stunning she'd be dressed for a formal event. But even if he could muster the nerve to ask her, he was pretty sure she would turn him down.

''Mr. Starke...'' Elaine was staring at him expectantly.

''Let me think about it,'' he hedged. ''I'll let you know tomorrow morning.''

''Sure. You've got so many to choose from,'' she teased. ''I guess it's hard for you to make up your mind.''

''Yeah, sure,'' he said, matching her banter. ''I'm a regular Tom Cruise. Women are beating down my door wanting to go out with me.''

Elaine's tone became serious. ''You're the best catch in central Florida, and you know it.''

He could have flippantly agreed and said they both knew why, but didn't. It sounded conceited, and he was not that.

He waved her away, repeating he'd let her know about the charity ball in the morning.

For a long time after she left, he sat there silently arguing with himself over whether to ask Carlee to go with him. He had avoided her as much as possible since that night when he threw caution to the wind and kissed her. Embarrassed, he'd felt it was best but couldn't help himself where Scotty was concerned. So he had stopped by to see him at the day-care center every chance he got, and the reward had been seeing him take those first precious steps straight into his waiting arms.

But it had also made him want to be with Carlee again, to be a part of her life, as well as Scotty's.

Bracing himself for rejection, Nick drove to her cabin, parking his car next to hers. He walked up on the porch and knocked. She didn't answer, and he couldn't hear her moving around inside. Nor could he see any movement through the screen door.

He looked toward the lake and saw Scotty. They were all the way over at the pavilion, so he walked around and as he drew closer, saw that she was coaxing Scotty to walk.

"Hey, isn't that something?" Nick called when he was close enough. "I wish you could've been there, Carlee. He took three steps, right into my arms."

"Now he doesn't want to slow down," she said, her hazel eyes frosty as she flicked a glance in his direction. "And, yes, I'd have liked to be there, too. Becky tells me you've been stopping by a lot lately, coaching him."

She was sitting on a blanket she'd brought, and he dropped beside her. "That's all it took. A little coaching. Becky said she didn't have a lot of time to work with him, and we both agreed he was slow because of his baby fat. He'll lose that now, I'll bet."

"I've been coaching him, too."

She sounded annoyed, and Nick was quick to say, "Well, it just happened that I was there at the right time."

"Why?"

He blinked, caught off guard. "What do you mean?"

"Why were you there? Why do you spend so much time with him, Nick?"

Nick did not like feeling the need to defend himself and

stiffly answered, "Because I've grown fond of him. Is that wrong?"

"It is if you're using him to get to me."

He bit back a laugh, because he'd never do anything like that. "Excuse me?"

Very cool, very controlled, she said, "I've made it plain to you that I'm not interested in any kind of relationship right now. Since the night you kissed me, you've avoided me, yet you visit my son, knowing Becky will tell me about it. I think you're doing it to get to me."

He did laugh then. "Carlee, forgive me, but I have to say that's about the most conceited thing I've ever heard. The reason I haven't been around is because I was embarrassed over that kiss. You did make it plain you're not interested in me that way. But it was nice. I enjoyed it, and if I had it to do over again, I would. But as for me trying to use Scotty to get to you, well, I'm sorry if you feel that way.

"Furthermore," he added, no longer smiling, "it's none of my business, but for his sake, as well as your own, I think you should stop being so paranoid. Every man you encounter is not like your husband. I know damn well I'm not."

Carlee felt like an idiot. She hadn't meant for it to come out like that, but then, she knew she didn't have any business saying anything about it in the first place. She was furious that Nick got to see Scotty take his first steps when he hadn't even wanted him to be born. So to hide that, she'd lost her cool and blurted out her accusation about Nick trying to get to her.

She also realized in that instant when she was out of control that she was angrier than she realized about Nick's avoiding her since their kiss, as if it had meant nothing.

But good heavens, what did she want it to mean? Was she totally losing her mind?

She held Scotty up on his feet, and he reached out for Nick, which wasn't helping the situation. He started crying, and she let him go, hoping he actually wanted to sit and play with one of the toys she'd brought. Instead, he teetered back and forth for a few seconds, then began taking short, faltering steps—straight for Nick.

Nick held out his arms to him and cried, "That's my boy!" and hugged him tight.

Carlee winced.

She did not want that. Heaven help her, she did not want Scotty crazy about Nick, and that was wrong. She had no right to feel that way. Especially when she was almost certain he would not only help with Scotty's support but also want to share in his life. And Scotty deserved to know his father. She could not try to keep it from happening. Further, if she didn't get hold of herself, it would only cause problems in the future.

"Carlee, listen to me…"

She had turned her back on him and stood wooden and silent.

"I have tried to talk to you about this before, but it hasn't done any good. It probably won't now. But I'm going to say it again, anyway. I want to be your friend. I want to spend time with your son, because I'm crazy about him. And I promise that what happened the other night will never happen again unless you want it, too. But the way you've hardened your heart to romance…to love…it won't.

"I don't know," he continued, "what happened to make you so bitter. It's none of my business. But as long as you're here, can't you just tolerate me a little bit?"

She felt ashamed, and her voice cracked a little as she

said, "Sure. And I'm sorry for what I said. You're right.
It was conceited of me. And not fair to Scotty. You've
been good to him."

She did turn to face him then and as she did so, thought
for probably the hundredth time that she could understand
how Alicia had so easily fallen in love with him. Not only
was he a very handsome man, he was also compassionate
and tender.

Tell him now, a voice within commanded. *Tell him and
get it over with. Why prolong the misery? Tell him what
you want and expect from him as Scotty's father, and then
run to the cabin, pack your things and leave.*

It was what she *should* do.

But what she could *not* do.

She had tried to tell herself it was because of the available work and the money to be made, but knew that was
not her total motivation.

It was her heart, betraying her and making her want to
remain and savor being with Nick as long as possible. She
would suffer for it later, but could not help herself now.

"I guess I was just jealous you were there and I
wasn't," she said finally.

He looked relieved. "Then you aren't mad about the
kiss?"

She hoped she was not blushing. "No, it's okay, really.
It was just a good-night kiss."

"Just the ending of a nice day," he was quick to agree.
"Nothing meant by it."

Maybe not for you, she thought. "Right. Just a friendly
kiss. No need to think about it."

"And you aren't mad about me spending time with
Scotty? I mean, you won't think I've got ulterior motives?"

"I was silly to say that. Spend all the time with him you like. He needs that."

Feeling things were okay between them again, Nick turned Scotty around and pointed him at Carlee. "Now walk to your mommy. You can do it."

She opened her arms to him and, after hesitating only a few seconds, he went to her.

They played sending him back and forth for several minutes. Then Scotty tired of it and wanted to go back to his toy.

Carlee felt a bit awkward then, not knowing what to say. She noticed that Nick also seemed uncomfortable.

Then he cleared his throat and said, "I had another reason for stopping by. I wanted to ask if you'd like to go with me to a charity function in Orlando in a couple of weeks. It's a children's charity. We use the money we raise to send underprivileged kids to summer camp. It's a nice affair. Dinner. Dancing. I think you'd enjoy it."

She was stunned. He was asking her to go to a formal affair, but there was no way she could accept. She had nothing to wear and couldn't afford to buy a gown for something like that. "I'm sorry, but I can't, Nick. Thanks for asking, though."

"Hey, wait a minute. I thought we'd settled things between us and that we're friends again." He searched her face anxiously. "So why can't you go?"

She hated to admit it, but knew he'd keep after her till she gave him an explanation. "Nick, I have nothing to wear."

He breathed a sigh to learn it was nothing serious. "Is that all? We'll go into Orlando this weekend and find something."

"I can't let you buy me clothes. I wouldn't feel right about it, and even if you wanted to loan me the money, I can't afford to spend it on things like that. I have bills to pay, and..." Her words trailed off to silence and she shrugged, not wanting to say too much about her financial situation. He might use it against her later if he contested her having custody of Scotty.

"Listen." He moved closer and took her hand.

As before, his touch ignited a heated rush, and she prayed he didn't notice.

"I've got to go to this thing, and I need to take someone. I'd like it to be you, Carlee, because I enjoy being with you. And I promise you'll have a nice time. So you might as well say yes," he warned with a mock frown, "because I won't give up."

She gave her head a stubborn shake. "I will not let you buy me clothes, Nick."

He sighed, let her hand go and reached out to pick a blade of grass and chew it thoughtfully as he stared out across the lake. Suddenly he snapped his fingers as an idea struck. "You wear an apron to put the oranges in when you're picking them, don't you?"

Bewildered, she nodded. "Yes. Then I climb down and empty them in the pick sacks, because the sacks are too heavy for me to carry up the ladder like the men do. What are you getting at?"

"And you wear gloves, don't you?"

"Yes, because I get blisters sometimes."

"Those things are mine—the apron, the gloves." The play of a smile touched his lips.

She was totally baffled. "So? If you think I've lost them, I haven't—"

"No, it's nothing like that. But you do agree that those things belong to Starke Groves, right?"

"Well, yes—"

"And you're just borrowing them."

"I guess so, if you put it like that, but—"

"So what's wrong with borrowing something else that, technically, belongs to Starke Groves?"

Carlee was fast becoming exasperated. The truth was, she did want to go with him, but would never allow him to pay for her dress.

"Come on," he coaxed, "play the game. Answer the question. Do you agree it's okay to borrow something?"

"I suppose so, but I have no idea what you're talking about." She got to her feet. "The mosquitoes are starting to get bad. I need to take Scotty in now."

Nick scrambled to his feet, taking Scotty with him. "Come on. You two are coming with me. I've got something to show you."

She picked up the blanket and started folding it. "Nick, it's time for me give Scotty his supper and his bath."

"He can wait a few minutes. This won't take long. Let's go."

He took her hand as if afraid she'd run if he didn't hang on to her. They walked across the grassy bank, with Carlee glancing about in hopes no one was watching. But then she decided it didn't matter. In another month or so she'd be leaving and never see any of these people again. So let them gossip all they wanted.

"Everybody into the buggy," Nick said merrily. "Hang on to Scotty. We aren't going far enough that he'll need the car seat."

Carlee balked "Nick, what's this about?"

"It's a secret. And I've got some cookies at the house that will tide him over till supper."

"Your house?" She took a step back, away from the beach buggy. "I'm not going there. Why—"

"You'll see why."

Those precious dimples were flashing, and Carlee felt her resolve slipping.

"Besides," he teased, "I've still got Scotty, and if you don't get in with us, I'm going to kidnap him."

She finally got in, not because of his threat but because her curiosity was overcoming her irritation.

He drove past the migrant cabins, and as luck would have it, Mamie was outside. She waved, grinning from ear to ear. Sandy was also on her porch and stared coldly as they passed.

Nick drove up the curving drive to his house and stopped outside the triple garage. Carlee had never seen the place up close, and it was even more impressive than she had imagined. A two-story stucco, it was painted a soft cream and trimmed in a shade of deep aqua. White wicker sofas and chairs, with bright floral cushions, were on the front porch, purple wisteria vines trailing about the columns. The yard was like a huge garden, with hydrangeas, hibiscus and daylilies all in bloom.

Nick led the way around to the back of the house and the kidney-shaped swimming pool with a rock waterfall at one end. A concrete deck surrounded it, and there was a gazebo and a barbecue pavilion to the side.

"You have a nice place," Carlee said in awe.

"Thanks. My great-grandfather built it nearly a century ago. I added the pool." He wasn't about to reveal that it had been Gina's project.

They stepped into a kitchen full of modern appliances. Carlee felt a little uncomfortable, but Nick was in a happy mood, and she wanted to find out why he was being so mysterious.

He paused to open a cabinet and take out a box of cookies. Scotty reached out, and Carlee said he could have two and that was it. "I don't want to ruin his supper."

"This won't take long. Come on." They walked down a hallway. "There's a big walk-in closet in what used to be my parents' bedroom. I use it for storage." He glanced at her over his shoulder. "Let's see, you'd be about a size six, right?"

She came to a complete stop and demanded, "Nick, if you don't tell me what this is all about…"

He took Scotty, who was happily munching on a vanilla wafer. "My mother was about your size, and she and my dad were very social. She loved to dress and had a lot of nice clothes. I gave most of them to Goodwill, but I kept her fancy gowns, thinking that sometime at a board meeting I'd suggest having one of those auctions of really nice things, you know? Like antiques, elegant clothes, jewelry, things people would donate. Only I never got around to it."

He continued walking, and Carlee had no choice but to keep up with him if she wanted to hear what he was saying.

Opening a door, he motioned Carlee inside a bedroom furnished in beautiful oak. There was a lace canopy over the bed with matching curtains at the windows. The blue carpet was so thick she felt as if she was going to sink right into it. Through another door she saw a marble bathroom, gold fixtures shaped like swans at the sink.

Nick sat Scotty on the floor and gave him his other cookie, then opened the closet. They were greeted with a blast of cedar-scented air. He made a face. "Whew, I need to air things out, but don't worry, whatever dress you choose I'll have cleaned."

"Whatever I choose…" she echoed, awed, and then he was pulling out several gowns in sequins and satin. "Oh, my gosh," she breathed. "They're beautiful."

"This one." He held up a green sequined creation,

strapless with a straight skirt and a slit up the side. "It looks like it might fit, and it'll go great with your hair."

Carlee checked the designer label. It was a size six, and if it wasn't a perfect fit, she was sure she could make alterations by hand. "Your mother had excellent taste."

"Yes, she did," he agreed, proudly adding, "She was only thirty-eight when she died, but she was the same size she was in college."

"That's so young," Carlee said, a catch in her throat as she thought of Alicia, also dying much too young.

"It was cancer. It hit suddenly and took her fast. My dad never got over it. They said he had a heart attack, but I think it was broken when she died and never healed."

"I'm so sorry, Nick." Carlee reached to touch him in a gesture of sympathy, then drew back. She was afraid to touch him, afraid he would take her in his arms in a moment of shared compassion, and she could not risk that happening. The situation they were in just then was much too intimate. And she sensed that talking about his parents had moved him deeply.

"So—" he drew a deep breath to bring him out of painful rumination "—do you want to try this one on or do you like one of the others better? I'll take Scotty and go outside."

She held up the dress. "Nick, I can't borrow this. It wouldn't be right."

He playfully tweaked her cheek. "Then you can't borrow my gloves and apron, either, which means you can't work for me anymore."

"That's blackmail," she said with a mock scowl. She could not deny she wanted to wear the dress and go to the ball with him, but still felt a little uneasy.

He crossed his arms and countered her scowl with his own. "That's right. So if you don't go, you're fired."

"Well...." She held the gown away from her, as though seriously considering the situation, then said, "Okay. I'll go. But only because I don't want to lose my job."

He looked as he had that other time when he was so happy she thought he was about to kiss her. "Great," he said, beaming. "And just remember the only reason I'm taking you is because I couldn't get another date."

They both broke into laughter.

And Carlee, even in the midst of her happiness, silently prayed that Alicia would forgive her.

Chapter Ten

Nick's mother had been larger in the bosom than Carlee, but other than needing to be taken in there, the gown fit just fine. She had to buy shoes to match, but found some that weren't too expensive. She had been making her quota every day and received a bonus, so she was able to make payments on all her debts and have a little money left over to buy the shoes.

Now that she had agreed to go to the ball, Carlee was counting the days. She was so excited she didn't even mind when Mamie found out—she'd seen Carlee taking the sequined gown out of her car and had come running to ask questions. So there was a lot of good-natured teasing among the female workers.

Nick began spending more time in the orchard near Carlee. He would stand beside her as they picked the oranges from the lower branches without having to climb ladders, and they would talk about everything. But Carlee was careful when he broached anything personal about her past. The less he knew the better. After all, their relationship was only temporary, and the most she could hope to forge from it was friendship where Scotty was concerned if— the fear continued to nag—he did not ultimately despise her.

He invited her out to dinner, but she always made excuses, also declining his suggestion that they spend another day at the beach. She did not want that kind of intimacy. What she did want, however, was for him to be with Scotty as much as possible. It did not matter whether he was using him to get to her. The important thing was that he become fond of Scotty, and Scotty like him, as well.

One afternoon it was particularly hot. The temperature soared toward a scorching one hundred degrees. The air was still and heavy, and midway through the afternoon Nick told everyone to quit for the day. It was too hot to work, and they were running ahead of schedule, anyway.

Carlee was disappointed. She'd have liked a few more hours of pay, and there was nothing to do but sit inside the cottage in front of the air conditioner.

She had just picked up Scotty from day care when Nick pulled up beside her in his truck. "How about going for a swim in my pool? Scotty will love it. I've got a little rubber float we can sit him on."

While Carlee tried to think of a plausible excuse to refuse, Scotty spotted Nick. He squealed and waved and kicked his legs, trying to go to him, which made the situation even more difficult.

"You can't think of a reason to turn me down, can you," he teased. "And besides, I think Scotty just answered for both of you."

There was nothing to do but give in. She decided there was no harm in it. Scotty was wide awake, and they'd be paying all their attention to him. There would be neither time nor opportunity for anything romantic. Besides, the thought of swimming in that delicious pool was much too tempting.

She told Nick she would drive to his house after she went home and changed into her swimsuit. She also wanted to get swim diapers from Becky to put on Scotty. Becky used them on all the toddlers who were not potty-trained before letting them play in the wading pool at the day care.

By the time she got to Nick's, he had set out cold bottles of soda and a tray of cold cuts, cheese, breads and even slices of orange-frosted brownies. "You did all this?" she asked, amazed.

"I'm afraid I can't take the credit." He gestured to an older, gray-haired woman who was coming out the back door carrying a bucket of ice. "This is Lily, my house-keeper. She only works a few days a week, because there's not enough for her to do full-time, but when she does, she bakes for an army. If I weren't careful, she'd have me looking like a blimp."

"What he needs," Lily said with a wink at Carlee, "is a wife to see to it he eats right. You won't believe the fast-food junk I have to clean out of the refrigerator."

Carlee was embarrassed to think Lily meant she might be interested in the position, but Nick saved the day.

"Now don't go baking a wedding cake, Lily. Carlee and I are just good friends, and I'm crazy about her little boy. That's all it is."

Lily made a face. "That's all it ever is. I might as well give up. You're going to wind up an old curmudgeon if you aren't careful. Just wait and see." She set the bucket on the table and turned to go back inside.

"And a fat one, too, if you have anything to do with

it,'' he called, then said to Carlee. "Don't pay any attention to her. She's always telling me I should get married again. She can't stand to see a man single, I guess. But I hope she didn't make you uncomfortable.''

"No, and I really appreciate your setting her straight. The teasing I get from the other women is bad enough.''

Suddenly, Nick asked, "Is it so bad? For people to think we're dating, I mean?''

For a moment Carlee didn't think she was going to be able to respond, but she finally managed to say airily, "I just like to keep my personal life private, Nick.''

With that, she dived into the pool, slicing into the water and swimming all the way to the end without surfacing. Scotty was sitting on the steps, Nick right beside him, so she had the freedom to escape...if only for a little while.

She was a good swimmer. Growing up near the ocean, she had spent as much time as possible in the water. Now it was a relief to have something to do besides address the delicate subject Nick's housekeeper had innocently broached.

When she finally surfaced, Scotty was waving his hands and bouncing up and down, wanting to join her. She picked him up and held him tightly as she began to swing him around in the waist-deep water of the shallow end. He loved it, and then Nick got in the pool to hoist him on his shoulders and ride him around. They were so caught up in having fun, the previous conversation was forgotten for the moment.

Still, even as they laughed and cavorted, totally focused on Scotty, Carlee was very aware of Nick and his all-too-masculine body. Chest bare and glistening with beads of water, shoulders broad and tanned, arms strong, legs sinewy.

It wasn't fair, she thought grudgingly. The man seemed

absolutely wonderful in every way. He appeared to be sensitive and caring to everyone around him, and extremely solicitous of her feelings and Scotty's welfare. Truly he seemed to be the ideal mate, father and family man.

How could it possibly be only an act?

Scotty grew tired, and she watched as Nick carried him to the side. He called to Lily and asked her to take him inside for a while, dry him off and give him some juice. He seemed to know instinctively what the child needed.

How, she wondered, could he have treated Alicia so callously? She hadn't been the sort to sleep around and had even told Carlee she would not have gone to bed with Nick so easily had she not loved him. Plus, he had made her believe they had a future together.

Maybe, Carlee reasoned, Nick had cared for Alicia in the beginning, but it hadn't lasted. Then, when he learned she was pregnant, he felt abortion was best so she could get on with her life and not have a child to raise alone, because he did not love her and did not want to marry her. But if that was the case, it still did not make it right. It would, however, make Nick seem less conniving, less of a womanizer.

She was standing in water to her chest, toward the deep end. She had not heard Nick sneak up behind her and turned around just as he slammed the flat of his hand on the surface, sending a sheet of water into her face.

Stunned, momentarily blinded, she stumbled backward to where the pool was over eight feet deep.

Nick moved fast to pull her back to the shallower water and quickly apologized, "I'm sorry, Carlee. I meant to splash your back, not your face." His arms were folded about her, holding her protectively, tenderly. Unconsciously or otherwise, he was rubbing a hand up and down her back, up into the fine wet hair at the back of her head.

Carlee willed herself to move but could not, the swell of her breasts pressing against his chest.

"Are you all right?" his voice was like a caress, wrapping her even closer in his spell.

She was drowning—but only in the warmth of his gaze. "Yes, yes, I'm okay. You just took me by surprise, that's all."

"I didn't mean to—"

But that was all he had time to say before Carlee caught him off guard, pushing him backward. Laughing, she sprang to duck him, intending to give one mighty shove and then leap away, only he was quick and kept her from escaping. Grabbing her, he took her down with him.

They were rolling over and over, legs and arms entwined, and somewhere along the way their lips met in a searing kiss. No longer were they playfully wrestling but drifting slowly upward, locked in each other's arms.

Carlee pulled away from him the instant she surfaced. She quickly swam to the ladder and hoisted herself up and out of the pool.

Nick watched in silence as she snatched up a towel and wrapped it around her, keeping her back turned.

He did not apologize.

He saw no need.

After all, she hadn't resisted in the water. It was only when they came up that she couldn't get away from him fast enough. Maybe she was afraid Lily would see. Or maybe she'd been so stunned at the time that she was unable to react sooner. But whatever her reason, Nick was through making excuses for what he was—a man drawn irresistibly to a woman. And if Carlee had a problem with that, then it was up to her to stay away from him. Sure, he'd pressured her into saying she'd go to the charity ball with him, but she could still have refused. As for swimming, she didn't have to agree. He might have kept trying to persuade her, but so what? The final decision was hers.

"I'm going to check on Scotty."

He could tell the cheeriness in her voice was forced.

In frustration, he slammed his hands down on the water again.

What kind of game was she playing? He had done everything he could think of to break through the invisible barrier she managed to leap behind when he tried to get close to her. She didn't care if he spent time with Scotty, but it was obvious she was uncomfortable as hell when they were alone together.

He told himself he should back off and quit wasting his time, then shook his head in disgust. After all, what difference did it make? He had relegated himself long ago to the idea that he was going to be single the rest of his life because he'd never be able to find the right woman. And since Carlee had let him know at every turn she wasn't interested in getting up close and personal, he needed to forget her.

The problem was he couldn't.

She was everything he desired. Cute, perky, fun to be with, intelligent, a good mother. And as far as Nick could tell they shared similar interests. She appeared to like citrus fruit and seemed to know a lot about it. And something told him she would never complain about living so far out or yearn for the excitement of a city as Gina had.

But what about more babies? How would she feel about his not being able to give her any? Would she want to adopt? Maybe use donor sperm if she felt really strong about having a baby of her own? He hadn't given that much thought, but maybe he should. Maybe...

He gave his head a vicious shake and did a surface dive

to take himself to the bottom of the pool, then swam all the way to the end.

When he finally surfaced, Carlee was coming out the back door.

"I think we'd better be getting home now," she said. She still had a towel wrapped around her and said she'd bring it to work tomorrow and give it back to him. "I should have brought one, but I didn't think of it."

"No problem."

She stood there a few moments before turning to leave. He had his back to her and could feel her watching him. She probably wondered about his sudden coolness, which he didn't understand himself. All he knew was that he was crazy about her, but feared he was heading down a one-way road to heartache.

She was almost to her car when she turned around and came back.

"We haven't talked about what to do with Scotty when we go to the ball. Do you think Becky would keep him?"

"I'm afraid not. She's got company for the next few weeks and has already told me she doesn't want to put in any more hours than she has to. Maybe Lily will do it. Wait here and I'll go ask her."

Carlee looked doubtful. "I don't know, Nick. She's much older than Becky, and she's probably not used to being around toddlers. I mean, she's very nice, but how good is she with children?"

"I don't think there's anything to worry about. He'll be asleep. You can bring him here and settle him down before we leave. It's not like she'd have to try to keep up with him during the day like Becky does."

Carlee was still not convinced. "Why can't she keep him at my place? He'd sleep better in his own bed."

"Because—" Nick wagged a finger and grinned

"—you don't have a satellite dish, and Lily is a TV fanatic. He'll be fine. I promise." Finally she gave in. Once Scotty went to sleep he was usually down for the entire night, anyway.

As she drove home, Carlee thought about Nick's kiss. Like before, it had been wonderful, only he had behaved a little strangely afterwards. He had not protested when she said she had to leave and had almost seemed relieved. Was he having doubts and fears, just as she was, over the way their relationship seemed to be heading?

Soon she would be leaving, and that was for the best.

The kiss had been her fault this time. She was the one who had coquettishly ducked him, and they couldn't help winding up with their hands all over each other. It was only natural that things happened as they had. So she had no reason to be angry with him. His reaction had been normal. So had hers. But she had to keep things under control, or it would only make for misery later for them both.

She arrived back at the row of migrant cottages to find an impromptu party in progress at the lake. The hot weather had driven several people into the cool water.

Mamie saw that Carlee was wearing a bathing suit and apparently figured out where she had been. "Hey, it's not as fancy as the boss's pool, but come join us, anyway."

Carlee was anxious to give Scotty his supper. "No thanks. I've got things to do."

She went on inside, groaning when she saw that Mamie had left the others and was following her.

"So how was it?" Mamie prodded, walking right behind her and into the kitchen. "It's a nice pool, I'm told."

"Yes, it is, and Mr. Starke was kind to invite us." She opened a cabinet and took down two jars of junior baby food—chicken-and-vegetables and applesauce. She had already put Scotty in his high chair, and he was banging his little fists on the tray in happy anticipation.

"That the first time you've been there?"

Carlee wished she would go away. "That's right. Now I hope you don't mind, Mamie, but I've got to get Scotty fed, and then I'm going to bed early."

"Well, you need to get out of that wet bathing suit. Here. Go change, and I'll feed him." She gave Carlee a gentle shove and took over spoon-feeding Scotty.

Carlee didn't argue. She did want out of the wet suit, and when she came back in shorts and a T-shirt, Mamie and Scotty were getting along just fine, so she let the woman continue feeding him.

"You know," Mamie said, "Mr. Nick must really like you. He took you to the beach, asked you to swim in his pool, and now he's taking you to that fancy charity thing in Orlando."

Carlee was making herself a cup of tea and politely asked if Mamie would like one, too.

"Me? Lordy, no. I'm no hot-tea drinker. But thanks, anyway. Now tell me something—how do you feel about him?"

"We're friends. That's all." She wished Scotty would eat faster...wished she hadn't let Mamie take over...wished she was alone. The last thing she needed was someone asking a bunch of personal questions about her and Nick.

"He's a fine man," Mamie continued, "and any woman would be doing herself proud to wind up with him for a husband, but you've got to remember who you are...and who you aren't."

Carlee's spine snapped to indignant rigidity. "And what is that supposed to mean?"

"Look, you're not one of those high-society types he usually takes to those charity things. And I saw that fancy gown you brought in, sequins and all. Has to be expensive. He bought it for you, didn't he?"

"It was his mother's! He loaned it to me because I can't afford to buy one and wasn't about to allow him to pay for it. She wore the same size as me and—"

"Oh, honey…" Mamie had got up to put her arms around Carlee. "I've grown real fond of you in the short time I've known you, and even though I started off saying you ought to latch on to him, I was just kidding. I'd hate to see you get hurt. Just be careful, 'cause Nick Starke is way out of your league."

Carlee was swept with bitterness. He had been out of Alicia's league, too. That was why he'd dumped her. And now here she was, on the edge of falling in love with him, pretending his son was hers. Dear God, she had to have been out of her mind to have come up with such a bizarre scheme. She should have gone to a lawyer and had him contact Nick, and—

Woulda, coulda, shoulda.

She was doing it again, and it was too late to turn back now.

"Thanks for the advice, Mamie, but I can handle it," she said woodenly, pushing her teacup away and moving to take over with Scotty.

"Well, I hope I didn't make you mad."

"No, no. Nothing like that." She waved her away. "Now really, I've got things to do, and you need to get back to your swim."

After Mamie left, Carlee put Scotty to bed, then went to sit outside on the porch in the twilight. The swimmers had left. All was quiet except for the rhythmic chirping of the grasshoppers and tree frogs.

She sat and stared into the darkness, pondering her situation, then realized there wasn't really anything to think about.

She had to leave.

And soon.

Or she was going to wind up with a broken heart—and too much guilt to bear, because she'd betrayed Alicia by falling in love with the man she was supposed to hate.

Chapter Eleven

Carlee knew how Cinderella must have felt.

Nick arrived to pick her up driving a classic Cadillac. He was drop-dead gorgeous in a black tux, and Carlee was speechless. She always had thought him handsome, but now he looked like a movie star on his way to the Academy Awards.

She felt equally glamorous, and from the way he looked at her, knew he thought the same. The dress was stunning. She was a little self-conscious about the fact that she had altered the bodice and she had some cleavage showing. She had styled her hair up, with a few tendrils curling down about her face. She hadn't had any nice earrings, but had found a pair of imitation emeralds in a store in Sanford the week before. From a distance, they looked real, especially glittering along with the green sequins.

Nick sucked in his breath as if he'd been slammed in his chest. "Carlee, you are beautiful."

"And so are you, kind sir," she said, determined to keep things light and breezy. No awkward silences. No tense moments. She had made up her mind to have a wonderful night, one she would always remember. Pointing to the car, she quipped, "Amazing what a fairy godmother can do to a pumpkin...or maybe I should say beach buggy."

"It belonged to my father." He was careful as they went down the steps to make sure she did not trip in the tight skirt. "I keep it in the garage and only drive it on special occasions. I like my buggy and the truck better."

He opened the door for her, and she got in to marvel at the plush velour seats. "Well, this is nice, but you're right about the buggy and the truck. This wouldn't do at the beach, and you sure can't haul oranges in it."

She had taken Scotty to Nick's earlier and asked if he had settled down after she left. Nick said he was sleeping when he left. "You don't have to worry. Lily will take good care of him. We won't be out terribly late."

Once Nick was settled behind the steering wheel and backing away from her cottage, he said, "I thought you might want to leave Scotty overnight. No need to wake him up. Tomorrow is Sunday, and you'll probably want to sleep late. I can feed him his breakfast and take him home later."

"No, I don't want to leave him." She saw the quick glance he cut and knew she'd spoken too sharply, and she instantly sought to smooth things over. "I mean, I appreciate the offer, but I wouldn't sleep a wink without Scotty."

"As you wish. But I don't mind." He was not about to get into a debate over Scotty or anything else. He wanted Carlee to have only pleasant memories of this night and remember it as being very special. He didn't want anything to come between them and intended to do everything possible to see that she had a good time. He didn't even plan to kiss her good-night, fearing that might spoil things, since she continued to make it clear she was not interested in any kind of relationship. Still, he could not help feeling that the two kisses they had shared had moved her almost as deeply as they had him.

The drive to Orlando took nearly an hour. Carlee didn't care if they ever got there. She was enjoying the ride, as well as the scenery and the music on the CD player.

They talked about work, which was a comfortable subject. Nick said he was going to try out a mechanical harvester. "It's called a trunk shaker. It clamps onto the tree trunk and shakes the fruit off into a catch frame."

"Wouldn't that bruise the fruit?"

"This one is supposed to be different. Of course, that's what all the machinery salesmen say. Right now, there's no cost advantage in using mechanical versus hand-harvesting, but I told the guy I'd give it a try. Besides, I'm going to harvest about a dozen blocks this fall just for juice, and it won't matter as much if there's a little bruising."

"I hope the mechanical harvesters never take over. That would put too many people out of work."

"Like you?" He raised a brow. "Not likely. You'll find something else to do, maybe a husband to take care of you and Scotty so you won't even have to work."

She felt a little tug of warning that they might be heading into the danger zone. She didn't want to talk about her future—or his—but she did feel driven to say, "If that were to happen, if I were to get married, I would still keep on working. I like staying busy, and I also like being around people. That's important to me.

"Maybe—" now she spoke more to herself than to him "—that's why I've enjoyed working in the groves so much. Of course, I like the gift shop better, because I like doing displays, helping customers find just the right souvenir to take home, and—'' She realized she was talking too much. ''Anyway, I'll be sorry when the Valencias are all harvested, but there will be other groves, other harvests.''

He could have kicked himself for asking, because he'd promised himself to steer clear of anything to do with her personal life, but could not resist. ''So you aren't going to hang around? Maybe find a temporary job till fall season begins?''

''No. I'll go back where I came from.''

''Gainesville? But that place where you worked before has gone out of business.''

Carlee was glad she was looking out the window when he said that, because she blanched to think he had actually checked out what she had written. The other migrants never filled out that much information and weren't expected to. She had only put all that down to throw him off in case she decided to leave and didn't want him to find her. Now she was surprised that he had bothered to look at her application at all. It only reinforced her suspicion of his interest in her—to add her to his list of conquests.

''We are fashionably late,'' Nick said as he drew to a stop before one of Orlando's poshest hotels. ''But I always hate arriving at these things too early. I find the cocktail hour chatter incredibly boring.''

Valets descended upon them, one opening the door for Carlee to help her get out of the car, the other sliding behind the steering wheel as soon as Nick got out.

Photographers were lining the sidewalk as they entered, flashbulbs popping. Nick kept a firm hand on her elbow and quietly explained, ''They're from the local papers and a few of the state's glossy magazines. We need all the publicity we can get for this charity, so smile.''

She already was, he noted, relieved that she seemed so at ease with the crowds and the attention, not at all nervous as he had feared she might be. It was quite a gala, and he had a feeling she'd never been to anything like it before. But that was one of the things he adored about being with Carlee, enjoying the things he was accustomed to through her eyes. It made all that he took for granted new and exciting. He also liked seeing her happy...*making* her happy.

He gave himself a mental shake.

Tonight, and that was it. He would not torture himself with hopes for any kind of future with her, regardless of how his heart kept urging him onward.

As they entered the hotel, heads turned to stare at Carlee, she was so stunning. Nick saw how she demurely pretended not to notice the admiring eyes as the two of them walked through the lobby with its grand furnishings, polished marble floors, glittering chandeliers and flowers, which made the air thick with scent.

''Nick, everything is gorgeous,'' she breathed as they entered the ballroom.

''No, *you* are,'' he could not help saying. ''And you make everything around you beautiful.''

Her whisper of thanks was lost in the swell of voices trying to rise above the orchestra. They paused at a table where names were being checked off. He introduced Carlee to a few people there. But he did not want to waste time with chitchat. He wanted to hold her in his arms, and the only way to do that was to get her on the dance floor.

They walked past tables lining the walls, skirting the dancers, as Nick escorted her to the head table. When he found the place cards before their seats, he said, ''You can leave your things here. I'd like to dance with you before they serve dinner.''

Carlee marveled at the elegant settings, crystal wine and water glasses sparkling beneath the lights next to shining china and silverware. The table was round, with seats for eight. A lavish centerpiece of roses and gardenias was too tempting, and she leaned over to inhale the heady sweetness.

''They always have a floral theme,'' Nick explained. ''I see tonight it's roses and gardenias. They're everywhere.''

''My favorites,'' she murmured.

Laying the little evening bag that matched her gown next to her plate, she turned back to Nick. Her heart was pounding madly as he led her onto the floor, and she bit her lip to hold back the tears that threatened to well in her eyes—tears of joy, as well as sadness—because the fairy tale she was living would not end like Cinderella's.

He swept her so easily into the rhythm of the music it was as though they had danced together all their lives. Carlee was mesmerized by the tender moment, her cheeks warm and flushed. She felt as though she were drowning in his embrace, and closing her eyes, she let the magic take her away to a world where there was no fear of what tomorrow might bring. She wished to remain there forever, lost in the music, the fragrance of roses and gardenias…and Nick holding her so very, very close.

When that dance ended, they waited motionlessly for another to begin, heated gazes locked, both oblivious to everything around them.

Nick fought to keep from kissing her then and there, afraid to let his emotions show.

Carlee could not tear her eyes from his, delicious tremors moving deep within her. Never had she known such an enchanting moment. She could only wish she did not know what she did about him. But the sensible part of her said it was best she did; otherwise, he might hurt her as he had Alicia. After all, this was the real world, and Nick Starke was no Prince Charming. He was wealthy, powerful and used to getting what he wanted by wit, charm or money. And right now she was helpless before him, glad they were surrounded by people, because she knew if he kissed her, she was his, regardless of the heartache later to bear.

They had another dance, and then the magical spell ended with the music and the announcement that dinner was being served.

Nick introduced Carlee to the others at their table, and she joined them in polite conversation. He was impressed at how she could discuss just about anything, from politics and current events to fashion and celebrities. Everyone seemed to like her, and Nick was proud. In the past, he'd brought merely "arm candy"—local models, debutantes. Carlee was positively dazzling in her own right, and he adored her all the more.

After dinner and too many glasses of champagne to remember, Carlee listened, fascinated, as Nick got up and delivered an impromptu speech of encouragement for the programs planned by the charity for the coming year. He was not only eloquent but entertaining, spicing his talk with warm stories of children that had been helped in the past. At the end, a man in the audience stood up and loudly declared his donation to kick off the drive for the new year. That was followed by another and another, and Carlee could only sit there and watch in amazement as the amounts grew higher and higher.

And once again she looked at Nick and wondered how on earth he could ever have done what he did to Alicia. It did not seem possible.

When dinner was over and all the speeches ended, so many people crowded around Nick that he could not get away. Carlee waited patiently to one side, impressed by his popularity and how he was obviously held in such high esteem by everyone.

An older woman, looking like a walking jewelry store, approached Carlee to clasp her hands and exult, "Oh, my dear, you don't know how I've been looking forward to meeting you. You are every bit as lovely as I'd heard, and I want you to know that you are absolutely the most stunning woman Nick has ever brought."

She was wearing a gown of beige brocade, the cuffs trimmed in what Carlee guessed was genuine mink. "That's very kind of you, Mrs...."

"Joanna Pipkin. My husband is Claude Pipkin. He's president of Nick's bank. They lunch together sometimes, as you and I must do. I'm so happy you could come tonight, Brooke. Claude said Nick told him you were out of the country, and he wasn't sure you'd be back in time."

"You obviously have me confused with someone else," Carlee said uneasily. She hadn't thought of the possibility that she had been Nick's second choice, because his usual date couldn't make it.

Joanna abruptly let go of Carlee's hand. Her face went taut, her rouge-dusted cheeks becoming brighter. She was visibly embarrassed. "I am so very sorry. I still think you are beautiful, my dear, and I'd love to have lunch with you sometime. Please tell me your name."

"Carlee Denton."

"Have you and Nick been seeing each other very long?"

Carlee felt as if she was on a hot seat. Now the woman was going to grill her to find out as much as possible so she could go back and tell her friends all about Nick Starke's new girlfriend.

Carlee hesitated, trying to think how best to respond. Nick had a girlfriend. She was out of the country. That explained why he'd been around the groves so much—and why he had tried so intensely to make a move on her.

She thought about Cinderella, wondering how she would have reacted had Prince Charming put someone else's glass slipper on her foot. Carlee responded, "Actually, Nick and I are just good friends. He invited me because Brooke couldn't be here."

Joanna gave a sigh of relief. "Oh, I am so glad to hear that. I was afraid maybe you were a new girlfriend and I had gotten him in trouble.

"So tell me," she rushed on, "when will Brooke be back? I've heard so much about her, I feel like I know her, that's why I was so chummy with you, dear."

"I really have no idea. I'm sorry." Like a lifeline thrown to someone drowning, Carlee saw that Nick was motioning to her. She quickly excused herself and made her way to his side.

He turned away from the group he had been standing with to whisper, "I thought you'd appreciate being rescued from Mrs. Pipkin. She's a nice lady, but she can drive you crazy with her nosy questions. I hope she didn't bother you too much."

"It's all right," Carlee said woodenly, then, "Can I borrow your cell phone? I'd like to call Lily and see if Scotty's okay."

"Sure. Just hit number three on memory dial. I never remember my own number so I saved it." He noticed how she suddenly seemed unnerved when earlier she had appeared to be having a good time. He squeezed her hand and asked, "Is anything wrong, Carlee?"

"Everything is fine," she said tightly, then took the phone and hurried out of the ballroom, through the lobby and outside the hotel in order to get a good connection. The warning light on the phone indicated the battery was getting weak. Carlee hoped it lasted long enough for just the one call.

After four rings, Lily finally answered, sounding as if she had just woke up.

"Lily? It's Carlee. How is Scotty? Is he okay?"

Lily yawned. "I haven't heard a peep out of him. He didn't want his supper and seemed kind of fussy, so I went ahead and put him to bed. But there's nothing to worry about. I'm sure he's fine."

"Well, would you check on him for me, Lily? We should be home soon. Give him a hug for me if he's awake."

"Sure, sure."

She laid the phone down.

Carlee waited anxiously, tapping her toe and listening to the ominous beep that the battery was fast going down.

And then it happened.

The phone went dead.

Carlee turned to go back inside and bumped into Nick.

"Hey, there you are," he said jovially. "How about one more dance before we start for home?"

"I don't think so." For Carlee, the magic had ended.

Apprehension crept up his spine. "What's wrong? Scotty's all right, isn't he?"

"Lily said she thought so and went to check, but before she got back, your phone went dead." She handed it to him.

"I have a charger in the car. It won't take long to recharge. Are you sure there's nothing wrong? You're acting strange, like you aren't having a good time. Has something happened?''

She did not want to talk about what Mrs. Pipkin had said and how she was his second choice to take to the ball. What did it matter, anyway? She had known all along nothing would come of the evening except an opportunity to glimpse a world she would never know again. "I'm just tired. I think we should go home now."

He sensed that something had happened here at the ball to spoil her evening. He had a pretty good idea of what it was.

He signaled to the valet to bring his car around.

They were almost home, and Carlee had not said a word. Nick had tried to make conversation, but she answered in monosyllables, if at all.

Finally he couldn't stand it any longer. They were passing the turnoff to a golf resort, and Nick turned in. He had played there a few times and knew the curving road well. It was a long way back to the clubhouse, with parklike settings along the way, and he drove into one and stopped.

Carlee, lost in thought, sat up straight to glance about. The night was lit by a half-moon, and she could see flowers, shrubs and a lot of grass. "Where are we? This isn't your house."

"No, it isn't. We're at a golf course a little ways from home." He switched off the engine, leaned back and drew a ragged breath. "Carlee, we aren't going home till you tell me what happened. What turned our very nice evening sour?"

Angry with herself for the disappointment she could not help feeling, she was not about to play coy. "Mrs. Pipkin thought I was Brooke."

He straightened and turned in the seat, then burst into laughter. "She what?"

Carlee didn't think it was funny. "She came up to me and called me Brooke. I know it's none of my business," she tartly added, "but I guess no woman likes feeling she was second choice."

"Hey, wait a minute. Hold it right there." He held up his hand, voice taking a sharp edge. "You've let me know many times over, Carlee, that you don't want to be my choice, period. But I asked you to go with me tonight because I wanted to spend some time with you, and because I thought you'd enjoy it."

"I did," she acknowledged, wishing now she'd kept her mouth shut, realizing she had come across as being jealous, which she was, only she didn't want him to know that. "It was just embarrassing, that's all, to realize everyone expected you to be with someone else."

"That's not true. Listen to me—" he cupped her chin, forcing her to look at him "—I don't care what anybody expected. I brought the person I wanted to be with—you."

"Because Brooke is out of the country," she said petulantly, hating herself all the more for not keeping her mouth shut. Dear God, right then she wouldn't care if the car did turn into a pumpkin, anything to escape making such a fool out of herself.

She pulled away from him. "Look, Nick, it's none of my business. I had a nice time. I shouldn't have said anything. Thank you for inviting me, and now I'd like to go home."

"I have no idea where Brooke is, and I don't care. It never occurred to me to invite her. All I thought about was you, Carlee." He grabbed her then, almost roughly, to pull her into his arms and hold her tight against him. "Dammit, don't you realize you're all I ever think about?"

He buried his lips in the sweet hollow of her throat. "I'm sorry. I know we had an agreement to keep things light, but, Carlee, I can't help feeling the way I do."

Carlee felt panic wisping over her like fog over a riverbank. This was not good. This was dangerous. She felt herself going weak and mustered what strength she had left to pull away from his embrace, but he would not let her go. "Please, stop it now. You promised—"

Her ragged gasp of denial was silenced as his mouth claimed hers.

He felt her resistance cease as her lips parted beneath his, allowing his tongue to slip between. His fingertips clutched her face, moving to trace tiny circle patterns in the sensitive hollow beneath her ear, igniting hot tingles throughout her body.

His hand moved down her throat, in burning anticipation of his lips. He wanted to taste all of her, inch by inch. He could feel her quaking beneath his touch, could hear the faint moaning sound that proved her own primal need was awakening.

Carlee's gown was designed to drape off the shoulders, and it was easy to hook his fingers inside and pull it down. "Tell me you want this as much as I do, Carlee..."

She could more easily have turned the tide than push him away. Heaven forgive her...Alicia forgive her...but she wanted him as she had never wanted any other man.

Nick was on fire as his mouth claimed her breasts, lips opening upon the soft tender flesh to assault one taut hard nipple between his teeth. Carlee writhed and twisted in pleasurable anguish, lost in the fevered moment.

He lowered the gown to her waist. Nick hated conversation in such a passionate moment but had no choice. It was so damn awkward. Like back in high school. And he didn't want it this way. Not with Carlee. It had to be special. Because she was special. He knew that now. Beyond all doubt.

He didn't know what to do. Suggest they get in the back seat like a couple of kids? He could not remember the last time he'd been in such a situation. There had always been a motel to go to or a blanket on the beach...

Blanket.

There was one in the trunk. He'd put it there when he'd had to carry a fragile wedding gift to a friend several months ago. He'd used it for wrapping and had not gotten around to taking it back in the house.

When he drew away, it was the awakening Carlee needed—but did not want. Too much champagne, she told her throbbing head. Tomorrow she would hate herself and knew she had to stop it here and now. "Nick, we mustn't..."

"But we both want it, Carlee. If you really don't want to, I'll understand, but I think you want me every bit as much as I want you." He lifted her, about to move her into the back seat. "I wish we were someplace else, but I want you so badly..."

And she wanted him, despite everything, and knew she would yield to her desire.

The phone rang. Nick had plugged the cell phone into the charger connected to the cigarette lighter and the battery was working again.

"Let it ring," he said hoarsely.

Instinct took over, and Carlee grabbed it to answer, afraid it might be Lily. It was, and Carlee heard the woman's voice, shrill and terrified, trying to tell her something, but she was so hysterical Carlee could not understand what she was trying to say.

"Lily, calm down," she commanded. To Nick she said, "Let's go! Something's happened."

Nick started the engine and backed out with a roar and a squeal of tires.

Carlee was tugging at her gown to cover herself as she spoke to Lily. "Please. What is it? What's wrong with Scotty?"

Lily was gasping, wheezing, overcome with panic as she struggled to explain. "When I went to see him, he was choking...couldn't get his breath. You'd hung up so I called 911, then I tried to call you back but couldn't get an answer. They just left with him. I've been trying to call you ever since."

"Dear God, no..." Carlee dropped the phone.

Nick snatched it up, shouted at Lily to repeat herself, and then said they were on their way to the hospital.

He looked at Carlee. She was pale and stricken, shaking from head to toe. "You hang on, honey." He reached to pat her hands, clenched tightly in her lap. "They'll take him to Sanford. It's the nearest emergency room. We're right on the way, and I'll get you there as fast I can."

Carlee was not listening.

She was too busy praying.

And as they reached the end of the drive into the resort, an ambulance streaked by, lights flashing and siren screaming.

Chapter Twelve

By the time Carlee and Nick arrived at the emergency room, paramedics had already taken Scotty inside. Nick dropped Carlee off at the ambulance bay and went to park the car. She rushed inside nearly hysterical and demanded of the first person she saw—a young man dressed in green scrubs—to be taken wherever the baby was that had just been brought in.

"Ma'am, I'm sorry," he said, eyes sweeping her sequined gown, "but you'll have to go the waiting room. You can't go back into the ER treatment area."

"I have to," she insisted. "You don't understand. I wasn't there when he got sick. The sitter called the ambulance. I don't know anything about his condition."

He repeated, "Ma'am, I'm sorry."

His badge identified him as an EDA—emergency department assistant—which was just another name for orderly. She realized he didn't have the authority to tell her anything about Scotty's condition, much less take her where he was.

She started by him, heading straight for the doors clearly marked No Admittance. And out of nowhere, a security guard appeared to also tell her how sorry he was, but he couldn't allow her to go back there and would escort her to the waiting room.

Carlee broke into fresh tears, and just then Nick walked in and crisply informed the guard that she was not going anywhere till somebody told her what was going on. With his hand firmly clamped on her arm, he declared, "We will stand right here until somebody comes through those doors with some information.

"I'm not trying to make trouble," Nick went on. "But I mean to find out about that little boy."

The security guard could see Nick meant what he said. "Okay. I'll try to get somebody to come out here to talk to you." He disappeared behind the doors.

"I don't mean to make a scene," Carlee said brokenly, melting against Nick as he hugged her to his chest. "I just can't stand not knowing how he is."

"You have a right to," he gruffly agreed. "And don't worry. I'm staying right here with you."

It was not long before a doctor came out. Like the EDA, he flicked a curious glance at Carlee's gown, as well as Nick's tux. "I'm Dr. Abbott. You're the baby's parents?"

"Yes," she said automatically, not about to waste time explaining about Nick.

But Nick amended, "Actually she's the mother. I'm her friend."

"I see." The doctor had a chart and began asking questions—what was Scotty's full name, age, what kind of medications he was on, his medical history.

Carlee told him about Scotty's illness of few months

earlier when he'd had the croup. "Is that what it is this time?" she asked, hoping against hope that's all it was.

"We're doing some tests. I'll know more when we get the results. Meanwhile I have to warn you that he is a very sick little boy, but I believe we have him stabilized."

Anxiously Nick asked, "So when can she see him, Doctor?"

"We're moving him to the pediatrics intensive-care unit. As soon as he's settled, you can go up. Meanwhile, I'll let you know when I find out anything."

Nick asked, "What about his babysitter? Didn't she come in the ambulance with him?"

The doctor looked at the chart he was holding. "I see a notation from the paramedics that she stayed behind to try and get in touch with you."

Nick took Carlee's hand. "Come on. Let's go get some coffee. It's going to be a long night."

"You don't have to stay," she said, hoping he would.

She needn't have worried. He said he was not about to leave her. "Let's find the cafeteria."

A nurse walked up just then to tell Carlee that she needed to go to the admitting office.

Carlee felt a sinking sensation, dreading the ordeal of having to reveal she had no hospital insurance. Only this time it was worse, because she didn't have a checking account, had no money with her, and the hospital would demand a deposit as it had before.

She told Nick she would meet him in the cafeteria.

"No way." He took her hand. "I'll go with you."

She hated for him to find out she was so destitute, but there was no time to worry about it. She just wanted this over with, so she could be with Scotty as soon as possible.

The night admissions clerk was taking a break, so they sat down to wait.

A few moments of stilted silence passed, and Carlee noticed Nick seemed uncomfortable as he crossed and re-crossed his legs, folding and refolding his arms across his chest. She was likewise uneasy, remembering what they had been doing at the time his cell phone rang. A little while longer and she knew she'd have been in that back seat, stripping out of her gown and…

Nick cleared his throat. Then, unable to keep his thoughts to himself any longer, said, "Look, Carlee, about what happened—"

"It's okay. We can talk about it later."

"No. I want us to talk about it now, because I don't want you blaming yourself for any of this."

"I don't, so there's no need." Carlee was picking nervously at a string of sequins that had come loose on her gown, probably when Nick had pushed the bodice down. She almost blushed but didn't. She was only human, and she had been fighting the desire growing between them for a long time. Her only mistake was thinking she could control it.

He looked relieved. "That's good, because what happened was natural, Carlee. I want you to know—"

She held up a hand. "I shouldn't have let it go that far. It's my fault, but right now I'm only thinking about Scotty. I don't blame you or me for him getting sick. It could have happened with me right there, like before. But of course I can't help wishing that we'd left for home sooner.

"And that we hadn't stopped along the way," she added tightly, because although she was determined not to add to her stress by faulting herself or anyone else, it did bother her to look back at how Nick probably had planned to set a scene for seduction.

As though he could sense what she was thinking, Nick slipped his arm about her as he said, "Carlee, I want you to know I didn't mean for that to happen like it did. I mean, I didn't plan it. I stopped and parked at the resort because I could tell you were upset about something and I wanted to find out what it was before we got home. I knew you'd never talk about it once we got there. Then one thing led to another... That's how it was, I swear to you.''

All of a sudden Carlee thought how tired she was of so many things—hiding the truth, worrying about what would happen when he found out, fears for the future. It was all too much. ''Please, Nick, I truly appreciate your bringing me here and staying with me, but I just wish you'd leave me alone right now. I don't feel like talking about this.''

She glanced around in annoyance. ''Where is that clerk? They should have somebody else on duty so people don't have to wait when they're anxious to get to their loved ones. And I can't keep just sitting here like this when I want to be with Scotty.''

''You're right.'' Nick stood and walked over to the guard seated behind a desk at the front entrance.

Carlee couldn't hear what was being said, but evidently Nick made his point, because the guard picked up a phone and within minutes a woman came hurrying up the hall.

''Sorry to keep you waiting.'' She took her position on the other side of the counter and got out some papers, her eyes widening slightly as she took in Carlee's gown. ''Goodness, I take it your evening was interrupted.'' She did not wait for Carlee to respond. ''I need some information and also need to make a copy of your insurance card.''

Carlee cringed. ''I'm afraid I don't have any insurance.''

Like the last time, she was told a deposit would be necessary. The woman made a phone call, then explained that since Scotty was being admitted to Peds ICU, a deposit of one thousand dollars was required.

"Well, I'm afraid that's a problem, because—"

Nick interrupted. He had been standing back but quickly moved to take a plastic card out of his wallet and hand it to the woman. "This is a bank debit card. Run it through for whatever you need.

"And we'd appreciate your hurrying this up," he beseeched. "She's anxious to get to her son."

"Of course." The clerk proceeded to ask Carlee the necessary questions, had her sign the papers, then pleasantly said, "That's it. And I do hope your son will be all right."

"We'd better get back to the ER." Nick took Carlee's hand again. "Maybe they'll let you see him now."

The phone on the counter rang as they were walking away, and a few seconds later the clerk ran after them to relay the message that Scotty had just been transported upstairs. "They've taken him to the fifth floor. The elevators are that way." She pointed.

Once alone in the elevator with Nick, Carlee stammered a thank-you for his posting the deposit. "I'll pay you back when I can." Right then she wasn't thinking about the future and how he might ultimately agree to be responsible for Scotty's medical bills, or at least help with them. All she cared about was getting the best possible care for Scotty then and there.

Once they reached the pediatrics floor, a nurse led them to a small waiting room while she explained that Scotty was being settled in. "I'll take you to see him in a little while."

The nurse went away and Carlee began to pace, but Nick urged her to sit down. "I need to call Lily and let her know what's going on, and I can't use my cell inside the hospital, but I don't want to leave you like this.''

"I'm okay. I'm okay." She sank onto a plastic-covered sofa. "Please, do whatever you have to do.''

He dropped to one knee so he could look her straight in the eye as he vowed, "I'm going to see you through this, Carlee. And I don't want you worrying about anything. I'll take care of the hospital bill and whatever medicine he needs. I want you to know—" he reached to cup her chin "—I'm here for you. You aren't alone, okay?''

She was about to cry and could only nod her head.

"I've got to go make that call now, but I'll be back as soon as I can." He brushed his lips across her forehead.

Alone, Carlee felt as if she'd explode if they didn't soon let her see Scotty. And finally, when she thought she couldn't stand it any longer, the nurse returned and said she would take her back.

"But only for five minutes. The doctor wants him kept in the ICU till morning, and then he'll be taken to a room where you can stay with him as much as you like. Till then, we just can't let parents stay in the unit. I hope you understand.''

Carlee didn't say anything. The reality was that she didn't understand a lot of things these days and figured it best not to try, especially in the state she was in right then.

When she saw Scotty, she had to stuff her fist in her mouth to keep from crying out. He looked so tiny and helpless in the white crib, his right arm taped to a padded board, an IV line running into the back of his little hand. An oxygen mask was on his face, EKG leads stuck on his chest, and an oxygen monitor was clipped to one of his fingers.

For the five precious minutes she was allotted, Carlee stood next to the crib, her arm stretched through the bars so she could keep her hand on Scotty's chest. She wanted to feel his every breath, silently praying as she did so.

She loved him so much, and as she hovered over him, she wondered painfully whether it would have made a difference if she'd been there with him when he was stricken. She might have seen the attack coming, recognizing symptoms she'd not known about the last time. But then, she knew she wasn't being fair to herself to think like that.

Carlee took solace in believing she had taken very good care of Scotty. He'd not been neglected at all. Still, she couldn't help wishing she hadn't been at a ball when he got sick, but that had nothing to do with Scotty.

The nurse gently told her the time was up. Carlee returned to the waiting room and wondered where Nick was. Then another nurse came in to hand her a paper sack and a take-out coffee.

"Your husband said to give this to you and to tell you he'll be back later."

"He's not my husband," Carlee said too sharply. The nurse gave her a strange look.

She set the food aside and curled up on the sofa to get as comfortable as possible. Fortunately Scotty was the only baby in the ICU, so there were no family members waiting. She was glad, not wanting to be around strangers. She also found herself wishing Nick hadn't left. After all, he had no idea—yet—that it was his place to be there as much as it was hers.

It was a pleasant room, painted in soft shades of blue and pink and yellow. The walls were decorated with drawings of teddy bears, lambs and other warm and fuzzy creatures. The floor was tile, but there were nice, cushy throw rugs. The lighting was soft, and there were many books and magazines scattered about.

She kicked off the high heels that had been punishing

her feet for the past few hours. She wasn't used to wearing them and wished for sneakers, jeans and a T-shirt. There was no telling how long she'd have to wear that dress, because she had no intention of leaving Scotty while he was in the hospital. Maybe in the morning one of the nurses would find a pair of scrubs for her. Anything was better than wearing the gown for another minute.

The night passed with agonizing slowness, and her mind began to wander, as always, back to Alicia.

She tried to think of everything Alicia had ever said about Nick. Though she had refused to identify him, she had described him as being handsome, exciting and fun to be with. He liked to spend money. Sometimes he would buy a round of drinks for everyone at the bar. Generous to a fault, she'd said.

Carlee could relate to that. He certainly hadn't minded spending money on her or Scotty.

She also recalled the wondrous splendor she'd found in his arms before that fateful phone call. There was no denying she had wanted him every bit as much as he'd wanted her.

And what, really, was the harm? she asked herself there in the pained stillness of the night. It had nothing to do with Nick's relationship with Alicia. It was easy for Carlee to justify the emotions she was experiencing. After all, he had come through for her in so many ways, and what woman in her right mind wouldn't be helplessly drawn to him?

Yearning to feel positive about the future when the present seemed so bleak, Carlee promised herself that she was going to make the most of every single day she had left at Starke Groves. Not that she planned to jump into bed with Nick. Far from it. She would do her best not to find herself in that situation again. But she did want to follow through on her original plan.

As for the guilt she continued to feel where Alicia was concerned, Carlee argued once more it was not her fault she had become enamored of Nick. She had fought against it. But so what? She was doing what she had promised Alicia. She was raising Scotty as her own and would continue to do so.

As the first fingers of dawn crept around the blinds at the windows, outside in the hallway were the soft sounds of the nursing shift changing.

Carlee sat up and managed to slip her shoes on her sore feet, then went to the rest room and splashed cold water on her face. The mirror above the sink told her what she already knew—that she looked a sight. Her hair was mussed, and her eyes were puffy. But none of that mattered. She didn't care how she looked or how people stared at the gown that now seemed so garish. She was totally focused on Scotty. Still, she couldn't help being a little surprised that Nick had left and hadn't returned.

She was more than a little surprised. Especially when just a short while earlier they'd been about to make love. But she told herself she had no right to be upset or angry. After all, he had paid the hospital deposit, so what more could she expect of him? Furthermore, he had a business to run, and they had no ties to each other. He didn't owe her anything.

Still, it would have been nice to have had someone to lean on through the dark hours.

At last the door opened and a man in a white coat walked in to introduce himself. "I'm Dr. Pelligrino. I'm sorry we had to keep your son in ICU all night. I know you want to be with him, but we needed to keep him under constant observation."

"Just tell me how he is," she begged.

Dr. Pelligrino explained that Scotty's prognosis was good. "He's definitely over the worse of it. He had a serious croup attack, and I see by the notes in his chart that you told the doctor in the emergency room that he had one a few months ago, as well."

"But it wasn't this serious," she said. "I can't help thinking that if I'd been home last night, I might have noticed some symptoms before he got so sick."

He shrugged. "You shouldn't feel that way. These things can strike without warning. What's important is that he's going to be all right. There is some infection in his bronchial tubes, and we're treating that with antibiotics. In addition, there is a small chance he might be asthmatic."

"Are you saying this will happen again?"

"Possibly, but next time you'll be better prepared. I'll give you prescriptions so you can start dosing him the second you see a sign he's in distress. But we can talk about all that when he's discharged."

"And when will that be?" She wanted the best possible care but couldn't help but think of the mounting costs.

"Probably not for a few days. He's still a sick little boy, and although he appears to be responding to treatment, we have to make sure before we discharge him. We can't risk a relapse."

"Of course. Do whatever needs to be done." She was ashamed to even remotely think of money at such a time. Scotty came first always—regardless.

"We should be able to move him out of ICU and into a room by lunchtime. You might as well go home for a while." He was looking at her gown as he spoke.

"I'm staying right here. Please let me know when he's moved."

She sat back down. To hell with sequins and high heels. She wasn't leaving the hospital without Scotty.

When Nick stepped off the elevator on the pediatrics floor, he went straight to the nurses' station where a doctor was going over some charts. "I'm Nick Starke, a close friend of Carlee Denton. I wonder if someone can tell me how her son is doing."

Dr. Pelligrino introduced himself and repeated what he had told Carlee.

Nick was relieved that it was mostly good news and said he wanted to make it clear that Scotty was to have whatever he needed, regardless of the cost. He didn't know whether Carlee's lack of insurance would make a difference, but wasn't about to take any chances. Dr. Pelligrino assured him he had nothing to worry about.

Nick had stopped by the hospital business office on his way in and signed for the responsibility of the bill. Regardless of what the future held for him and Carlee, he wanted to do this for Scotty. He had come to love him, and if he failed to win Carlee's heart, he hoped she would at least let him stay in touch and perhaps visit Scotty from time to time. But that was just a pipe dream. Sooner or later she would fall for someone and remarry, and her husband wouldn't want Nick hanging around.

He shook Dr. Pelligrino's hand and went in search of Carlee.

She was huddled in a chair in a corner of the waiting room. Another family had come in, distraught over an infant who'd been injured in an automobile wreck. They had taken over the room, and Carlee had moved to get as much out of their way as possible.

At the sight of Nick, she bounded to her feet. "You

came back. Oh, Nick, I'm glad. I would've understood if you hadn't, but I'm glad you're here.''

"I'm just sorry I took so long, but I had a flat tire on the way home and thought I'd never get it changed." He was elated she was glad to see him, but reminded himself it was only natural she'd be happy to see a familiar face walking through that door. He set down the overnight bag he was carrying. "I wanted to get you a change of clothes. You need to get out of that gown, and I knew you weren't about to leave the hospital.

"And," he added with a smile of relief, "I just saw Dr. Pelligrino out in the hall, and he gave me the good news that Scotty seems to be doing okay."

"Yes, he is. They should be moving him into a room in a few hours." She was deeply touched that he had gone to the trouble of bringing her some clothes and eyed the bag eagerly. "That was so nice of you, because I'm getting a little tired of people staring at me. It's like they're thinking I was out partying while my son got sick. Which," she feebly added, "I guess I was."

"Don't start that. It only makes the situation worse. I talked to Lily. She was still at my house when I got there, waiting to hear how he's doing, and she told me exactly what happened. Go change. We'll run down to the cafeteria, and have some breakfast, and I'll tell you all about it."

Fifteen minutes later they were sitting opposite each other at a table in the corner of the hospital café. Carlee had filled the biggest cup she could find with black coffee. And though Nick urged her to fill her plate with bacon and eggs, she took only a bagel, insisting she didn't have any appetite. He went ahead and got pancakes and sausage, which he really didn't want but hoped would tempt her. It worked. He was able to coax her to take a few bites as he recounted Lily's story.

"As you already know, when she went to check on Scotty when you called, she saw that he was breathing funny. What she didn't say when she called in a panic was that when she felt his forehead he was burning with fever. She ran back to tell you, but as we know, the cell phone went dead. So she called 911 and then kept putting cold washcloths on his face to try and bring down the fever while she waited for the ambulance.

"And, yes," he hated to relate, "she admits it had been a few hours since she'd looked in on him, because she got interested in a movie on TV and then fell asleep."

"Which explains why she sounded like I woke her up when I called," Carlee said, and couldn't help being peeved. "Nick, I don't blame her for Scotty being sick, but I can't help thinking she could have kept a closer watch on him."

"Carlee, nobody is going to watch him as closely as you do. Nobody is going to take as good care of him as you do. You're his mother. It's only natural. Lily feels real bad about this, but I don't think it's fair to blame her."

"I don't," she said quickly, "and I'll never say anything to her about it, believe me. I remember when Scotty got sick last time. I blamed myself for not noticing earlier how serious it was. But I won't leave him with Lily again."

"That's okay." He cut into a pancake with his fork, dipped it in syrup, then held it for her to eat. "Besides, we'll try to do things in the future where we can take him, too.

"And I do want to keep seeing you," he added, wishing they were alone so he could put his arms around her and try to kiss away the furrows on her brow. She looked exhausted. "I know you didn't feel like talking about it last night, and maybe this isn't a good time, either. But I want you to know that what happened—what almost happened—was because we both wanted it. I didn't plan it, I swear. And you have to believe that. Don't think that's all I'm after. It isn't. I like you, Carlee, and I love Scotty. I enjoy being with both of you."

He wished he could tell her how he really felt. The terror of Scotty's sudden illness had made him realize just how much he did care about him. Nick already knew he was falling in love with Carlee. And now he was determined to do everything in his power to make them a part of his life and his future. He had thought of nothing else as he had rushed about finding her clothes at her place and while changing the damn tire.

Carlee looked at him over the rim of her coffee cup, her eyes red and swollen from lack of sleep and crying. Finally she said, "We enjoy being with you, too, Nick, and for whatever time I've got left at Starke Groves, it would be nice to spend as much of it as possible with you." She meant it, having made up her mind, as well, to seize as much happiness as possible before the time came when they would, undoubtedly, be at odds with each other.

"Great." He slapped his palms on the table, making her jump. "How about a trip to Disney World as soon as he's well."

She laughed. "I don't think he's old enough to really enjoy it, Nick. About the only thing he'd get out of it would be riding in a stroller all day. Besides, it's too hot right now, don't you think?"

"I think," he said with a smile and a wink as he caressed her cheek with his fingertips, "that anything you want to do is fine with me. We can spend time at my pool, go to the beach, whatever."

"For now I just want to go back upstairs and be with Scotty."

She rose and he joined her, sliding his chair under the table, then picking up their trays.

"I'll call Becky in a little while," Carlee said as they walked out. "I want to ask her if she's going to mind having him in her care when we first get back. He'll have to have a lot of medicine, and it's going to take up a lot of her time."

"That's no problem," Nick said, putting their plates and cups in the garbage, then stacking the trays on top. "You can stay home with him."

"I think you're forgetting I have to work for a living."

"You can afford to take a few days off, Carlee." He held the door for her to pass through, then fell in step beside her. He wished he could take her hand, but was afraid to push things too fast.

"No, I can't, and don't you dare say you won't let me. Scotty will be fine with Becky once he's out of the hospital, because I have an idea they aren't going to release him till he's a hundred percent over this."

Nick was equally as stubborn. "A few days' pay won't make that much difference. You need to stay with him. After all…"

Despite Nick's many kindnesses to her, despite how he'd just said he wanted them to spend more time together, Carlee's ire was raised to think he dared tell her what she needed to do where Scotty was concerned. Not now. Not ever. She was perfectly able to make those decisions with Scotty's best interests at heart.

She stopped walking to glare at him, her jaw firmly set. "I won't leave Scotty if he needs me. Understand that. But I will make the decision, Nick. Okay?"

"Okay," he said with a shrug, miffed that she'd obviously taken offense. "I was just trying to help."

"And your help is always appreciated, but *I* make the decisions about Scotty."

They continued on their way, with Nick wondering why she got so defensive any time he voiced an opinion about Scotty's care. He was only trying to help.

With a soul-wrenching sigh, he wondered if it was futile to continue to try to break through that wall she had around her.

But he knew he would.

He couldn't help it.

He was falling in love with her.

Chapter Thirteen

Scotty stayed in the hospital for three days, with Carlee beside him all the while. Nick brought clean clothes daily and kept vigil while she showered and changed in the nurses' locker room. He was also able to coax her into going with him to the cafeteria at least once a day for a decent meal. The rest of the time she snacked from the vending machines if she was hungry.

The hospital was used to parents insisting on staying with their children and provided comfortable recliners that could be made into beds. With a blanket and a pillow, Carlee was able to rest.

She could see improvements in Scotty with each passing day. Because of the infection in his bronchial tubes, he had been plagued with raspy breathing, periodic coughing and gasping spells. But soon he was playing with toys and walking around in his crib. Then he demanded to get out, because he was feeling better and becoming bored.

It was a relief when Dr. Pelligrino at last said Scotty was well enough to be discharged. He was to remain on his medications for another week, then be checked by his regular pediatrician. When Carlee explained he did not have one in the area, Dr. Pelligrino said he would be glad to have him as a patient and had the nurse make the appointment.

The night before, Nick had insisted she take a break and leave Scotty in his care for a while. Scotty was being a handful, restless and anxious to get out of the tiny room, and Carlee had been staying with him constantly, not about to leave the nurses to try and entertain him. So she had enjoyed getting some fresh air as she took a leisurely walk on the hospital grounds. She was now by herself but not worried about finding a way home, since Nick had kindly had her car delivered to the hospital, anticipating he would not be around when Scotty was discharged in the morning.

Dr. Pelligrino wrote out several prescriptions and had the nurse send them downstairs to the hospital pharmacy. The amount would be added to Scotty's bill. All Carlee had to do was go to the business office, pick up the discharge slip, and Scotty was ready to go.

She wished it was that simple and dreaded going to the office with every step she took. What if they wouldn't accept monthly payments? Surely she wasn't the only person in the world with no insurance and no money.

The business office was not crowded, and a man ushered her right in. Before he even took his seat behind the desk, Carlee nervously began to explain her situation. "I'm a single mom. I have no insurance. But I do have a job. I can make monthly payments. Not a lot, but I promise you I'll pay the whole amount no matter how long it takes."

She was still standing, and he motioned for her to sit down. "Ma'am, I can assure you the hospital will work with you in every way possible to make things easy for you, but first let's take a look at your child's account and see what we've got. My name is Ron Ballentree, by the way.''

"Carlee Denton." She shook his hand, glancing at the sign on his desk to note that he was the assistant manager of the billing department. She sank into a chair. "This is all so embarrassing, and I can't emphasize enough that I'll take care of this. It might take a while, but—''

"Please, hold on." He tossed her a smile then focused on a computer screen. "Give me your child's name."

"Scotty Denton." She hated admitting she was broke. It was all so humiliating. In fact, she had been sorely tempted during the past few days to go ahead and admit everything to Nick and ask for even more of his help, but was glad she had resisted. Something told her she would know when it was the right time to tell him, and it wasn't now.

Mr. Ballentree punched his keyboard. A screen appeared, and he looked it over and said, "Well, Ms. Denton, it appears you have nothing to worry about. Your son's bill is all taken care of.''

Carlee was sure she'd heard wrong. "I beg your pardon?"

"His bill is taken care of."

It had to be some kind of mistake, a cruel joke of fate. "You must have the wrong record. His full name is Scott Lee Denton. He's in pediatrics.''

"I know, I know." Mr. Ballentree tapped the screen with his pencil eraser. "I see it right here. You are listed as his mother, and your address is Starke Groves over in Snow Hill. Your son was admitted Saturday night with croup and a bronchial infection. Two prescriptions have just been posted.'' He hit a button, and a printer on the other side of the room came to life. "I'll give you a copy of everything."

She did not have to ask.

She knew even before she was handed the printout of the bill.

Scanning down to the line denoting financial responsibility, the name leaped out at her.

Nick Starke.

"So—" Mr. Ballentree was saying as he handed her a discharge slip, "all you have to do is take this slip upstairs, and you're all done. Mr. Starke has given us carte blanche on his bank debit card to take care of any and all expenses connected with your son. We have the bank's approval for any amount necessary."

Carlee was a maelstrom of emotions as she returned to the pediatrics floor and began getting Scotty ready to leave.

Would she ever truly know the kind of person Nick was? He had signed to be accountable for a bill for thousands of dollars; yet he had turned his back on a woman who told him she was pregnant with his child.

Nick just did not fit the picture of a man who could do such a thing.

Unless he was a damn fine actor and even more cunning and deceitful that she could imagine.

By the same token, Carlee was jolted to think that could be why he had pursued her so strongly. He had found it intriguing that she blew him off so many times when he was used to women falling all over him.

Whatever his motive, Carlee told herself it didn't matter. She wanted him for Scotty's sake. Beyond that, he would eventually break her heart, which she helplessly seemed to be wearing on her sleeve lately, anyway.

Arriving home, Scotty clapped his hands and giggled to see the dozens of balloons tied to the front porch railings.

There was a note from Nick pinned to the door saying he had called the hospital that morning and learned she had already left with Scotty. He said not to worry about dinner. He was having something delivered. She was to settle down with Scotty and not even think of reporting to work. They would talk about that later.

She was warmed by his thoughtfulness, more than a little impressed, but as for when she went back to work, there was nothing to discuss. She had asked Dr. Pelligrino about leaving Scotty at the day-care center, and he saw nothing wrong with that. Scotty was fine; otherwise he would not have been discharged.

Once inside, she put Scotty down on the floor and he took off running through the cottage, happy to be home. He fell, got back up and continued toddling around, enjoying himself. He was, she gave thanks to acknowledge, in good health once more. Tests, however, had confirmed that he might be developing asthma, which would need to be monitored, but Dr. Pelligrino had assured her it was nothing to be too concerned about. The worst was definitely over.

Once Scotty had his lunch, Carlee brought him to bed with her, planning to take a short nap. Evidently having her slumber interrupted throughout the night and being in a strange bed had taken a toll. She wound up sleeping the rest of the afternoon and awoke only when Scotty rolled over and began cooing and patting her face.

It was just then that she heard a car door slam. Bounding to her feet, she looked out the window and saw it was Nick, loaded down with bags. Scooping Scotty up, she met Nick at the door. "You didn't have to do this. You've done so much already." She could feel that Scotty needed changing and turned back to the bedroom. "I'll give you a hand in a minute."

"Don't need one," he said cheerily. "I've got everything under control."

By the time she finished with Scotty, Nick had unpacked the bags and was setting the table. He had brought barbecued chicken and all the trimmings—coleslaw, potato salad and fresh-baked rolls. There was even an apple pie. "Compliments of Lily. She still feels bad about what happened. She sent whipped potatoes for Scotty."

"Well, tell her thanks for me. It all looks wonderful." She put Scotty in his chair. He insisted on feeding himself, and in no time she and Nick were laughing over the dollops of potatoes on his nose and chin.

Everything was delicious, and Carlee ate more than she normally did, because it was wonderful to eat something besides hospital food. There was even a huge pitcher of lemonade, sweet and frosty.

With Scotty banging his spoon on his tray and making a happy mess, there was no chance for serious conversation. Carlee got her chance afterward, when they walked down to the lake to watch the ducks in the sunset.

"I want to thank you for everything you've done, Nick," she began, feeling very awkward. It was even worse to harbor such a deep dark secret, but it could not be helped for the time being. "I don't know what I'd have done without you—taking care of the deposit, bringing me clothes, just being there for me. That was all so kind of you. But then to find out you've also paid the hospital bill is just overwhelming."

They were walking slowly side by side, with Nick holding Scotty to keep him from taking off after the ducks and winding up in the lake. Nick reached to give her hand a squeeze. "I'm glad to do it, Carlee. I'm your friend, and I think you know how I feel about this little boy of yours."

"But that's a lot of money. I could have arranged to make payments."

"There's no need. Like I said, I'm your friend, and I'm crazy about Scotty."

"Well, it's appreciated," she said. The moment was still awkward, and she was glad when Scotty began fussing. "I guess he's still tired from the hospital and all the excitement of coming home. I should turn in early, too, since I'll be going to work tomorrow." She darted a glance at Nick to see his reaction.

He frowned, but only slightly. "If you think it's okay to leave him, Carlee, then I won't object. After all, you're the mommy."

"Mah-mee," Scotty said, reaching to pat her face with his hand. "Mah-mee..."

She was thrilled just as she was the first time he'd said the precious word. She kissed his fingertips, then his cheek. "Mommy loves Scotty. Can you say 'Scotty'?"

It came out "Kah-tee," and she and Nick laughed till tears ran down their cheeks as he kept saying it over and over, giggling.

Carlee gave him his bath, then tucked him in bed, Nick beside her all the while. Impulsively she asked him to stay for another glass of lemonade.

"Thanks, but I really need to get home. I've got to be up real early. A factory rep is bringing in one of those mechanical harvesters for me to try out, and I invited him for breakfast."

"And you're going to cook?" she said, surprised at the thought.

"Well, yeah," he said, cocking his head and grinning. "You think I can't? It doesn't take a rocket scientist to whip up scrambled eggs, pop a frozen coffeecake in the oven and pour a glass of orange juice."

"I think that's admirable. Especially when you have a housekeeper."

"Don't tell anybody—" he lowered his voice conspiratorially "—but I love it when she's not around. Then I can fix what I want."

"Which is?" Carlee couldn't help being curious.

"Spaghetti. Pizza. And I love to grill steaks."

"Those are my favorites, too." They were standing just inside her door. "Well, I'll be anxious to hear how you like the harvester. Do you think I could see it in action? Maybe climb aboard?"

"Sure. Just let me make sure Mike and I know how to operate the thing first. Otherwise, you might get shaken to pieces."

She walked him to the door. Before opening it, Nick turned to say good-night, but could only stand there gazing at her and wishing he didn't have to leave. Not ever. He wished they were home, together, and that her head would rest on his shoulder all night long. And in the morning, there'd be the three of them, having breakfast, laughing together as they did so well so often, looking forward to the day...to the future.

He could hold back no longer and pulled her against him, his lips mere inches from hers as he gazed down at her in question. He did not want to force her to kiss him. He had given much thought as to how to proceed in his quest to make her love him. He did not want her to think she owed him anything just because he had signed for the hospital bill. Whatever she gave had to be of her own free will, and that was why he held her so gently, waiting to see what she wanted to happen next.

Shyly, so very shyly, she raised her lips to brush them against his, softly touching, only the slightest pressure, something to be tasted and savored with no rush, as though there was all the time in the world.

He drew her closer, sliding his arms around her shoulders. The kiss went a little deeper, the tip of his tongue skimming the delicate seam of her lips, searching for more, probing ever so gently at the corner of her mouth, coaxing, teasing…waiting for a sign that she wanted the kiss to deepen.

Opening her mouth, she gave a soft moan as he took complete possession.

His hand slipped downward, his palm filling with the weight of her breast. Tenderly his fingers kneaded the soft flesh. Suddenly her fingers closed over his, not to pull them away but to press him yet harder against her. From his throat came a low sound of arousal as he found her nipple and rubbed it with his thumb through the soft T-shirt and bra she was wearing.

She ended the kiss, arching her throat, instead, for the sweet assault of his mouth.

"Carlee, I want you," he breathed, tongue licking downward. "Say you want this, too, please…"

She was so overcome with desire that she could not speak, could only surrender by leaning into him, offering all she had to give.

He lifted her easily into his arms and carried her to the sofa. Laying her down, he dropped to his knees and kissed her once more as his fingers trailed to the zipper of her shorts. He eased it down, then slid his hand inside her panties and began a rhythmic massage. "I want you, Carlee. Please say you want me, too…"

She was dizzy, swept away on a torrent of desire unlike anything she'd ever experienced. But as she felt him sliding her shorts down, along with her panties, she mustered the strength to say, "I do want you, Nick, but I—" she hesitated ''—I don't take the Pill. You need to use something.''

He had learned long ago to carry a condom in his wallet, not about to admit there was no need to worry about him making anyone pregnant. Besides, there was always the matter of safe sex.

''Trust me,'' he whispered raggedly.

For one frozen instant Carlee wondered whether he'd said the same to Alicia, but then it melted away as Nick stroked the most feminine part of her, driving her mad with want and need.

She closed her eyes, and her breath caught as she felt the last of her restraint slipping away. She was overcome by sensation and raw, ragged passion.

He turned from her momentarily, undressing, making himself ready, and then he gently lowered himself on top of her.

''I've never wanted anyone more, Carlee,'' he whispered fervently, lips nuzzling her cheek and trailing downward. ''And I think I wanted you from the moment I first saw you.''

His chest was bare, and she began to massage the muscles, tracing ridges, her fingertips twining in the mat of dark hair.

In one swift movement he lifted her arms, removing her T-shirt, and bra, rendering her naked. Then, lowering his mouth to her breasts, he circled her nipples with his tongue in turn, evoking a gasp from her that was between pleasure and tortured need.

''Nick—''

He silenced her with a kiss, then continued his sweet assault upon her body, trailing kisses across her belly.

She clung to him, willing herself to empty all thought from her fevered brain. She did not want to contemplate anything but this wondrous pleasure. For this crystallized moment in time, neither the past nor the future mattered. Only the wonder of the here and now. All that counted was the joy, the deep, soul-shuddering ecstasy at hand.

Nick wanted it to last forever and told himself that even though the doubts were there, he might be offering his heart to be slashed into little pieces, he knew it was not just sex. He could have that whenever he wanted. This was different.

He told himself he was crazy. His life was fine as it was. He reveled in his business. He was financially secure. But it wasn't enough. He wanted more. Wanted what he could have with Carlee if only she felt the same.

Yet, if this was to be all they would ever have, if she later left him never to return, then he wanted her to look back on this night as the most wonderful of her life.

He was aroused to fever pitch, calling on all the inner strength he had, every ounce of self-control, to keep from entering her and taking himself to glory. Instead, he continued to kiss her, caress her, wanting her to be as crazy with want as he was. He wanted her to beg for the release only he could give her. And focusing on what he wanted in the long run, concentrating on what hopefully might be if the gods smiled down on him, helped him to hold back.

Shamelessly, Carlee could stand it no longer. His tongue, his hands, the caress of his lips, all combined to ignite fires that burned hotter and hotter, rushing toward helpless explosion. She spread her thighs, inviting him to enter.

"You want this," he said in wonder. "You want it as much as I do."

"Yes," she whispered against him. "Now—take me now, Nick, please…"

With his hands clutching her buttocks, he drove into her,

filling her with one mighty push. He could feel her tight and hot around him, her fingertips digging into his back.

Faster and harder, he moved in and out of her, and she moved with him, rhythmically and sensuously, her hips pumping to meet his every thrust.

She cried out as her climax ripped through her, holding on all the tighter, flesh against flesh, perspiration pouring from their bodies as they called each other's names. And only when Nick was sure she had reached that pinnacle of joy did he allow himself to come in a hot rush.

He held her for a long time afterward, their breathing harsh and ragged, hearts pounding like jackhammers.

When they calmed at last, Nick tenderly brushed a hand over her hair, brushed a kiss to her forehead, then shifted sideways to hold her close.

In the light filtering from the kitchen, he looked at her in complete adoration. Her face was still flushed, and he could feel her heart beating against his chest like a frightened bird. She didn't know it yet, but she had nothing to fear from him and never would.

Suddenly, because he had to know, he raised his head to look at her as he asked, ''Carlee, do you care for me at all? Do you feel anything?''

She returned his intense gaze, but he could not tell what she was thinking. And when at last she drew a deep breath and let it out oh, so very slowly, he steeled himself for words he did not want to hear, words that would pierce his soul to release whatever seeds of hope were harbored there.

''It's not the time,'' she said, her voice so low he almost didn't hear her.

He tightened his arms about her. ''What better time than now, when we're as close as a man and woman can possibly be?''

She shook her head, and he saw how her eyes glimmered with tears. "I...I don't know, Nick. I just know I can't talk about it now."

"But surely you feel something."

"Yes." The word fired like a bullet, sharp, cracking. And then she closed her eyes, turning her head so he could no longer see her face.

He thought that his very soul was smiling. "Then everything will work out, Carlee. It has to." He hugged her and kissed the top of her head and her forehead and as much of her face as he could reach. "There's so much I need to tell you, that I *want* to tell you—"

"Not now. Please, Nick, not now."

He was alarmed by how her voice cracked, as if she was about to burst into tears. He realized he might be pushing too hard, too fast. They'd just made love, and it had been wonderful, and though he wanted to revel in the magic, he sensed that for her it was over.

"Later," he whispered, gently extricating himself and getting up from the sofa. "We'll have lots of time later to talk. I know you have to be tired."

She did not speak, keeping her face turned into the sofa.

He felt heat rising again at the sight of her nakedness, the small of her back, the high, perfect curves of her buttocks and taut, slender thighs. She was beautiful, not only in body but also in spirit, and he knew he wanted her to be his in every way for always and ever.

Suddenly, from the other room, the cry came.

"Mah-mee. Mah-mee."

Carlee bolted upright, reaching for her clothes and fumbling in her embarrassment. Nick, in gentlemanly fashion, told her that he'd see to Scotty while she got dressed, and hurried to do so, pulling on his own clothes as he went.

A night-light shaped like a yellow duck bathed the room

in a mellow glow. Nick could see Scotty standing in his crib, clinging to the railing and happily pulling to and fro. Seeing Nick, his little mouth spread in a wide grin.

"Dah-dee…"

Nick froze, his heart slamming into his chest.

Scotty let go of the railing to hold out his arms, stamping his feet impatiently. "Dah-dee. Dah-dee."

It was a name Nick had thought he would never hear in his life, and here it was, spoken by a little boy he loved as if he were truly his very own son.

Behind him, Nick heard a soft gasp and Carlee's stunned question, "Did you tell him to call you that?"

With a start, he detected what sounded like accusation and quickly said, "No. Never."

"Then why…?" She went to Scotty, but he was still beckoning to Nick and calling to him. "I don't understand."

Suddenly Nick did and hastened to give her his theory about it. "The other kids at the day care all have daddies. Evidently he's seen them come and go and heard their children call them Daddy. I'm the only man who ever spends any time with him, so it's only natural he would call me that, too."

Carlee thought about the theory, then allowed, "I suppose that might be it."

She sounded shaky, doubtful, and Nick decided things really were happening too fast, daring to hope that when she heard Scotty call him Daddy, it got her to thinking that maybe one day it could be for real. Now she must be all twisted up inside trying to sort out how she felt about things. Based on that, it was probably best he leave her to do so.

"I'd better go now." He went to Scotty, lifted him in his arms for a hug and a kiss, then set him back down.

Carlee was still standing there, looking on in wonder, lower lip trembling ever so slightly.

Nick kissed her cheek. "I'll see you tomorrow. If you need me for anything, I'm only a phone call away."

Then he remembered.

There were no phones in the cottages. Lines had never been run because migrants had no need for them. There was a bank of pay phones outside the office, and they used those. But Nick wanted Carlee to be able to reach him if she needed to. He took his cell phone from his pocket and gave it to her. "I'll bring the battery charger by tomorrow."

And then he left.

Carlee stared at the phone, still unable to spring back to life from the shock she'd just been handed—Scotty had called Nick *Daddy.*

It was spooky.

Did Scotty actually sense that…?

No.

She gave her head a vicious shake.

It was like Nick said—Scotty had seen other men go into the day care and pick up their kids, heard them say Daddy, and with childlike reason, called Nick the same. Like saying puppy or kitty or duck when he recognized pictures in a book. To Scotty, Nick was a picture of a daddy. It would never have occurred to him to refer to Nick by any other name.

Carlee changed Scotty's diaper, then she held him and rocked him till he went back to sleep.

And even then she continued to hold him, not wanting to let him go. He meant so much to her, and she loved him with every fiber of her being. But now, in the stillness, her body still warm from Nick's caresses, her lips kiss-swollen, she had to acknowledge the reality that she had tried to push away and not think about.

Nick loved Scotty, too.

She could see it in his eyes and hear it in his voice when he talked about him.

She had also been aware of his deep concern and distress when Scotty was so sick. He was at the hospital almost constantly for the first two days till they could be sure the little boy was out of the woods. No father could have worried or cared more about his ailing child than Nick.

Then, too, Carlee was moved by how tender Nick had been when they had made love. It was all about her, because he had wanted her satisfaction even more than his. Women could sense things like that, and she was no exception. Nick cared for her. How much, she had yet to learn. But it was there.

And she cared for him. Oh, yes. Much more than she wanted to admit.

So now it was time to do something about it, time to find out just what the future held for all of them.

Because, after what had just happened, it was time to tell Nick he was Scotty's father.

Chapter Fourteen

When the alarm went off, Carlee felt as though she hadn't slept a wink. She was tortured trying to figure out how to tell Nick about Scotty. It was not going to be easy. In fact, it was probably going to be the hardest thing she'd ever had to do in her whole life. She was so afraid of how he would react, and a few times during her long restless night she'd been actually tempted to leap out of bed, pack their things, and run away and not look back. But she couldn't do that, because regardless of how Nick had treated Alicia, there was no getting around the fact he'd been good to her, Carlee, as well as Scotty.

Then there was also the matter of her heart. Maybe last night had just been sex to Nick, but it had meant much more to her. She couldn't just walk away and pretend it hadn't happened. Yet she knew that once she told him everything, there was a good chance he was going to be absolutely furious. He might agree to pay child support, but would consider her his mortal enemy for having deceived him. It could put a terrible strain on their relationship regarding Scotty. But if he wanted to put up a fight, she was ready. Maybe she didn't have money to hire a big-shot lawyer to duke it out, but what she did have was Alicia's witnessed note, and she was almost certain Bonnie Handel would be willing to testify as to how Nick had abandoned Alicia when she told him she was pregnant with his child.

She rolled out of bed and crossed to Scotty's crib. He was sleeping on his stomach, face turned toward her. Suddenly his mouth spread in a smile. She had once heard that when babies smile in their sleep, it's because an angel is talking to them. Was that angel Alicia? Carlee wondered, tears welling in her eyes.

With a heavy heart she knew it would probably be a futile battle if Nick wanted sole custody. The natural father always had the edge in situations like this. It was also her word against his, and he could always lie and say he never knew Alicia was pregnant, that they had just broken up, as couples do. He could claim he did not hear from her again and deny that she didn't know how to contact him. He had the upper hand, all right, if it came right down to it.

But that was the chance she was going to have to take. She had no other choice and had come too far to back down now.

She patted Scotty on his back and gave him a little shake. "Come on, honey. Time to start waking up. Miss Becky and all your little friends are going to be waiting to play with you."

He blinked sleepily, yawned, then rolled over to look up at her. Again he smiled, and this time happily cried, "Mah-mee," and held out his arms.

She picked him up and hugged him so tightly he squealed. "You're mine," she whispered, tears streaming down her cheeks to think how much she loved him. "And no one will ever take you away from me. I swear it."

Then and there she resolved that if Nick gave even the slightest hint he wanted custody, she would take Scotty and run away.

She carried Scotty into the kitchen and put him in his high chair. It was time for their morning ritual of seeing how much oatmeal she could get into his mouth and how much wound up on his face and the floor.

"It's going to be a good day, little guy," she told him, "because no matter what happens, we'll always be together."

"The workers aren't going to like having a short season, Mr. Starke," Mike Thurston said as they had coffee together in Nick's office. "They're going to be upset they passed up the chance for longer work elsewhere."

Mike had told Nick what he didn't want to hear—that the Valencias were almost completely harvested, and it was only the first of June. Everyone had counted on at least four more weeks of work. "Well, it can't be helped. The groves just didn't produce as many oranges as last year. It was the drought, and we didn't get enough water to the back blocks of trees. We'll make sure to do that next year."

Mike gloomily pointed out, "Next year the oranges might rot on the ground, because we probably won't have the workers to pick them after this. They'll head on out to do other crops like all the other migrants when the regular season ends."

Nick hated to agree. "Well, maybe that new mechanical harvester we're trying out today will solve the problem."

Mike laughed. "Lots of luck. I haven't seen one of those things yet that can do the job as good as humans."

"I know, and I'll probably ultimately decide that, but the salesman has been hounding me to give it a chance, so I finally agreed—anything to get him off my back."

"So when do you want to tell the workers they won't be needed after this week?"

Nick dreaded having to do it. "Tell you what. I'll have Elaine get a picnic together for Friday night. I'll talk to them then and give them all a week's wages to help out a little till they move on to where they can find work."

Mike gave a long low whistle. "That's going to cost a lot."

Nick was well aware of that fact and knew it would mean a big loss in the season's profits, but the way he saw it he had no choice. "Starke Groves has always taken care of its workers, and I'm not going to send these people off without compensating in some way for their disappointment."

"Okay, it's your money. I'll just go along the rest of the week like nothing's wrong."

Mike finished his coffee and left, and Nick was glad to be alone, wanting time to gather his wits before seeing Carlee again.

After he had returned home the night before, he had gone to bed but could not fall asleep. So he had gone out to the pool and swam laps in the moonlight, trying to wear himself out. But it hadn't worked. He kept reliving the evening and how wonderful it had been making love to Carlee. It was as though she had been smoldering for a long, long time, the heat of her desire just below the surface of that icy facade she had so often taken refuge behind in the past. The spark had ignited, triggering an explosion unlike anything he'd ever experienced. He could feel that she had given her all to him. Held nothing back. She had wanted it as much as he had.

He had not seduced her or pressured her into anything. Her pleasure, her enjoyment, was complete. Her eyes as she gazed at him afterward said it all.

It was only when Scotty had called him Daddy that Nick sensed she was pulling behind that curtain of ice once more.

Not that she was coldly unfriendly or made him feel repulsed.

Far from that.

But there was something that swept her away from him and the closeness in which they had been languishing. Until he discovered what it was, their relationship could not progress any further.

And God help him, he wanted so much more.

Now the situation was even more crucial. He had been so enamored with her and with Scotty that he hadn't paid much attention to harvesting, leaving everything to Mike. Normally Nick kept up with things and would have known they were reaching the end of Valencia season earlier than anticipated. Not that he could have done anything about it, but it was still his place to keep abreast of things like that.

Worse, it meant no more work for Carlee, and he did not want her moving on. They needed time—*he* needed time—to see if what was happening between them was real, if it could grow into something more. But if she left…

He couldn't let that happen.

He pushed the buzzer on his desk that brought Elaine, and he got right to the point. "What's the situation with the gift shop?"

She raised her brows. "What do you mean? It never

opens till the first of November when the snowbirds start flocking in.''

She meant the people from the north who took up temporary residence in Florida to enjoy the warm winter months and escape the bitter cold. They were the ones who came to the groves to order baskets for Christmas shipping, packed not only with oranges but jams and jellies and other items available in the gift shop. Nick had never worried about it too much, because the big money came from selling citrus to distributors for resale to grocery stores and other outlets. The gift shop was just a sideline, only now it dawned on him that it could be the key to keeping Carlee. He had only hinted at it before, but now was the time to get serious.

''I was thinking we need to expand and make the shop like the big ones along the Indian River between Vero Beach and Melbourne. Call somebody to give an estimate on renovation.''

Elaine did not look at all enthused. ''Sure. I can get somebody to do that, but I don't see how I can take over the gift shop when I've got so many other things to do in the office. You know we usually hire somebody to work there when the season starts, and that's months away.''

''Don't worry about it, Elaine. Just get me that estimate, and I'll take care of finding someone to take over the shop and run it for me.''

The corners of her mouth twitched as she asked, ''Do you have anybody in particular in mind?''

''I don't know,'' he hedged. ''I'll have to think about it.''

Impishly she persisted, ''Well, I just happened to remember that the young woman you hired on last, the one with the cute little boy, wrote on her application that she had some experience working in a grove gift shop. You could ask her. Maybe she'd be glad for the job, since Mike told me this week will be the last of midseason harvest."

"I suppose I could talk to her," Nick said, trying to appear nonchalant. He had a good idea that there was talk going around about his interest in Carlee. After all, it was common knowledge he'd taken her to the charity ball and had also driven to Sanford every day while Scotty was in the hospital. Still, he liked to keep his personal life to himself as much as possible, which wasn't easy.

But Elaine persisted. "I can find time to do that, Mr. Starke. After all, you've got other things to do. I'll just send word for her to come in to see me and—"

"It's okay." He was also having a hard time holding back a grin. He looked her straight in the eye. "I appreciate the offer, but I'll handle it."

"Whatever you say, sir." She turned on her heel and walked out.

But not before Nick saw she'd lost the battle to hold back that smile.

"That is undoubtedly the weirdest thing I have ever seen," Carlee declared, hands on her hips as she stared in wonder at the mechanical harvester. "It looks like a giant one-armed robot."

"Yeah, I'd say so." Nick tried to sound cheerful when actually he was worried about why she'd been avoiding eye contact the few times he'd seen her during the day. "Are you ready to see how it works?"

"Sure." She shrugged as though it didn't matter.

He had been wanting a chance to speak with her all day about managing the gift shop, but the factory representative for the harvester had hung around. By the time Nick got rid of him, it was late in the day and the workers were finishing up. The rep said he'd return in the morning to

either firm up the sale or collect the harvester. Nick could
have told him then and there he wasn't buying, but wanted
to use it as an excuse to be alone with Carlee. He reasoned
if he went to her cottage to talk to her, she might think
his real motive was to get her into bed again.

He showed her how the arm clamped onto the trunk of
an orange tree, then set the switch and drew her to one
side to watch. "It's set just long enough to shake the fruit
off an average-size tree, and— What the…?"

Something was wrong. The harvester was shaking too
fast, becoming violent. The oranges were falling so hard
they were splattering on the ground, and some of them
bounced back up to hit Nick and Carlee.

He ran to shut it off, but it kept on going. "It's like that
damn drum-beating bunny," he cursed. "Going and going…"

Carlee, although pelted by oranges, could not help
laughing. "My gosh, Nick, it's like one of those machines
in old-fashioned motels where you put a quarter in to make
the bed jiggle, only it won't stop jiggling."

An orange smacked her shoulder, and she retreated out
of range as Nick continued trying to shut down the harvester.

"It's no use," he said, joining her to watch from beneath a nearby tree. "It's going to have to run out of gas
before it stops. I think I'll make the salesman pay for all
the fruit that's ruined. Good grief, I'd never buy one of
these things."

"Oh, I think it's kind of fun," she said.

Just then an orange bounced off the frame and burst,
part of it careering through the air to hit his cheek. Carlee
burst into gales of laughter.

"Oh, you think it's funny, do you?" He gave a mock

growl. "Let's see how *you* like it." Scooping up one of the smashed oranges, he smeared it on her face.

Carlee retaliated and threw one at him, and soon it was all-out war, ending only when she tripped and went sprawling on the ground with Nick falling on top of her to pin her down.

Laughing so hard he could hardly talk, he held a smashed orange directly over her face and warned, "Give up, or I'll wash your face in it."

"Never," she cried, rolling sideways.

He caught her, pinning her arms above her head with one hand while still threatening her with the orange.

Suddenly he found himself gazing into her hazel eyes, flecked with gold and shining with the desire she could not conceal. His heart began to beat harder, and his breath came in quick ragged gasps as he drank in the sight of her. He had unbuttoned his shirt, for it was an extremely hot day. Hotter still, with her breasts touching his flesh with each breath she drew.

He let go of her wrists and, her arms, as though with a will of their own, instantly twined about his neck.

Her breath was warm on his face, and he felt himself growing harder with each passing second. He wanted her. So badly it was like a knife to his soul. They were at the far borders of his land, with no one anywhere nearby. The workers were gone. The trucks, the haulers, everything.

The wind picked up, blowing their hair about their faces. Clouds drifted across the sun, and they were painted in silvered shadows.

Yet neither of them moved.

Then, with a last frantic shake, the harvester abruptly shut down, and the sudden silence jolted them from their trancelike state.

"It…it ran out of gas," Nick said awkwardly, still not moving away from her.

"Thank…goodness," she said tremulously, shivering despite the waves of heat washing over her.

"Carlee, I…" Nick did not know what he was about to say, only that he needed to speak, to do…something.

And then his body spoke for him.

Parting her lips, he slid his tongue between them and into her mouth, plunging deep, probing, withdrawal slow and rhythmic, raw and primal and carnal.

She rose to meet him in answer to her own hunger, her body melting against his. They rolled sideways, and his hands began to roam over her, caressing her breasts in turn, then sliding downward.

Abruptly he pulled back. "Not here…" He stood, pulling her with him, then lifted her in his arms and carried her to where his truck was parked. There was a custom cover over the bed, complete with a small door in back and windows on both sides that opened for ventilation and a rubber liner on the floor.

Inside, they were hidden away from the world. All the workers had left, and no one would happen to venture so far back in the groves.

Opening the door, Nick helped her inside, then followed. Both were eager to peel out of their orange-stained clothing, and once they were naked, fell into each other's arms in wild abandon. Carlee tried to cry his name, but was silenced by his eager lips.

She loved how his hands roamed so possessively over her body, leaving a trail of fire everywhere they touched. She wanted to touch him, to feel him. Her fingers boldly danced down his taut belly and below, twining in the soft mat of hair, then tracing the hard, long length of him. She wanted to savor every second, committing it all to memory, for this would undoubtedly be the last time they would be together.

Her insides cringed at the thought, and she willed it to go away. There would be time later for grieving. Right now she wanted to relish the splendor of the moment.

Nick had moved his lips to her breasts, feasting on each in turn, his tongue circling her nipples greedily. He could feel her gentle shuddering, could hear her soft whimpering as she arched to get closer to him. Over the blood rushing in his ears and the hammering of his heart against his ribs, he thought how he had not wanted it this way. Not now. He had wanted to talk to her, to tell her just how much he cared, then beg her to stay so they could get to know each other all the better and discover if they had a future. And, oh, how he prayed they did. Only it had not worked out that way. Passion had ruled, and he had to have her then and there.

Maneuvering her beneath him, they rocked together, with Carlee raising her hips to undulate and thrust wildly, wantonly, and it was becoming more than Nick could bear. It was sweet anguish, but he held back, not about to rob her of release in preference to his own.

At last, he felt her quivering against him, and he took them both to shattering climax together.

Afterward he rained kisses over her face and gasped, ''I don't believe it. We're in such complete unison, Carlee. It's wonderful. *You* are wonderful.''

Though silently agreeing that the experience had been earth-shattering, sending her into celestial bliss, Carlee came back to earth like a falling star, streaking down to land with a thump on reality.

She could wait no longer.

She had to tell him.

Nick was likewise plummeting back to earth, but anxious to do so in order to make his offer to Carlee. Rolling on to his side, he propped himself on one elbow and said, "Honey, listen. After this week the Valencias are all harvested, but I can't stand the thought of your leaving. I want you to stay on and help get the gift shop remodeled. You can be the manager and run it any way you want. It'll mean a job for you and a place for you and Scotty to live.

"And," he rushed to continue, pausing to kiss the tip of her nose, "it will give us a chance to really be together and find out what the future holds. Because the truth is, Carlee—" he hesitated, hoping he wasn't going too far, too fast "—I think I'm falling in love with you, and I can only wish that you might be able to say the same about me."

She turned away, then reached for her clothes and struggled to put them on. The top of the cover was too low for her to stand.

Nick tensed, warning bells ringing in his head. This was not good. She was slipping behind that wall again, and it was even more maddening in the wake of such wondrous passion. He reached for her, but she moved away, busy trying to get her shorts zipped. "Carlee, what's wrong with you? All I said—"

"It's not what you said." Her lower lip began to tremble. "It's what I've got to say to you."

"Then talk to me, honey. Tell me what's wrong. Please. I care about you so much. And Scotty, too. But I've sensed so many times that there was something preying heavy on your mind...your heart. You've been hurt, I know, but I swear I'll never hurt you."

He had been dressing as he spoke. Carlee waited till he finished, then sat down cross-legged. She cleared her throat. She looked upward and closed her eyes for a few seconds, then took a deep breath and faced him squarely.

"It hasn't got anything to do with me, Nick. It's about Alicia."

Nick blinked, then frowned and echoed, "Alicia? Who's Alicia?"

"Alicia Malden," she said calmly, evenly. "She worked at the Blue Moon Lounge in Cocoa Beach."

He gave a helpless shrug. "Carlee, I don't know anyone by that name. Am I supposed to? And I've never heard of that place. I don't hang out in bars."

Carlee couldn't help it. She was flooded with anger—at him, as well as herself. She had just given herself to him wholly and completely and knew she had fallen in love with him. But those actions, those feelings, were for the person she had come to know. Not the lying stranger who sat before her with wide innocent eyes, pretending to be astonished.

"You do know her," she said through clenched teeth. "Granted it's been nearly two years, but surely you don't forget leaving a woman pregnant."

"Carlee, that's crazy. I never—"

Again he reached for her, and as before, she pulled away, only this time she hissed, "Don't you touch me. I don't know what I expected, but certainly not that you'd deny even knowing her."

"I swear to you, Carlee. I have no idea what you're talking about. I've never met anyone named Alicia Malden, and I've never been to the Blue Moon Lounge, either. What the hell is all this about, anyway?"

"Want me to refresh your memory? You were in Cocoa Beach at one of your citrus-growers' meetings. She was a waitress at the Blue Moon Lounge. You kept seeing her after the conference, driving from here to there almost every night. And when she told you she was going to have your baby, you told her to get an abortion and walked out and never went back.

"So do you remember her now?" Her voice rose shrilly as she raised herself on her knees to get right in his face. "Nick, don't you dare lie about this. I was ready to forgive and forget because I gave you the benefit of the doubt since I didn't know your side of the story. But you are crazy if you think you can deny it."

Nick's head was in a spin. "Now let me get this straight." He touched his fingertips to his temples. "You're saying I dated this woman, got her pregnant, then walked out on her. Why are you telling me this? What kind of sick joke is this?"

"It's not a joke." Carlee slammed her fists on the floor. "Alicia was my best friend, and she died a few months ago. And when she knew she was dying, she signed a paper giving me custody of Scotty—"

"Scotty isn't your son?" Nick cried, rocking back on his heels.

"No," she said in a low, fierce whisper. "But he's *yours.*"

"That…can't be." He leaned back, resting his head against the side of the truck bed. This was a nightmare. None of it made sense.

"I don't blame you for wanting to be sure. Paternity tests will prove you're his father." She sat back, commanding herself to calm down. He was showing his true colors, reverting to the same selfish, callous creep he'd been when he turned his back on Alicia. Only Carlee was not about to let him get away with it as Alicia had.

Nick tried to blink away the tears that sprang to his eyes as he beseeched her with outstretched hands. "Please listen to me. I wish Scotty were my son. I'd give anything if he were, but it's not possible. Why are you doing this to me?

I thought I knew you, Carlee, yet here you are, trying to railroad me, no doubt trying to nail me for child support. But you didn't have to. I mean, dammit, you should know by now there's nothing I wouldn't do for him...for you. If you really needed anything, all you had to do was ask.

"I was even trying to give you a full-time job," he rushed on, staring at her like she was a total stranger. "And I just got through telling you I was falling in love with you. What more do you want?" He brushed a tear away with the back of his hand. He knew he should be ashamed but wasn't. Men weren't supposed to cry, but they could be crushed and hurt just as women could, and right then he felt as if he was dying inside.

Icily she retorted, "Maybe you tell that to all your women. Maybe you even said it to Alicia. As for helping me financially, you can afford it, and it was probably all part of your seduction, anyway."

"Seduction? Wait a minute, Carlee. You wanted it every bit as much as I did, and you know it."

"I'm only human, but that's not the issue here."

Nick's face was flushed with outrage. "I thought I was a good judge of character, Carlee, but I guess not, because I never thought you'd stoop to something like this."

"Stop trying to make me out to be the villain!" she cried in frustration, anger and disgust. "Scotty is your son, and while I can understand that you'd question that fact without proof, don't sit there and tell me you never slept with Alicia, that you never told her to have an abortion. You even lied to her, claiming you were going through a divorce when you already *were* divorced."

She moved to get out of the truck, unable to stand being in such close quarters with him. If she stayed there another second, she was afraid she'd explode.

"Hold it." His hand snaked out and caught her ankle.

Flipping her over, he pinned her down, eyes burning like hot coals, nostrils flared, lips tight and set. "There's something very wrong here, Carlee, but I'm not responsible. I swear to you I have never known anyone named Alicia Malden, much less told her or any other woman to have an abortion."

"Just let me go, damn you," Carlee ground out, fists clenched to keep herself from raking her nails down his face. Silently she cursed herself for thinking she could ever have allowed herself to love him, much less have given herself to him with such wanton abandon.

"Not till you let me explain. We've got to settle this before it goes any farther. And how many people have you told this to?"

"No one but you. I was a fool to think that a man who could do what you did would take responsibility for his child. I'll find a way to take care of Scotty without any help from you, mister."

She was struggling against him, and he did not want to hurt her by continuing to restrain her.

So he let her go.

She opened the door and was about to crawl out when he called to her. She almost kept on going, but there was something so heart-wrenching in his tone that she could not help but hesitate.

"Scotty can't be mine, Carlee," Nick said, every word a dagger to his heart. "Because I can't father children. I'm sterile."

She whipped her head about to stare at him incredulously, then spat, "Nick Starke, you are without a doubt the most pathetic excuse for a man I have ever encountered. And all I can say to you is...*go to hell.*"

He sat there, numb, as she bolted from the truck. He struggled to think of what, if anything, he could say or do

to make her believe him. A paternity test would prove
Scotty wasn't his, and he could get a letter from his urol-
ogist confirming his sterility. That would not solve the
mystery of just who Scotty's father was, but it would prove
his innocence at least.

He got out of the truck. He wanted to find Carlee and
tell her his plans to prove his innocence, but couldn't see
her anywhere. Figuring she was taking a shortcut by cutting through the trees, he would just have to drive slowly
and try to spot her along the way. It was a long walk, and
she wouldn't make good time winding her way through
the grove.

First, however, he needed to secure the mechanical harvester. The shaking arm had to be disconnected from the
tree trunk and folded back. He also didn't want to leave
the key in the ignition should some mischievous kids happen by. It wasn't likely, but until the salesman came back
and got it, Nick was responsible for the expensive piece
of equipment.

He was up inside the harvester when he heard the engine
of his truck roar to life. Scrambling down, he was not in
time to stop Carlee from driving away, tires spinning sand
into his face.

He took off walking as fast as he could, but it was hard
going, and he was exhausted after working all day and,
yes, he burned to think, making love. But with each plod-
ding step he took, his determination to prove he was not
lying deepened.

Trying to take a shortcut, he got turned around and
cursed himself for getting lost in his own groves. By the
time he hit the right path and made it back to the office,
nearly an hour had passed.

His truck was parked at the office, and he jumped in
and drove like mad to the migrant cottages.

It was like a fist slammed into his stomach when he realized her car wasn't there.

And his first glimpse inside her cottage was like a knife to his soul.

Her things were gone. And so were Scotty's.

He heard a sound and whipped around, hope springing. Maybe she'd decided to hear him out, after all, and—

"Mr. Nick, are you looking for Carlee?"

It was Mamie.

"Well, you're wasting your time," she continued. "She lit out of here like a bat out of hell. Never seen anybody pack so fast. I tried to talk to her, asked her what was wrong, but she wouldn't say a word. Just took off."

Nick didn't say anything. What could he say? He wasn't about to tell Mamie or anyone else what had happened. It was too humiliating—and also unbelievable.

He could only stumble, sick and heartbroken, from the cottage and into his truck.

She was gone.

But God help him, he intended to move heaven and earth to find her, because he figured he owed it to himself to set her straight.

If what she said were true, if she actually believed he was Scotty's father, he would prove otherwise.

But on the other hand, if she'd been playing games all along in an effort to get money out of him, well, he had a score to settle there, as well.

Carlee could hardly see through her tears. She kept wiping her eyes with the back of her hand. Beside her, strapped in his car seat, Scotty was howling. She knew he was both hungry and scared. She had rushed into the day-care center and grabbed him out of his playpen with a brusque nod to Becky. Then when she got to the cottage, she had packed in a frenzy, throwing things in the car as fast as she could while Scotty had watched wide-eyed from his crib.

She had tried to reassure him as she moved about, telling him everything would be okay—words he did not understand, but she felt talking was better than ignoring him in her panic.

There had been no time to think about where she was going and what she was going to do. She had been focused on getting away from there, away from Nick, as fast as possible. Because underlying her fury at having him so brazenly deny everything was fear. He'd practically accused her of extortion, so she couldn't be sure he wouldn't quickly devise a plan to call the police and have her arrested and put in jail. Then later he would pretend to be magnanimous, and offer to adopt Scotty to keep him from being placed in a foster home. Nick would then have custody of his son with not a breath of scandal. She was not about to let that happen, and that was why she was running as though her life depended on it.

And maybe it did.

Because Scotty was her life.

"Oh, baby, please stop crying." She tried to pat his leg, but he was kicking wildly, screaming so loudly his face was red. "Honey, I know you're hungry and tired, and I promise I'll stop as soon as I can."

She hated that she could not do more to comfort him, but needed to put some miles between her and Starke Groves. It would take Nick a while to walk back to the office to retrieve his truck and then discover she had left. At best, she figured she was an hour ahead of him if he did try to follow, and once she reached Interstate 95, felt she could relax.

She really hated having to lose her last week's pay. She

needed the money, but there was just no way she could have stayed around long enough to collect it. She'd done the only thing she could do and would have to make the best of it.

Finally Scotty cried himself to sleep. She kissed her fingertips and pressed them to his forehead. "I'll make it up to you, sweetie. I swear I will."

She kept driving till he woke up, then pulled into an interstate rest area and parked. She changed his diaper before digging into the food bag for a jar of food and a can of formula. It was awkward, but she managed.

Once he was fed, he settled back with a toy and seemed content.

"Now what?" she asked.

Scotty looked at her and laughed.

"It's nothing to laugh about, honey. We happen to be homeless and almost broke."

He laughed again, and Carlee thought, what a blessing to be so young and regard life so frivolously. She wished she could do the same, but worry and responsibility came with growing up.

She knew if they stayed in the rest area for very long, a security guard would ask questions. There were signs posted everywhere saying No Overnight Parking.

Then she spotted the phone booth. She got out of the car and went to the other side to lift Scotty out. "There's only one person who might help," she told him. "It's a long shot, but it's all we've got."

She found change in her purse for the phone and dialed the number from memory.

When she heard Ben Burns's voice, it was all she could do to keep from breaking down. In the calmest voice she could muster, Carlee explained that the job she had told him about had not lasted as long as she hoped. "So now

I'm afraid I have a bit of a problem, Mr. Burns. I not only don't have a job, but I don't have a place to live, either. It wouldn't be so bad if it were just me, but you know I have Alicia's baby and—''

That was all she had time to say before he cut her off. ''Carlee, don't you worry. You've got a home here. Mrs. Burns and I will be glad to put you both up for a while. And I'll find some kind of work for you to do. Now, where are you? Can you make it here tonight?''

''I'll be there,'' she said, laughing and crying both at once as she tried to keep Scotty from choking her with the phone cord.

''Good,'' he declared, the warmth in his voice making Carlee think of all things fuzzy and warm. ''I'll tell Mrs. Burns to keep some supper warm for you. Drive carefully now.''

Carlee hung up the phone and stepped out of the booth.

And that was when she saw the penny on the ground.

''It's an omen, Scotty,'' she said as she maneuvered to pick it up with him in her arms. ''When you find a penny, it means it fell from heaven—a message that an angel is watching after you.

''And that angel,'' she said chokingly, covering his face with kisses, ''is your mommy. We're going to make it, honey. You and me.

''As for your daddy,'' she added fiercely, hurrying to the car, ''we'll just pretend he never existed. We'll forget all about him.''

And, oh, how she hoped she could.

But the cruel truth was, she had left behind more than her last week's pay at Starke Groves.

She had left part of her heart, as well.

Chapter Fifteen

Nick was lying on the sofa in his office, staring up at the ceiling and figuring he had to be the most confused human being in the whole world.

And maybe the loneliest, as well.

The workers had all left. Elaine and Mike were taking their annual vacation. Starke Groves was shut down and would be until September when it would be time to get ready for fall harvest.

He had even given Lily the rest of the summer off, wanting to be completely alone in his misery.

He was especially glad Elaine was not around. She had asked too many questions, worried, she said, about how depressed he seemed. She had guessed it had something to do with Carlee, wanting to know why she had left without collecting her last paycheck. Nick had shrugged and said he had no idea, but if she called about it, he wanted to talk to her. Elaine had seized on that, as it seemed to her suspicion that things had been getting serious. She got real nosy then. He'd had to politely tell her to butt out. Talking about Carlee was like pouring salt into a wound.

His first impulse that day had been to go after her, and he had actually driven all the way to the interstate thinking he might overtake her. He could only guess that would be the direction she would go, recalling how anything east of the groves around Sanford or Orlando seemed alien to her.

There had been nothing to do but turn around and go home. He had then sat up the entire night going over and over that frenzied conversation in the back of his truck. None of it made any sense, and he couldn't understand why she had gone totally ballistic when he said he never knew a woman named Alicia Malden. There had been no reasoning with Carlee after that.

But then, as he had thought back to all the times they had been together, he wondered if there had ever really been any reasoning. The way she could turn so instantly cold, how little things he said—or didn't say—had triggered that damn curtain to fall between them, all pointed to the belief that she'd had something against him from the beginning.

Now he knew why.

Maybe he shouldn't have accused her of trying to get money out of him, but at the time, it was the only explanation he could think of. Why else would she have claimed he was Scotty's father?

He had hated having to bare his very soul then and there and confess his sterility, but at the time saw no other way to try to make her believe him. And when she had glared at him, hatred blazing in her eyes, and told him to go to hell, it had hurt worse than anything Gina had ever said or done.

That was when he realized just how deeply he had fallen in love with Carlee.

Torturing, also, was the worry over what was going to happen to her and Scotty. He was well aware she had money problems.

And just who the hell was Scotty's father, anyway?

So many thoughts whirling around inside made him dizzy.

Finally he sat up and wearily shook his head to try to clear it. He had slept in the office, because after doing some paperwork to get his mind off things, he'd been unable to muster enough energy to go to the house.

He knew he had to get hold of himself and stop brooding, because there didn't seem to be anything he could do about it. Sure, he could hire a private detective to find her. He had her social security number. It was difficult for anyone to hide these days. But then he asked himself what he would do if he did track her down. If she hadn't believed him before, she was not going to believe him now.

Still, right after she'd left, he'd tried to figure out where she would have gone. It took a lot of doing, but he had managed through the Citrus Growers' Association to find out the name of the owner of the grove where she claimed to have worked before it went out of business. He had then called him—a man named Seth Barklee. Seth told him sorry, but he'd never heard of her, and laughingly said from the way Nick described her he was sure he would have. Nick knew then she had lied on her application in order to keep him from finding her if her scheme didn't work.

And by then, he had to painfully acknowledge that was what it had been—an extortion scheme. It certainly explained why she had run away so fast, not bothering to collect her pay. When he had told her he was sterile, she had realized her plan had backfired and there was no way he would pay her off. And sure, she had said he could have a paternity test done, but was no doubt banking that he'd just settle quietly rather than face all the gossip and scandal.

So he told himself that if he could achieve that mindset about Carlee—that she was a schemer and a crook— his love would turn to hate.

Only it wasn't working.

He paced around the office a few minutes to get the stiffness out from being cramped on the sofa. He supposed he should find some good, hard physical labor to help combat the stress. Maybe a few laps in the pool. A couple of rounds of golf.

A sudden roll of thunder sent him to the window. The skies were dark, and the wind was whipping the fronds of the palm trees into a frenzy. Another summer storm was about to strike, so there was nothing to do but stay right where he was till it passed.

His desk was covered in paperwork he needed to tend to. He had let things pile up. He wished for a cup of hot black coffee to give him a jump start, then thought about the pot Elaine kept in the outer office.

He went to make some, but could not find any coffee. He rummaged around out there, then went back into his office to search. When he met with wholesalers' representatives or conducted business meetings, she sometimes brewed a pot in there so if he or his guests wanted refills, they wouldn't have to take time to ask her to take care of it. Maybe she had left one of the little filter packs she used.

He searched the bookcases, his desk drawers, then noticed a stack of things on top of a file cabinet. Shuffling through them, he came across a big brown envelope that was unfamiliar and thought again how he really needed to

straighten up things. His office was starting to look as if a
pack rat lived there.

Thinking Elaine might have put the filters in the envelope, he dumped the contents on his desk. Then he realized
it was the items the Brevard County Sheriff's Office had
returned to him, items that had been stolen by the pickpocket two years earlier. He had meant to throw everything
away, but had tossed the envelope on top of the cabinet
that day so long ago and forgotten all about it.

He took the credit cards into Elaine's office and stuck
them in the shredder. They weren't any good to anyone,
hadn't been ever since he'd reported them stolen and had
new account numbers and cards issued, but the pickpocket
had sure had a good time with them for a while. There
had been charges for expensive clothing and restaurants,
huge bar bills and five-star hotels on the beach. The culprit
had obviously tried to spend as much as possible before
Nick reported the credit cards stolen, thinking he would
ultimately get away with it once he stopped charging.

But as things turned out, Nick had been slower to report
the theft than he should have been. He could not recall the
credit-card accounts or the numbers to call to report them
stolen. It had happened on a weekend and Elaine was not
working, so he could not phone her to look everything up.
So several days passed before he could do anything about
it.

The charges were stopped, but it had been several weeks
before the police caught up with the man responsible for
the theft, and only then due to a traffic violation that had
turned tragic. It had happened on the interstate. A highway
patrol tried to pull a man over for speeding. It was later
surmised that the man thought they were after him for the
theft, so he had refused to stop and tried to outrun the
patrolman. A high-speed chase ensued, which ended only

when the man lost control of his car. It flipped over, and he was thrown out and killed instantly.

Added to the catastrophe was the mix-up in his identity. While the patrol traced him through his license plate, the confusion came when a rescue-squad member, responding to the accident, took out the man's wallet and saw Nick's driver's license.

Nick winced to remember what had happened next.

He had been in Orlando on business, and when he got home, he was stunned to see all the cars crowded into the parking lot, as well as on the road leading to his house. He had to park his own a ways back, and when he walked into the office, the first thing he saw was Elaine with her head down on her desk sobbing.

Then someone saw him and screamed.

Then *everybody* saw him and started yelling and screaming.

Somebody shouted he was supposed to be dead, and slowly, amidst the hysteria, it all came out how someone with his driver's license had been killed, and the authorities had called the grove office to pass the information on. Word had quickly spread. People had gathered. And Nick knew what it felt like to witness his own wake.

It turned out the dead man's name was Danny Tolar. He was twenty-eight, lived in a mobile home park in Titusville and had no family. He worked for a catering company, which was how he managed to pick Nick's pocket as he passed through the crowd at the growers' meeting in Cocoa Beach. He had no previous criminal record, and had he not panicked and tried to outrun the patrol car, he would have maybe done a couple of years or might even have been put on probation. Sadly, he had lost his life, instead.

Nick had worried for a while that he would hear Danny

Tolar had done other things in his name that might have repercussions, but nothing else ever came up.

And then, as Nick stood there feeding the credit cards into the shredder, it hit him like a thunderbolt.

Dates started flashing in his head, and suddenly it all added up.

The period during which Danny Tolar had assumed his identity was around the same time Scotty's mother became pregnant.

Dear God.

No wonder Carlee had believed he was Scotty's father. And now he knew the reason he had sometimes seen such hatred and loathing in her eyes, why he'd sensed she didn't like him even before they'd met.

Nick threw himself into his chair and spun around to stare out at the heavy downpour of rain. The thunder rolling above was nothing compared to the emotions churning within as the pieces of the puzzle started to fit.

Carlee had come to the groves under false pretenses, acting as though she was only looking for work. Her real plan had been to hit him with the news that he was Scotty's father when she felt the time was right. No doubt she had wanted to get to know him in order to predict what his reaction would be.

It was obvious she loved Scotty as much as she would her own child. So it was reasonable to assume she had never intended to just turn him over. If that had been her plan she could have left him on his doorstep with a note pinned on his chest.

Carlee's intention, he was positive, had been to ask him for financial support. Sure, she had been prepared that he would want to have a paternity test done.

The slammer had been the news that he was sterile.

That was why she had run away. Already disgusted to

think he was lying when he denied knowing Scotty's mother, she'd just thrown up her hands when he'd said he was sterile. Of course, she didn't believe him and considered him the scum of the earth to lie about himself that way in order to shirk his responsibilities.

She had no clue that he would have given anything for Scotty to be his biological son.

But she was going to find out.

Nick leaped out of his chair so fast it hit the desk with a bang. He rushed to the outer office and the bank of file cabinets where Elaine kept the employee records. He found Carlee's and took it back to his desk and, after making a few phone calls, was able to confirm that every bit of the information she had given was false. But that did not make sense. She knew too much about citrus growing not to have worked around it before.

He took out his directory for the state Growers' Association. Even though it was going to take some time to phone every single grower in the state of Florida to ask if anyone, anywhere, knew her, it was quicker than hiring a private detective to do it. Besides, it was something he wanted to do himself.

He reached for the phone again, then hesitated to ask himself why he was even bothering. After all, once he proved there was no way he could be Scotty's father and backed up his theory with police evidence of Danny Tolar's pretending to be him, what then? Carlee's quest would be over, because Scotty's real father was dead.

She might also think Nick's motive in tracking her down to tell her all this was to remind her she owed him money for Scotty's medical bills. But that had nothing to do with it. Nick had never intended to let her repay him and had to admit having dared to hope that by some miracle they would one day be a family.

The bottom line was, he loved her and wanted to marry her. She might again tell him to go to hell, but that was the chance he had to take.

He snatched up the phone.

Carlee was sitting on the floor of the Jupiter Groves gift shop painting the shelves of one of the display cases. Ben had said she could pick all the colors, and she had chosen a bright shade of blue, because it was cheerful. And she needed cheering up desperately. Not that her present situation was miserable. Far from it. She had a job cleaning, helping Vera Burns around her house, as well as getting the shop ready to open for the fall season. She and Scotty also had a place to say—a little mobile home behind the grove office. And she had also found a day-care center nearby that was funded by the state. Vera had helped her fill out the necessary paperwork so that she could receive free care for Scotty. And Ben had taken her to see his lawyer to help her get the ball rolling to be awarded legal and permanent custody of Scotty.

So life would have been good except that Carlee was still smoldering over what had happened with Nick. Bad enough to have found out what a lying creep he was, but she also had to live with the pain and humiliation of having fallen under his spell just as Alicia had.

And the story he had quickly made up about being sterile had been the frosting on the cake. He had carried condoms in his wallet, but when he found himself backed into a corner, he had come up with that preposterous lie to deny fatherhood. There was no end to what the man was capable of doing. He had absolutely no honor! How glad she was to have gotten away, because the more she thought about it, the more it seemed likely he might have charged her with extortion, and she would have wound up in jail and lost Scotty.

She kept telling herself not to look back, to count her blessings, instead. After all, she did have Scotty to love, and Ben and Vera were helping her in every way possible. She had much to be thankful for and hoped that with the passing of time, she would stop feeling like such a fool. After all, she had done what she thought was right, and never in her wildest dreams could she have imagined the outcome.

Leaning back, she inspected her work. The cabinet had been white before, but now it would be a nice background for the dishes, with their orange-blossom design, that she planned to display.

"Carlee, that really looks good."

She turned to see Ben and scrambled to her feet. "Do you like it? I wasn't sure you'd want me changing all the colors around, after all."

"Anything you want is fine with me." He set the box of jars of orange-blossom honey he was carrying down on the counter.

"I got a letter from the business school this morning," she said, "and I can start night classes when the fall session begins. That way I can work and still go to school."

"Well, don't push yourself too hard. Me and the missus worry about you, Carlee. You work all the time."

"I have to," she said with a shrug and a smile. "I've got a family now, remember?"

"How can I forget? He's some boy." Ben began unpacking the box. "By the way, things must be moving right along with your petition for custody. I had a call early this morning."

She was glad, because she would not rest easy till Scotty was legally hers. "So what did the lawyer say? I hope it does go through quickly and smoothly, because he said that once I was official guardian, I could then think about adoption, and I would really like that.''

"It wasn't the lawyer." Ben wiped some dust off one of the jar lids. "Fellow didn't say who he was. He just asked if you had ever worked for me. I said yes, and then he wanted to know if I knew where you were now."

Carlee felt a little frisson of fear, but told herself not to get all worked up. It was probably somebody with Social Services checking her out. "So what did you tell him?"

"I told him, of course that I know you and that you're working for me now, doing a great job, and there were no problems. Trust me, you don't ever have to worry when it comes to me giving you a good recommendation."

"Thanks," she murmured, still a wee bit concerned. "But didn't he say why he was asking about me?"

"No. And I didn't ask. I knew what it was about." Ben set out the last of the jars. "Me and Vera are going into town. Want us to pick up Scotty on the way back?"

Carlee grinned and wagged a finger. "Now you and I both know that's not necessary. The day care is a five-minute walk from here. You just want to pick him up and spoil him all you can before I get home."

He snapped his fingers. "Shucks, you guessed. Okay, I confess."

"Then pick him up." Carlee's brow furrowed in a mock frown. "But I warn you, when he gets so spoiled I can't stand being around him, I'm going to send him to live with you."

"Suits us," Ben called breezily, almost out the door.

Carlee busied herself again, and a couple of hours later had finished her painting. Then she turned to the boxes of vegetables from Vera's garden that Ben had brought in earlier. He wanted to open the outdoor portion of the fruit stand for any tourists that might happen by, and she wanted to make a nice display.

He had also bought some Valencias, thinking a fruit stand at a grove should offer citrus even if it hadn't been grown there. With a flash of bitterness, Carlee had bitten back the impulse to say she hoped the oranges weren't from Starke Groves, because that would surely have caused questions she didn't want to answer.

She had her back to the door, putting the finishing touches on a small gift basket. She did not hear anyone come in until her blood ran cold to hear the familiar voice.

"Hello, Carlee."

She turned so fast she thought her heart twisted in her chest.

It was Nick.

"What…what are you doing here?" she stammered, her fingers tightening about the oranges she held in each hand. She looked beyond him and out the door to the parking lot, fearing that he had the police with him.

"I've been looking all over for you." He took a step toward her.

"Stay right there." She held up an orange as though it was a hand grenade. "Don't you dare come any closer. Just turn around and get out of here. I don't want anything to do with you."

"Sorry. I can't do that. I'm not going anywhere until you listen to what I have to say."

Carlee was stunned by how sad he looked, his eyes downcast, mouth a thin line, no hint of the dimples she had once adored. And his shoulders were slumped, as if he was very, very tired. "No," she whispered, determined to resist whatever act he planned this time. "Just go. We've nothing to say to each other."

He stopped his approach but firmly declared, "Well, I

have something to say to you, Carlee, and you've got to hear me out.''

Quickly, nervously, she said, ''Forget everything I told you that day, Nick. I wasn't trying to make trouble, I swear. Now leave me alone.''

He continued as though she'd not spoken. ''Scotty's father's name was Danny Tolar. He'd stolen my wallet and was using my identification, passing himself off as me. He used my credit cards, and—''

Carlee lost control then. First he had denied knowing Alicia, then claimed he was sterile, and now he was trying to say someone else had assumed his identity. She couldn't take it anymore and threw the only things she had her hands on—the oranges.

One hit him in the chest; the other sailed right by him.

Nick sprang to grab her wrists and push her gently back against the wall, holding her so she would have to listen. ''I'm not making this up. Danny Tolar was killed in a high-speed chase. When they searched his body, they found my wallet with my driver's license in it. Everyone thought I'd been killed. It turned out he was the one who had stolen my wallet a few weeks earlier.

''I can prove this,'' he rushed to continue ''just like I can prove I'm sterile. I have my medical records with me in the truck, verifying that childhood mumps is the cause.''

Carlee stared at him in wonder that he would go to so much trouble to continue to lie. ''Nick, will you just stop it?''

She twisted so hard in his grasp he feared he might hurt her and let her go. ''Carlee, please listen,'' he begged.

She moved quickly away from him. ''Why are you doing this? Maybe you got more attached to Scotty than I thought, but I swear you aren't going to take him away from me, so what kind of sick joke is this?''

"It's no joke, Carlee. I'm telling the truth."

Her eyes narrowed thoughtfully. He was the image of a deeply tormented man, and if he did have proof, if he *was* telling the truth, then what difference did it make? She was out of his life. So was Scotty. "What's your point, Nick?" she demanded, heart leaping into her throat. "Why are you here? To make trouble for me? To mess up my life because you thought I was trying to get money out of you for Scotty? Well, I wasn't. I really believed you were his father and wanted your help, but now it's over. It doesn't matter whether you are, because I never want to see you again. How did you find me, anyway?"

"By calling every grower in the Association directory till I found one who said you worked for him. That was early this morning. I didn't give my name. I was afraid he'd tell you I called and you'd run again. So I drove here as fast as I could. And I promise I'm not going to make trouble. I just want you to know the truth."

Carlee bit down on her lower lip. For some reason, she felt like crying and couldn't understand why. Maybe it was because he looked so sad, so beaten down, and it was more than she could bear. "Then why are you here?" she asked tremulously.

"Because I love you, Carlee. And I couldn't stand the thought of your believing what you did of me. I'd never turn my back on a woman I got pregnant—if I could get her pregnant," he added wistfully, "regardless of the circumstances. I wish I could call Scotty my son. Just like I wished it were so when he called me Daddy. You don't know how that made me feel. If you want to see the papers, I'll go get them and—"

"No, Nick. You don't have to do that." With love shining in her eyes, she went to him. "I don't need your proof.

I can see— No," she amended, "I can feel it in my heart that you're telling the truth."

He grabbed her and hugged her tightly. "Oh, honey, I am, and you can also believe it when I tell you I love you beyond belief. And I want to marry you, if you'll have me, and be Scotty's daddy. We'll be a family, and..." His voice trailed off, then holding her away to search her face, he said, "That is, if you don't mind that I can't give you any more children. You need to think about that, Carlee."

"I don't have to think about it, Nick. It doesn't matter, because there are lots of babies out there just like Scotty who need parents to adopt and love them. We can fill the house with them if we want to."

"And we'll do just that," he said huskily. "We'll fill it with kids...and with love. Marry me, Carlee, and let me prove how much you and Scotty both mean to me."

"I will," she cried, tears streaming down her cheeks as she raised her lips for his kiss.

"Carlee, what's going on?"

They sprang apart and saw Ben walking in the door, Vera right behind him and holding Scotty by the hand.

Before Carlee could say anything, Scotty recognized Nick. Jerking his hand from Vera's, he cried, "Dah-dee!" and ran straight for him, grinning from ear to ear.

Nick dropped to his knees to meet him, hugging him to his chest.

Carlee, smiling all the way from her heart, said to Ben and Vera, "I want you to meet Scotty's Daddy." She hastened to add, "I'll explain everything later."

Then, as she knelt to be included in Nick's embrace, something on the floor beside them caught her eye.

It was a bright, shiny penny.

*   *   *   *   *

Silhouette presents an exciting
new continuity series:

**When a royal family rolls out the red carpet
for love, power and deception, will their
lives change forever?**

The saga begins in April 2002 with:

The Princess Is Pregnant!

by Laurie Paige (SE #1459)

**May: THE PRINCESS AND THE DUKE by Allison Leigh
(SE #1465)**

**June: ROYAL PROTOCOL by Christine Flynn
(SE #1471)**

Be sure to catch all nine Crown and Glory stories: the first three appear in
Silhouette Special Edition, the next three continue in Silhouette Romance
and the saga concludes with three books in Silhouette Desire.

───────────────

And be sure not to miss more royal stories,
from Silhouette Intimate Moments'

Romancing
the Crown,

running January through December.

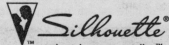

Where love comes alive™

*Available at
your favorite
retail outlet.*

Silhouette® —

where love comes alive—online...

eHARLEQUIN.com

your romantic
books

- ♥ Shop online! Visit Shop eHarlequin and discover a wide selection of new releases and classic favorites at great discounted prices.

- ♥ Read our daily and weekly Internet exclusive serials, and participate in our interactive novel in the reading room.

- ♥ Ever dreamed of being a writer? Enter your chapter for a chance to become a featured author in our Writing Round Robin novel.

your romantic
magazine

- ♥ Check out our feature articles on dating, flirting and other important romance topics and get your daily love dose with tips on how to keep the romance alive every day.

- ♥ Learn what the stars have in store for you with our daily Passionscopes and weekly Erotiscopes.

- ♥ Get the latest scoop on your favorite royals in Royal Romance.

your
community

- ♥ Have a Heart-to-Heart with other members about the latest books and meet your favorite authors.

- ♥ Discuss your romantic dilemma in the Tales from the Heart message board.

LINDSAY McKENNA

continues her popular series,

MORGAN'S MERCENARIES

with a brand-new, longer-length single title!

She had never needed anyone before. Never ached for a man before. Until her latest mission put Apache pilot Akiva Redtail in the hot seat next to army officer Joe Calhoun. And as they rode through the thunderous skies, dodging danger at every turn, Akiva discovered a strength in Joe's arms, a fiery passion she was powerless to battle against. For only with this rugged soldier by her side could this Native American beauty fulfill the destiny she was born to. Only with Joe did she dare open her heart to love....

"When it comes to action and romance, nobody does it better than Ms. McKenna."
—Romantic Times Magazine

Available in March from Silhouette Books!

Silhouette®

Where love comes alive™

Visit Silhouette at www.eHarlequin.com   PSDW

This Mother's Day Give Your Mom A Royal Treat

Win a fabulous one-week vacation in Puerto Rico for you and your mother at the luxurious Inter-Continental San Juan Resort & Casino. The prize includes round trip airfare for two, breakfast daily and a mother and daughter day of beauty at the beachfront hotel's spa.

INTER·CONTINENTAL
San Juan
RESORT & CASINO

Here's all you have to do:

Tell us in 100 words or less how your mother helped with the romance in your life. It may be a story about your engagement, wedding or those boyfriends when you were a teenager or any other romantic advice from your mother. The entry will be judged based on its originality, emotionally compelling nature and sincerity.
See official rules on following page.

Send your entry to:
Mother's Day Contest

In Canada	**In U.S.A.**
P.O. Box 637	P.O. Box 9076
Fort Erie, Ontario	3010 Walden Ave.
L2A 5X3	Buffalo, NY
	14269-9076

Or enter online at www.eHarlequin.com

PRROY

HARLEQUIN MOTHER'S DAY CONTEST 2216
OFFICIAL RULES
NO PURCHASE NECESSARY TO ENTER

Two ways to enter:

• **Via The Internet:** Log on to the Harlequin romance website (www.eHarlequin.com) anytime beginning 12:01 a.m. E.S.T., January 1, 2002 through 11:59 p.m. E.S.T., April 1, 2002 and follow the directions displayed on-line to enter your name, address (including zip code), e-mail address and in 100 words or fewer, describe how your mother helped with the romance in your life.

• **Via Mail:** Handprint (or type) on an 8 1/2" x 11" plain piece of paper, your name, address (including zip code) and e-mail address (if you have one), and in 100 words or fewer, describe how your mother helped with the romance in your life. Mail your entry via first-class mail to: Harlequin Mother's Day Contest 2216, (in the U.S.) P.O. Box 9076, Buffalo, NY 14269-9076; (in Canada) P.O. Box 637, Fort Erie, Ontario, Canada L2A 5X3.

For eligibility, entries must be submitted either through a completed Internet transmission or postmarked no later than 11:59 p.m. E.S.T., April 1, 2002 (mail-in entries must be received by April 9, 2002). Limit one entry per person, household address and e-mail address. On-line and/or mailed entries received from persons residing in geographic areas in which entry is not permissible will be disqualified.

Entries will be judged by a panel of judges, consisting of members of the Harlequin editorial, marketing and public relations staff using the following criteria:
- Originality - 50%
- Emotional Appeal - 25%
- Sincerity - 25%

In the event of a tie, duplicate prizes will be awarded. Decisions of the judges are final.

Prize: A 6-night/7-day stay for two at the Inter-Continental San Juan Resort & Casino, including round-trip coach air transportation from gateway airport nearest winner's home (approximate retail value: $4,000). Prize includes breakfast daily and a mother and daughter day of beauty at the beachfront hotel's spa. Prize consists of only those items listed as part of the prize. Prize is valued in U.S. currency.

All entries become the property of Torstar Corp. and will not be returned. No responsibility is assumed for lost, late, illegible, incomplete, inaccurate, non-delivered or misdirected mail or misdirected e-mail, for technical, hardware or software failures of any kind, lost or unavailable network connections, or failed, incomplete, garbled or delayed computer transmission or any human error which may occur in the receipt or processing of the entries in this Contest.

Contest open only to residents of the U.S. (except Colorado) and Canada, who are 18 years of age or older and is void wherever prohibited by law; all applicable laws and regulations apply. Any litigation within the Province of Quebec respecting the conduct or organization of a publicity contest may be submitted to the Régie des alcools, des courses et des jeux for a ruling. Any litigation respecting the awarding of a prize may be submitted to the Régie des alcools, des courses et des jeux only for the purpose of helping the parties reach a settlement. Employees and immediate family members of Torstar Corp. and D.L. Blair, Inc., their affiliates, subsidiaries and all other agencies, entities and persons connected with the use, marketing or conduct of this Contest are not eligible to enter. Taxes on prize are the sole responsibility of winner. Acceptance of any prize offered constitutes permission to use winner's name, photograph or other likeness for the purposes of advertising, trade and promotion on behalf of Torstar Corp., its affiliates and subsidiaries without further compensation to the winner, unless prohibited by law.

Winner will be determined no later than April 15, 2002 and be notified by mail. Winner will be required to sign and return an Affidavit of Eligibility form within 15 days after winner notification. Non-compliance within that time period may result in disqualification and an alternate winner may be selected. Winner of trip must execute a Release of Liability prior to ticketing and must possess required travel documents (e.g. Passport, photo ID) where applicable. Travel must be completed within 12 months of selection and is subject to traveling companion completing and returning a Release of Liability prior to travel; and hotel and flight accommodations availability. Certain restrictions and blackout dates may apply. No substitution of prize permitted by winner. Torstar Corp. and D.L. Blair, Inc., their parents, affiliates, and subsidiaries are not responsible for errors in printing or electronic presentation of Contest, or entries. In the event of printing or other errors which may result in unintended prize values or duplication of prizes, all affected entries shall be null and void. If for any reason the Internet portion of the Contest is not capable of running as planned, including infection by computer virus, bugs, tampering, unauthorized intervention, fraud, technical failures, or any other causes beyond the control of Torstar Corp. which corrupt or affect the administration, secrecy, fairness, integrity or proper conduct of the Contest, Torstar Corp. reserves the right, at its sole discretion, to disqualify any individual who tampers with the entry process and to cancel, terminate, modify or suspend the Contest or the Internet portion thereof. In the event the Internet portion must be terminated a notice will be posted on the website and all entries received prior to termination will be judged in accordance with these rules. In the event of a dispute regarding an on-line entry, the entry will be deemed submitted by the authorized holder of the e-mail account submitted at the time of entry. Authorized account holder is defined as the natural person who is assigned to an e-mail address by an Internet access provider, on-line service provider or other organization that is responsible for arranging e-mail address for the domain associated with the submitted e-mail address. Torstar Corp. and/or D.L. Blair Inc. assumes no responsibility for any computer injury or damage related to or resulting from accessing and/or downloading any sweepstakes material. Rules are subject to any requirements/limitations imposed by the FCC. **Purchase or acceptance of a product offer does not improve your chances of winning.**

For winner's name (available after May 1, 2002), send a self-addressed, stamped envelope to: Harlequin Mother's Day Contest Winners 2216, P.O. Box 4200 Blair, NE 68009-4200 or you may access the www.eHarlequin.com Web site through June 3, 2002.

Contest sponsored by Torstar Corp., P.O. Box 9042, Buffalo, NY 14269-9042.

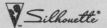

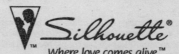